Four young women, fresh out of college, pursue their careers at a new ski lodge at Lake Tahoe's Incline Village during the winter season.

The Christmas Miracle by Jeanie Smith Cash
Bethany Stillman, RN, is only interested in her career until she meets paramedic Cole Beckman on the flight to her grandparents' ski lodge in the Lake Tahoe area. But Cole has a secret that could destroy any chance of a relationship with the nurse. As a teenager, he was responsible for the accident that crippled Bethany's grandfather. Will the Christmas season bring a miraculous healing of hearts and minds?

No Thank You by Lena Nelson Dooley
Scarlett McKaye takes a job as social director in a ski lodge but doesn't plan to go out on the slopes. She lost her first love because he took too many dangerous chances. So when daredevil skier Derrick Greene shows an interest in her, Scarlett wants nothing to do with him. Can Derrick convince Scarlett to trust him. . .and trust him to God?

Tinsel, Tidings, and Time-share by Jean Kincaid
Stephanie St. John meets Darrin Hart before the first time-share session she conducts at the Snowbird Lodge. After overhearing Darrin's negative comments to her boss, Stephanie avoids him like the plague. Garnering information he needs concerning his lodge in Colorado becomes more of a task than Darrin bargained for. Will Stephanie and Darrin find that sharing time with each other clears up major misconceptions?

Dating Unaware by Jeri Odell
While pursuing her love of photography and her accounting career, Michaela Christiansen has sworn off men, deciding they aren't worth the pain they evoke. But her college friends and eleven-year-old Lynzie Brooks are determined to change her mind. Will Michaela stand firm in her decision to avoid the opposite sex, or will she fall for widower Jonas Brooks, the attractive forest ranger who pines for her presence?

CHRISTMAS LOVE AT LAKE TAHOE

LENA NELSON DOOLEY

Jeanie Smith Cash / Jean Kincaid / Jeri Odell

BARBOUR
PUBLISHING

©2009 *The Christmas Miracle* by Jeanie Smith Cash
©2009 *No Thank You* by Lena Nelson Dooley
©2009 *Tinsel, Tidings, and Time-share* by Jean Kincaid
©2009 *Dating Unaware* by Jeri Odell

ISBN 978-1-60260-563-3

This book is a work of fiction. Names, characters, places, and incidents are either products of the author's imagination or used fictitiously. Any similarity to actual people, organizations, and/or events is purely coincidental.

Interior Illustrations: Mari Small, www.thesmallagencynj.com

Published by Barbour Publishing, Inc., P.O. Box 719, Uhrichsville, OH 44683, www.barbourbooks.com

Our mission is to publish and distribute inspirational products offering exceptional value and biblical encouragement to the masses.

 Member of the
Evangelical Christian
Publishers Association

Printed in the United States of America.

The Christmas Miracle

by Jeanie Smith Cash

To Jesus my Lord and Savior, who made this all possible.

To my own special hero, Andy. You are always there for me, and I love you so very much.

To my family for their love and support.

To my sweet sister, Chere Snider, for your love, prayers, and support in everything I do, including my writing. I thank the Lord for you. You are the best sister anyone could ever ask for and I love you so much.

I'd like to thank Lena Nelson Dooley, Jeri Odell, and Jean Kincaid for writing with me and especially Rebecca Germany, our editor, for her time, patience, and hard work.

Bear with each other and forgive whatever grievances
you may have against one another.
Forgive as the Lord forgave you.
COLOSSIANS 3:13 NIV

Chapter 1

Bethany Stillman zipped the top of her carry-on bag closed. She could hardly wait to board the plane that would take her to her grandparents' ski lodge at Lake Tahoe. She had thoroughly enjoyed a week she had spent at Snowbird Lodge celebrating her grandparents' anniversary, and she was looking forward to working there for the winter with her three best friends.

Just thinking of the ski trip she and her friends had planned years ago, to take place after they graduated from college, had kept her focused throughout four years of college with its long hours of studying. She couldn't believe it was finally time to go. She took one last glance around the living room of her small apartment, located above the garage of her parents' home, to be sure she had everything she'd need—suitcases, purse, coat, and her emerald cross, a gift from her parents. She always wore it around her neck.

"Oh no! Where is my airline ticket?" Wracking her brain, she couldn't remember where she'd put it. She dumped her purse upside down, checked her coat pockets, the kitchen drawers, and everywhere else she could think of, but it was nowhere to be found. In a panic, she cried, "Oh Lord! Please help me find it. I've looked forward to this trip for so long."

She started opening suitcases. Finally, at the bottom of the very last one, she found her ticket. "Thank You, Lord." She hugged it against her chest, breathing a sigh of relief. It was a good thing the Lord knew where she put things. How could she be so scatterbrained? She picked up the phone and called for a taxi. Stacking her bags, she strapped them on the wheels with a bungee cord. After slipping her backpack over her shoulders, she pulled the bags behind her and headed out the door. She bumped awkwardly down the stairs and waited at the foot of the steps for the cab that would take her to the airport.

Taking a taxi turned out to be a wise decision. After misplacing her ticket, she wouldn't have had time to park her car and still catch her flight. The driver would drop her off at the door, and she could go directly to the check-in counter.

Once the plane leveled out at cruising altitude, the flight attendants served the passengers a snack. Bethany finished eating and had just opened the new Christian romance novel she'd bought for the trip, when a loud *crash* behind her caused her to nearly jump out of her seat. A flight attendant ran by her, and, unsnapping her belt buckle, Bethany leaned over to look down the aisle. An older gentleman lay unconscious on the floor. Bethany jumped up and reached the stricken man just as a young man stooped down beside him.

"I'm an RN, Bethany Stillman. Can I help?" She knelt down in the narrow aisle.

The man looked at her and frowned, then unbuttoned the older man's shirt and placed his ear next to his chest. She thought his reaction odd but didn't have time to think about it for long.

"Colton Beckman, I go by Cole, and you can assist me with CPR." He pulled a mouthpiece from the duffel bag he had on the floor next to him and positioned it over the man's mouth. Bethany placed her hands on the patient's chest in the correct location. She began CPR compressions, following each time after Cole breathed air into the man's mouth.

"Do you have a defibrillator on the plane?" Cole asked the flight attendant between breaths.

"Yes, Mr. Beckman, we have a portable unit. I'll get it." She rushed off toward the front of the plane and returned moments later with the unit.

Cole opened the box, placed the paddles against their patient. "Clear," he said as he hit the switch, and the man's body jerked from the jolt of electricity. They both watched the machine, but there was no change.

He said, "Clear," again and hit the switch a second time. This time as they watched, the man's heart began beating rhythmically, and Bethany and Cole both sighed with relief. Cole removed the mouthpiece, and placed an oxygen mask in its place.

He glanced at Bethany and she couldn't help but notice he had the bluest eyes she'd ever seen. His smile revealed even, white teeth, softening his craggy features. Her heart did a little flip in her chest.

As he looked down at their patient, she studied Cole for a moment. Her gaze focused on his dark hair and tanned features. He was gorgeous. There was no denying it, and she had to tell herself that she wasn't interested. She had a career to pursue, not to mention that she'd probably never see him again.

She wondered what Cole did for a living. He certainly knew CPR and how to handle a defibrillator, and he carried a mouthpiece in his duffel bag. But he wasn't a doctor. The flight attendant had called him *Mr.* Beckman. Despite that, he'd had extensive medical training. He didn't learn how to use a defibrillator in a CPR class; he had to be in the medical field.

"He's stable for the moment." Cole turned to the flight attendant. "But tell the pilot to land at the nearest airport. If we don't get him to a hospital right away, he might not make it. He needs more help than we can give him here."

The flight attendant came back from the cockpit a few minutes later.

"Here's a blanket." She handed it to Cole and he laid it over the patient. "The pilot radioed the nearest airport and received permission to land. We'll be on the ground in about ten minutes. You really should be strapped into your seats."

"We can't leave him. If he goes into cardiac arrest again we'll need to be close by." Cole slid his bag under the nearest seat as the flight attendant went to the front of the plane and fastened herself in securely.

"You're an RN, huh?" he asked as he watched their patient.

"Yes." Bethany settled back against the frame of one of the seats. "I graduated from a nursing program in May. What do you do?"

"I'm a paramedic with a fire department. You sure got a chance to exercise your skills today."

"I'm just thankful we could help him." They braced themselves the best they could for the landing, while also holding the older man securely in place on the floor. The plane taxied to the terminal.

The pilot's voice came over the intercom, "Please do not leave the plane, folks. As soon as the patient has been cared for, we will continue on to our destination. We apologize for any inconvenience this unexpected stop may have caused you."

Bethany noticed that no one complained. Two paramedics brought a stretcher aboard for their patient. The two men lifted him gently from the floor and placed him onto the narrow bed. Cole explained what he and Bethany had done for the man, and the paramedics left as quickly as they had arrived.

Bethany waited while Cole handed the defibrillator unit back to the flight attendant, who headed toward the front of the plane. Bethany watched the paramedics as they carried the man off of the plane. "I wonder if we'll ever know if he made it."

"I don't imagine we will. But we did all we could for him. Now we should pray and leave him in the good Lord's hands."

Bethany glanced up at him. He was a Christian, a definite point in his favor. What was she thinking? She was glad he was a Christian, but she didn't have time to think about an attractive man.

"It was nice meeting you, Cole." She offered him her hand.

His tan Dockers and dark blue shirt were well pressed. He stood tall, at least six-three, and had a muscular build. At her height of five-four, he towered over her.

"It was my pleasure." Cole shook her hand and watched her walk back to her seat. The blue jeans and red plaid top she wore fit her slender figure well. Waves of thick auburn hair hung halfway down her back, and large golden brown eyes dominated her small face. She was lovely, and he found himself attracted to her. He wouldn't mind getting to know her. She hadn't hesitated to jump in and help, and she knew what she was doing. He'd been a little concerned at first as to whether she would have enough strength to keep up the chest compressions, but she hadn't faltered even for a second.

Cole doubted she'd want to get to know him if she realized who he was. He was surprised she hadn't recognized his name; he'd recognized hers right away. But it had been ten years. He'd only been sixteen at the time, and she couldn't be more than twenty-two now, so that would have made her only about twelve. He certainly remembered it. A person didn't forget something like that. He'd been involved in an accident that crippled her grandfather. Her father blamed him for the fact that his father, Charles Stillman, would never walk again. If she realized who he was, she wouldn't want anything to do with him. It didn't really matter. He'd probably never see her again.

He picked up his bag and went back to his seat.

As the plane taxied to the terminal at the Reno airport, Bethany put her book away. A few minutes later, the captain's voice came over the intercom and gave clearance for the passengers to depart.

Bethany slipped into her jacket and grabbed her purse. She slid her backpack straps onto her shoulders and followed the other passengers off the plane. When she'd made it to the end of the long hallway leading to the inside of the terminal, she walked up to the ticket agent.

"Excuse me, can you please direct me to baggage claim?"

"It's down the escalator and to the left." The young man pointed across the terminal from where they stood.

Bethany thanked him, walked across to the escalator, and took it to the ground floor. She quickly located the baggage-claim belt for her flight and had just sat down on a bench to wait when she saw Cole Beckman coming down the escalator. She should have realized he also would have luggage to pick up. She sighed; the man was just too good looking. It was a good thing she wouldn't be seeing him again after today. She didn't need someone like him complicating her life. She had set a goal, and she didn't intend to allow anything, or anyone, to keep her from achieving it. She feared he could weaken her resolve, so that made him off limits.

Chapter 2

Bethany stood up just as Cole stepped off the escalator. He was carrying what looked to be a fiddle case.

"Well, we meet again," Cole said as he walked up to her.

"Yes. The bags have just begun to come through." Bethany walked over to where she could see them as they dropped onto the conveyer belt.

Two elderly ladies stood beside them. When their luggage came around, Cole lifted it off for them, and they thanked him.

"I'll get yours, too, if you'd like." He smiled that million-dollar smile, and her heart nearly skipped a beat.

Oh, brother—this would never do. She was glad she wouldn't have to spend any more time around him; she'd be in trouble for sure. The thought hit her, *Why isn't he married?* Well, maybe he was. Why did she just assume he was single? A ridiculous assumption, given the fact that she didn't know a thing about him.

They stood watching the luggage as it came around.

Eventually they had located all of their bags, and Cole lifted each of them off the belt.

"Thanks for your help," Bethany said.

"My pleasure."

"So, you play the fiddle?"

"Yes, ever since I was a little guy. My grandfather plays, and he taught me as soon as I was old enough to hold one. My brother plays the guitar, my father the banjo, and my mother the mandolin. We're a musical family." He grinned.

"Sounds like it. So what does your grandmother play?"

"She plays the bass. Occasionally we play and sing gospel at bluegrass festivals."

"I love bluegrass music." Bethany placed her bags on the set of wheels and fastened them with the bungee cords. She pulled the luggage behind her as she walked away. "It was nice talking to you, Cole," she called over her shoulder.

"You too, Bethany. Take care."

As she left him, Bethany experienced a mixture of disappointment and relief. Colton Beckman was a man who could easily distract her from her goal, and she couldn't let that happen. She was glad the temptation had been removed—she wouldn't be seeing him anymore.

Bethany walked over to the candy machine she had spotted on the way down to the terminal. She bought two bags of Peanut M&M's and dropped them into her purse. Her mother always teased her, saying they were her crutch, because she always munched on them when she was nervous or uncomfortable about something.

Adjusting her backpack, she headed through the double doors to locate the shuttle her grandmother told her would be waiting when she arrived. The doors had just closed behind her when she stopped in her tracks; she couldn't believe this. Standing next to the shuttle to the ski lodge was Cole Beckman. *Oh Lord! What am I going to do now? Please tell me he isn't going to the lodge.* But no divine intervention seemed to take place, and Bethany knew in her heart that the lodge was exactly where he was headed. She didn't like it, but she had little choice in the matter; she headed for the van.

"Cole, are you going to Snowbird Lodge?" Bethany slipped the backpack from her shoulders and handed it and her luggage to the shuttle driver.

"Yes. Looks like you are, too," Cole said.

Bethany was more than a little annoyed as he followed her into the shuttle and took a seat across from her. But she knew this wasn't his fault. She'd just have to avoid him as much as possible while he was there. After all, he had as much right to be going to the ski lodge as she did, and surely he wouldn't be staying more than a few days.

"Are you taking a skiing vacation?" she asked.

"No, I'm on a leave of absence from the fire department. I lost my partner—my best friend—in a fire four weeks ago." He stopped for a moment and swallowed, making Bethany realize this was hard for him to talk about.

"My boss thought a change of pace would be good for me for a while. I saw an ad on the Internet for winter jobs at this ski lodge. I e-mailed the owners a résumé, and they called me for an interview. I flew out two weeks ago, and they hired me for the winter as a ski instructor."

He glanced out the window and then back over at her. She could see the anguish on his face.

"I'm so sorry about your friend. That would be an awful thing to go through."

"It's not easy. We'd been friends all through college, and then became partners at the fire department." He glanced out the side window again before continuing. "He died in my arms."

Cole cleared his throat, and Bethany suspected it was to cover up the emotion he obviously was having a hard time controlling. She wasn't thrilled about him being at the lodge all winter, but she did feel bad for him. Losing a friend would be unbearable. She couldn't imagine losing one of her three best friends—they meant so much to her. They would soon be joining her at the lodge, and she could hardly wait to see them.

He interrupted her thoughts when he spoke again, changing the subject. "So why are *you* headed to the lodge. Vacation?"

"No. My grandparents own the lodge." Bethany glanced over at him.

"Mack and Elizabeth Langston are your grandparents?"

"Yes. My mother's parents. In fact, that's the reason my mother named me Bethany." She glanced at him. "It's derived from my grandmother's name."

"They're nice people. I really appreciate them giving me the job." Cole set his carry-on bag on the floor next to him.

"Yes, I can relate. They gave my three friends and me jobs also. Since we just graduated from college, Gram and Papa are allowing us to work in our new professions for some experience while they get the lodge up and on its feet, so to speak."

"I take it you're the live-in nurse."

"Yes. Since the lodge is out from town a ways, my grandparents thought it would be good to have medical staff on the premises."

"That's a good idea. Well, looks like we've reached our destination," Cole said as the shuttle pulled up in front of the ski lodge. "Can I help you with your luggage?"

"Thanks, but I can get them. You have enough of your own to carry."

Bethany started to take her bags from Sean, the driver, but he told her he'd take them inside for her. She slipped her backpack onto her shoulders and headed into the lodge. She couldn't wait to see her grandparents. When she started to open the door, Cole reached around and held the door for her and Sean, as Sean rolled her luggage inside.

She thanked Sean. He smiled and politely refused the tip she offered since she was an employee of the lodge. Just then her grandmother saw her. She rushed over and enveloped Bethany in a big hug.

"Hi, sweetheart. I'm so glad you made it okay. Hi, Cole—I see you've met my granddaughter."

"Yes. Actually, we were on the same flight." Cole smiled at Bethany.

Her heart did a little flip and she chided herself; she needed to get a grip. This was going to be a long winter if she reacted this way every time he flashed that killer smile in her direction. No one should have a smile with such a devastating effect. Well, she would do her best to avoid him. Her career had to come first, no matter how much she was attracted to Cole Beckman. She just had to convince her heart of that fact.

"It's good to finally be here, Gram. Where's Papa?"

"He was getting antsy for you to arrive; you know how he worries. I sent him to town to get the mail and to run a few errands. He'll be back before dinner."

"Yes, I know how protective he is, and I love him for it. I can't wait to see him. Are the other girls here yet?"

"No. I got a call from them yesterday. Stephanie will be here Saturday morning, Scarlett and Michaela, Saturday afternoon."

"Well, I'm disappointed, but I guess I'll just have to wait a few more days. If you don't need me for anything and can point me in the right direction, I think I'll go to my room and freshen up a bit before dinner."

"Sure, honey—there isn't anything you or Cole need to do. You can both relax and enjoy this week before you start working. Take the elevator there." She indicated a set of doors opposite the entrance through which Bethany and Cole had entered the lodge. "It'll take you to the top floor, and your room is to the right at the far end of the hall. Yours is to the left at the end, Cole. Dinner is at six o'clock in the main dining room."

"Thanks, Gram. I'll be down in plenty of time."

"Thanks, Mrs. Langston."

"*Elizabeth* will be fine. We aren't formal around here." She smiled. "I'll see you both at dinner."

Chapter 3

Bethany frowned. *Great! We're on the same floor.* Cole interrupted her thoughts when he said, "After you, milady," indicating with his hand that she should walk in ahead of him as the elevator doors opened.

Bethany stepped in and rolled her luggage to the back to make room for Cole's. She decided that she would go on as if she'd never met him and do what she had come here to do. The first thing on the agenda was to find her room, unpack, and change clothes before dinner. Cole pushed the button, and the elevator whisked them quickly and smoothly to their floor. When the doors opened, he motioned again for her to step out ahead of him.

"See you at dinner, Bethany." Cole turned and headed down the hall in the opposite direction.

Bethany pulled her suitcases behind her, looking for the room Gram had assigned her. How in the world was she going to avoid Cole when they would often meet at the elevator and be at the same table during meals every day?

When she found her room, she slid the key card into the slot and opened the door. She stopped and gaped in awe of the large suite before her. It was gorgeous. A large rock fireplace graced the far wall, oak bookcases from ceiling to floor on each side. To the left was a huge window overlooking the ski slopes. They'd be able to watch it snow and enjoy a fire at the same time. Navy, forest green, ecru, and burgundy plaid curtains hung on the big picture window. A sofa, love seat, and three chairs in matching fabric were arranged in front of the huge fireplace. Oak end tables with green lamps, and an oak coffee table completed the decor. She could imagine flames licking and flickering against big logs in the fireplace. The room was warm and welcoming.

Bethany walked down the short hall that led to four bedrooms. Each had a separate bath with shower. The only difference in the rooms was color scheme. All four queen cherry-wood poster beds had a beautiful quilted bedspread. Bethany knew by looking at them that her grandmother had made all four quilts herself. The valance over the vertical blinds shading the picture glass window matched each room's quilt. An old-fashioned armoire resided against one wall, and a matching dresser with mirror sat against the opposite wall. Each room had a small dressing table with a chair. At the foot of each bed was a hope chest. Bethany chose the room done in tiny pink flowers with green leaves on a white background, with a pink ruffle at the bottom of the spread. The other three rooms were done in the same print—one in yellow, one in purple, and the other one in turquoise. The rooms were lovely, warm, and cozy. She took a minute to call her grandmother and thank her for the beautiful room before she unpacked.

Once Bethany had everything she would need for tonight unpacked and put away, she took a quick shower, dressed, and headed downstairs. She was getting hungry, and dinner would be served soon. When she walked into the dining room, she found her grandfather sitting at the table with a cup of coffee. He glanced up and smiled; as she walked over to him he stood and gave her a hug.

"Hi, sunshine. How's my girl?"

Bethany hugged him back. He was a big man—over six feet tall, with a sturdy build. She had to stand on her tiptoes with him bending down, for her to reach him. "Hi, Papa. It's so good to see you!"

He pulled out a chair next to him. "Sit down and chat with your old grandpappy for a few minutes." He sat back in his chair and sipped his coffee.

Bethany fixed herself a cup of hot chocolate from the beverage buffet and sat down next to him.

"Did you have a good trip?"

"It was fine for the most part. I'm just glad to be here. You know flying isn't my favorite thing."

"Yes, I remember. I'm glad you're here safe." Her grandfather stood up and smiled.

Bethany glanced behind her to see who had come into the room. It was Cole; he walked up behind her to shake her grandfather's hand before he sat in a chair across from them. *Great,* she groaned silently. She knew he'd be at dinner, but she hadn't counted on him being here this early. She had hoped for a few minutes alone with her grandfather.

"I think I'll go see if your grandmother needs any help." Bethany's grandfather slid his chair against the table.

"Why don't you let me go and help Gram?" Bethany started to stand up.

"Not this time, sunshine. You're on vacation. Next week will be soon enough for you to start working. Relax and enjoy yourself until then. You can keep Cole here company. The rest of the guests will be coming in soon, and we'll be serving dinner shortly."

"Did you get all settled in?" Cole asked after her grandfather had left the room.

"No, but enough to get me by for now." Bethany glanced at him. She didn't like the attraction she felt for Cole; it made her uncomfortable. She reached into her purse and opened one of her bags of Peanut M&M's. She held the bag out to him. "Like some?"

"Uh, no thanks. It's almost dinnertime—are you really going to eat M&M's now?" He looked at her quizzically, and Bethany knew he wouldn't understand her need for Peanut M&M's when she was nervous. And he definitely made her nervous. He'd probably just think she was strange.

"I'll just have a couple." She took two and put the bag back into her purse.

Before Cole had a chance to say anything more, the guests started arriving. Quite a few guests were already checked in. She was surprised at the number that would be staying through Thanksgiving. When she had talked to Gram earlier, her grandmother had told Bethany that several more families with children would be checking in this weekend. From the looks of things, every room would be filled. This was their first winter season, and she was thrilled for her grandparents that the lodge was doing so well.

Cole discreetly observed Bethany as she interacted with the guests during dinner. Her beautiful brown eyes lit up when she talked about nursing. Anyone could see she loved her profession and working with people. She'd be a good nurse. He'd experienced a bit of her expertise on the plane, and the guests related to her well.

"Bethany, since we don't start working until next week, would you be free to go on a snowmobile ride with me tomorrow afternoon?" Cole asked softly.

"Thanks for the offer, but I can't tomorrow. I plan to spend the day getting unpacked and organized."

"Maybe later in the week then." He reached to take the bowl of mashed potatoes she handed to him. The lodge served family style, so each dish was passed around. It was like having a home-cooked meal at your own table. He liked the idea. It gave everyone a chance to get to know each other.

Cole had the feeling Bethany was avoiding him. She obviously hadn't recognized his name, so that wasn't the reason. He wondered if it was him in particular or men in general. He'd bide his time and ask her out again later; maybe she really was going to be tied up all day tomorrow.

He finished his dinner and picked up his fiddle case. The Langstons had asked him if he'd play a couple of numbers after dinner to entertain the guests. He unfastened the case and lifted his pride and joy from it. This fiddle had belonged to his grandfather; he'd given it to Cole a year ago, when Cole's grandmother gave his grandfather the one *he'd* been eyeing, for Christmas. This was a beautiful fiddle, and it meant the world to Cole that his grandfather had chosen to give Cole a prized possession.

Bethany listened as Cole played. He wasn't just good; he was exceptional. It was obvious that he loved to play—he felt the music, became a part of it. She really enjoyed hearing him play. The other guests did, too, if their applause was any indication. He came back and sat down next to her.

"That was incredible, Cole. I've heard a lot of fiddle players, but never have I heard one play the way you just did. You're very talented."

She didn't want to be impressed. She wanted to get this man out of her head and forget about him. Fat chance *that* would happen, given that her heart seemed to beat twice as fast as it should every time she ran into him. Well, she couldn't be dishonest. He was good, so she'd given him a compliment, and that was that.

"Thanks, Bethany. I enjoy it, but the talent comes from the Lord. I'm just His instrument." He carefully placed his fiddle back into its case and snapped it closed. "I think I'll call it a night. See all of you in the morning."

"Good night, Cole." Bethany watched as he walked toward the elevator. It sure would be easier to ignore him if he wasn't such a nice person. The fact that he wasn't hard to look at didn't help either. She sighed. "Gram, Papa, I think I'll say good night, too. I'll see you in the morning."

She kissed each of them on the cheek and headed to the elevator. It'd been a long day, and she was ready for bed.

Chapter 4

The next morning, Bethany got up early and headed down to the workout facility to walk the treadmill. As she stepped through the doorway, she saw Cole using the weight machine. *Great, just the person I wanted to see.* She said hello as she stepped up on the treadmill.

"Good morning. I see you work out before starting your day, too." Cole raised the weight bar over his head, then lowered it again.

"Yes, I read my Bible and devotional and work out every morning," she said as she adjusted the speed and started to walk on the machine.

"It sounds like we have a similar routine," Cole said, glancing her way.

Bethany tried to ignore the fact that Cole was in the room. Not an easy feat. Her eyes kept drifting toward him of their own accord, drawn to muscles that rippled when he lifted the weight bar over his head. How could one man be so attractive in every way? His personality, his looks, and his build were hard to get past. She continued to remind herself that she needed to focus on her career and not on Mr. Cole Beckman, but she was losing the battle.

Cole must have been in the workout room for a while before Bethany arrived, because he placed the bar in the holder and picked up his bag a few minutes later. "I'll see you at dinner this evening. Hope you get all of your unpacking done." He flashed that gorgeous smile that sent her heart into high gear as he walked out the door.

"Thanks. I'm sure I will." Bethany finished her workout an hour later and headed back to her room; she wouldn't get her unpacking done if she didn't get started on it.

Everywhere Bethany went that week she seemed to run into Cole. And every time she saw him, he asked her to go snowmobiling with him. She'd make an excuse, and he'd say maybe another time, smile, and walk away. Then the next time she saw him, he'd ask again. The man just wouldn't take no for an answer. Of course, the thing she didn't want to admit was that every time he asked, her resolve would weaken a little more. She found herself actually wanting to say yes. If he kept at it, one of these times he'd catch her at a weak moment, and she'd agree to go. She couldn't allow that to happen. She'd just have to try harder to avoid him. Gram had been no help at all when Bethany had talked to her about it. She said she didn't understand why Bethany didn't go out with Cole; after all, he was a very nice young Christian man.

It was Saturday, and Bethany was excited that her three friends would be arriving momentarily. She had talked to them on the phone, but she hadn't seen them since they'd all graduated from college six months earlier.

Bethany took the elevator to the lobby. She was sure Stephanie would be here by now. Bethany walked into the dining room, and when she called Stephanie's name, Stephanie turned around and rushed toward her. They embraced, hugging each other and laughing.

"I've missed you so much! It's so good to see you," Bethany cried.

"I've missed you, too. I'm glad to finally be here—the lodge is even more beautiful than the brochure pictured it."

Before Bethany could answer, Cole stepped into the room. Stephanie glanced at Bethany, and Bethany could easily read that look. *Who is he?* she was asking.

"Cole, this is my friend Stephanie St. John. Stephanie, Cole Beckman."

"Hi, Cole, it's nice to meet you." Stephanie smiled at him.

Bethany watched Stephanie's reaction when Cole flashed that attractive smile back at her. He laid his skis down and shook her hand.

Bethany didn't like the way Stephanie looked at Cole. But why should that bother her? Stephanie glanced at her again, and she could read that look, too. *Hands off? Are you interested in him?*

Was she interested? She didn't want to be, but if she were honest with herself, she couldn't deny he made her heart do flips every time he came into the room. Was this a case of *I don't want him, but no one else can have him? Come on, Bethany get a grip. You need to be concentrating on your new job that will be starting in two more days, not on Cole Beckman. How many times will you have to give yourself this lecture before the truth sinks in?* But no matter how hard she tried to convince herself that she wasn't interested, she knew it wasn't true. Cole had gotten under her skin. Well, she'd just have to try harder. She reached into her pocket for her bag of Peanut M&M's. She offered Cole and Stephanie some. Stephanie looked at the bag and raised her eyebrows at Bethany.

Cole glanced at Stephanie and then back at Bethany. She could see that he clearly realized something was going on that he wasn't privy to, but she was thankful he didn't ask. "No thanks. I think I'll head out and try the slopes for a while."

"It was nice to meet you, Cole."

"My pleasure, Stephanie. I'll see you both at dinner this evening." Cole picked up his skis and headed out the door.

"Okay, Bethany. What's up with Cole Beckman?" Stephanie looked her right in the eye.

"He's the ski instructor for the lodge," Bethany said, glancing away.

"Don't give me that—I know you too well. You're trying very hard not to show it, but you're attracted to him. Others might not see it, but I can read you like a book."

"There's nothing going on, Stephanie. I don't have time for anything right now but getting my career off the ground. I'm not looking for a relationship with anyone."

"Okay, he obviously makes you nervous, because you and I both know that's the only time you scarf Peanut M&M's. But if you want to try to convince yourself there's nothing between the two of you, then we'll play it your way for a while. Now show me to our gorgeous rooms that you e-mailed me about! I can't wait to see our suite."

Bethany was relieved that Stephanie let it drop. She probably knew Bethany better than anyone, and Bethany wouldn't be able to hide her feelings from Stephanie for long.

They went up to the suite. Stephanie was as excited about their rooms as Bethany had been.

"Oh, wow! Bethany, I've never stayed anywhere as beautiful as this."

"It is lovely, isn't it? I took the pink room." Bethany grinned. "I figured you'd want the turquoise one."

"You figured right. I love this room. And we already know Scarlett will choose the purple one, and Michaela will want the yellow one."

"Yep. So we'll all be happy. Gram did a good job choosing colors, considering she didn't know what you three would like."

"She sure did. It's so good to see her and your grandfather again. I always enjoyed it when they came to visit us at college."

Bethany glanced at her watch. "Oh, goodness. Speaking of Gram and Papa, we'd better head downstairs. It's almost time for lunch."

Bethany wondered about Cole when he didn't return for lunch. She hoped he was all right. She knew she shouldn't even be thinking about him, much less worrying about him. He'd said just before he left that he'd see them at dinner, so obviously he hadn't planned to return for lunch. This was ridiculous. She'd been fretting about seeing him, and now she was fretting about *not* seeing him. She had to gain control of her emotions.

Bethany and Stephanie could hardly wait to get downstairs.

Scarlett was due to arrive any minute and Michaela would be here about an hour or so later.

"Do I look all right, Bethany?" Stephanie came out of her room wearing a navy blue dress with red accessories.

"You look wonderful as usual. But we'd better go, or we'll be late." Bethany was dressed just the opposite of her friend—she wore a red dress with navy blue accessories.

They barely made it downstairs on time. Bethany grabbed Stephanie by the arm and said, "There she is—Scarlett." They made their way across the room and exchanged hugs with their friend, who was dressed much as Bethany and Stephanie were.

"Where are your suitcases?" Bethany asked.

"The shuttle driver left them at the concierge desk for me until after dinner."

"Why don't we go over and sit by the fire to wait for Michaela. She'll be here soon." Bethany suggested.

They each poured a cup of coffee from the carafe in the dining room and sat down to wait. It seemed like an eternity to Bethany but was actually only an hour and a half until Michaela walked in the door. The young women hugged, laughing and excited to see each other.

"It's so good to see all of you!" "Michaela's face brightened. I couldn't wait to get here."

"It's so good to all be together again." Bethany said. "Michaela where is your luggage."

"I left it at the concierge desk. He said he'd bring it up when we're ready for it."

"Good he can bring yours and mine at the same time then." Scarlet smiled."

After dinner, Bethany introduced Scarlett and Michaela to Cole. When he'd walked in this evening, she had been relieved to see he was back and safe. After the introductions were completed, the new arrivals announced they were tired, so they all went up to their suite. Just as Bethany and Stephanie had guessed, Scarlett chose the purple room and Michaela the yellow one.

Bethany looked at Michaela when she noticed she only had one small suitcase. But before she could ask, Michaela explained. "I just had this one suitcase brought up with what I'd need for tonight. I met a little girl named Lynzie in the restaurant when I stopped for lunch. She and her father, Jonas Brooks, live with his parents next door. Her mother died a few years ago. She wanted so bad to come over and help me unpack, I didn't have the heart to say no. She and her father are coming over after church tomorrow to bring up the rest of my luggage and boxes."

Sunday morning dawned cold and blustery. Bethany listened to the weather forecast as the other three girls finished getting ready for church. "The weatherman said the roads wouldn't be bad before evening. We should be able to make it to the service and back without too much trouble." Bethany shut off the TV and grabbed her coat and purse. "I'm ready if you guys are."

"Well, Scarlett and I are," Stephanie said as she slipped her coat on. "Michaela, how much longer before you're ready? We need to leave."

"Here I am. I'm ready."

Bethany held the door open for her friends. They took the elevator down to the lobby. As the doors opened, they saw Cole standing with Bethany's grandparents. Bethany experienced a moment of displeasure at seeing him, but she chided herself. That wasn't a very Christian response. She should be happy he would be attending church. If she were honest with herself, she would have to admit she *was* glad he was going with them. She just didn't want to be, and that's what was causing her displeasure. *I'm sorry, Lord, for my first reaction. I'm glad Cole is coming to church. Please forgive me.*

They all greeted one another and went out to her grandparents' Cadillac Escalade, which had all-wheel drive. She knew it should get them to town and back without any trouble.

Papa pulled into the parking lot and found a space fairly close to the front doors of the church. The pavement wasn't icy yet, but it was covered with a dusting of fresh snow. They made their way carefully in case it was becoming slick. Cole was the first to reach the door, and he held it open for everyone. Bethany waited in the foyer until everyone else was inside, and they all went into the auditorium together. The minister greeted them as they walked in.

"Good morning, Mack, Elizabeth. I see you have company this morning." The minister smiled.

"Yes, Brother Adam, this is our granddaughter, Bethany Stillman, and her three friends, Scarlett McKaye, Stephanie St. John, and Michaela Christiansen. They've come to work for us at the lodge for the winter." They shook hands. Mack then turned and said, "And this is Cole Beckman. He's working for us also, as a ski instructor."

"It's nice to meet all of you. I'm glad you've come. I hope you'll continue to join us each week."

"It's nice to meet you, too, Brother Adam." Bethany waited while the others spoke to the minister, then they all walked down the aisle and sat down about halfway back from the front. This was a small, old-fashioned church that was beautifully done with stained-glass windows, a balcony with white railing up above them, and white pews with deep red velvet cushions.

"Nice church," Stephanie whispered.

"Yes, it is. According to Gram, it's been here for over a hundred years. It's been kept up very well over the years by the parishioners." Bethany shared quietly what she'd been told by her grandmother.

"That's amazing," Scarlett whispered back. Michaela nodded.

Bethany glanced around. It *was* amazing that the church had been here so long and was still in such good condition. The pulpit was made of dark wood that matched the organ and piano. It was a quaint little church, warm and welcoming. It reminded Bethany of the church on the front of the Christmas card she had received from her parents the day before. It pictured a white chapel set out in the snow with pine trees all around, and had a white steeple with a bell tower just like this one. The bell had been ringing as they drove into the parking lot this morning, sending a charming greeting to everyone close enough to hear.

The message that morning touched Bethany. It was about counting your blessings, putting your priorities in order, and realizing what was most important in life. It really made her think, on the way back to the lodge, about how blessed she was.

Chapter 5

The following morning, Bethany went downstairs to start her new job. She had just walked off of the elevator when her grandmother met her.

"Bethany, I was just going to call you. There's been an accident out on the bunny slopes. One of the children has been injured."

"I was just about to go out and take a look around. I'll go right now, Gram." Bethany grabbed the first-aid kit Gram and Papa had packed and went out the door. She took one of the snowmobiles up the hill. When she arrived, Cole was there with the injured child, a little boy who appeared to be about eight years old.

"How is he, Cole?" Bethany knelt down beside him in the snow and opened the first-aid kit.

Immediately she felt the ice-cold wetness soak through her snow pants, and she realized they needed to take care of this child quickly so they could get him in where it was warm. Cole was holding a handkerchief against a cut on the child's head.

"It's not bad enough to need sutures. If you have antiseptic, antibiotic ointment, and butterfly bandages in that kit, we'll be in good shape."

"I have all three in here." Bethany took out a gauze pad and a bottle of antiseptic while Cole talked to the parents. He assured them that Bradly would be just fine, that his cut wasn't anything serious. Bethany and Cole quickly cleaned up and bandaged the boy, and he and his parents were on their way back to the lodge within minutes. Bethany was touched by the kindness Cole had shown Bradly and his parents. They were scared, and he'd put them at ease with just a few words. She could see why he was a good paramedic; he worked well with people during emergencies. Bethany was impressed with Cole's compassion. She could see Christian love in the way he'd dealt with this situation, and it also had been evident on the plane when he'd cared for the older gentleman. Her grandparents were fortunate; they'd received two for one in Cole—a paramedic and a ski instructor.

The following week, Bethany, Scarlett, Stephanie, and Michaela spent the days working and the evenings in their suite playing games and putting a puzzle together in front of the fire. Bethany and Cole had helped Scarlett to set up puzzles and organize games in between Cole's ski lessons and Bethany's doctoring of cuts and bruises. Cole had asked her to go snowmobiling, to the movies, and out to dinner. Each time she had politely refused. She hoped he'd eventually realize it wasn't personal; she just wasn't interested in dating anyone right now.

On her way to the elevator that evening, one of the guests

stopped her and asked for some antiseptic and a Band-Aid; she had cut her hand. Bethany took her to the infirmary and helped her clean and bandage the hand. She thought afterward, on the way up to her room, that treating the injury had at least taken her mind off of Cole for a little while.

Thanksgiving Day dawned overcast with snow falling steadily. Bethany rushed downstairs with Stephanie, Scarlett, and Michaela to help Gram and Papa serve a big turkey dinner to all of their guests so the food-service staff could be home with their families. Bethany was setting tables when she saw Cole enter with her grandfather; they had brought in the last of the wood for the fireplace that had been stacked outside. Scarlett told Bethany that an order of wood, along with a Christmas tree for the main room, was to be delivered the following morning. Obviously Cole had offered to help her grandfather carry in the wood, she realized.

He flashed that smile again that caused her heart to beat double time. She tried to ignore him but it was hard to do. He pulled off his jacket, and the medium blue sweater he wore brought out the blue in his eyes, as if they needed any enhancement. They were gorgeous. *Bethany, you shouldn't even be noticing Cole Beckman, much less how beautiful his eyes are. Get your mind back on what you're supposed to be doing.*

When dinner was served, she and Cole wound up at the same table, with him sitting right across from her, so she had no choice but to talk to him. It didn't help that she found, after spending an hour eating Thanksgiving dinner with Cole, that she really liked him. After everyone had been fed and the games they'd had in the lobby after dinner were finished, Bethany and her friends stayed to help clean up.

Later that night, Bethany sat down with Stephanie, Scarlett, and Michaela at the folding table they had placed in front of the fireplace in their room. On the table was a puzzle of Busch Stadium she had bought. She was an avid St. Louis Cardinals fan, and they'd been working on the puzzle for the last two evenings. When they were finished, Bethany planned to glue it to a board, put it in a frame, and hang it on her bedroom wall.

She'd just found a puzzle piece to fit into one of the spaces, when Stephanie said, "Okay, Bethany, why do you keep turning Cole down? From what you've told us, he's a good Christian, he's very nice looking, he has a great personality, and he seems to be genuinely interested in you. It's got to be because of what Roger did, but you have to realize that not all guys will cheat on you. You can't avoid relationships forever because one guy betrayed you. Roger is an ex-boyfriend, for crying out loud. You need to put him in that slot, leave him there, and go on with your life."

Bethany looked at Stephanie. "He was a little more than an ex-boyfriend. We were engaged to be married." She reached into her pocket for her Peanut M&M's.

"We know, Bethany, but Stephanie is right." Scarlett patted her hand gently. "You have too much love to give. You need a good man in your life. You can juggle your job and a relationship— that's just an excuse, and we all know it."

"Okay, I might as well put in my two cents," Michaela said with a caring smile. "We love you, Bethany, but you already know that. We just want to see you happy. You haven't been truly happy since that jerk broke your heart. It's been two years, Bethany—it's time you let it go. The Lord has someone out there for you. Who knows, maybe it's Cole. If you don't give him a chance, you might miss the great future the Lord has planned for you."

Bethany looked at all three of her friends. She couldn't bring herself to be upset with them, because she knew they meant well. She popped a couple of M&M's into her mouth. "I know, but I'm just not ready yet."

"Well, you'd better get ready, because that hunk of a guy isn't going to hang around forever. He'll eventually give up, figuring it's a lost cause," added Scarlett.

Bethany glanced at her friends, knowing they had her best interests at heart. "I can't promise I'll change my mind, but I will pray about it." Bethany found the place for her puzzle piece and fitted it into the slot.

"Well, we can't ask any more than that, and we'll continue to pray with you." Stephanie smiled and took a couple of the M&M's Bethany offered.

"Not to change the subject or anything," Bethany said with a smile, "but thanks for helping today. My grandparents couldn't have done it by themselves."

"We were glad to help," Scarlett said, and Michaela and Stephanie nodded.

"You guys are the best." Bethany hugged each of them.

"Yeah, well, the feeling's mutual. Now put away those M&M's and let's go to bed and try to get some rest tonight." Stephanie stood and pushed her chair in.

Bethany put the M&M's into her purse and they went to their rooms.

The next evening, Scarlett, Stephanie, and Michaela decided to go shopping, but Bethany opted to stay at the lodge and have dinner with her grandparents. She was sitting at the table visiting with them when she noticed Cole at the table right behind her. He was with three guys about his age and two teenage boys. She became aware of bits and pieces of their conversation and realized they were discussing Bible verses; Cole was giving them the plan of salvation, along with relevant scriptures. One of the teens asked several questions, and Cole had an answer for each one. Cole certainly knew his Bible. Bethany noticed that her grandparents had become quiet. They were listening to Cole, too, so she turned her attention completely to what he was saying.

"Shane, are you ready to accept Jesus as your Savior?" Cole asked softly.

"I'd like to. Can you can show me how, Cole?"

"You just need to ask the Lord to forgive your sins and to be your Savior. I'll help you by saying the prayer, and you repeat the words after me, okay?"

"Okay." The teen bowed his head.

Together they prayed, "Lord, I know I've sinned. I ask You

to please forgive me and to come into my heart as my Lord and Savior. I want to live for You. Please help me and guide me, Lord, in all that I do throughout my life. Thank You, Lord. Amen."

"Wow, Cole! I can't believe how great I feel. It's like a huge weight has been lifted from my shoulders. I can't even begin to explain this feeling." He grinned, and Bethany couldn't help but look his way and be excited for him.

"I'm sorry, we didn't mean to eavesdrop, but we couldn't help but hear. We're so excited for you!" Bethany smiled.

"Welcome to the family, Shane," Mack said, reaching over to shake his hand. "As Christians, we're all part of the family of God."

They were sitting in the back corner of the room, so the other guests didn't realize what had just taken place. Once again Bethany was impressed with Cole's Christian witness.

"Thanks, Mack. Carl and I have been best friends since we were in grade school. He and Cole have been talking with me about God for quite a while."

"Bethany, this is my little brother Carlton. He and his friend Shane Benson, and three of my best friends—Chancelor Huntington, Scott Chambers, and Hunter Nelson—checked in this afternoon. Your grandparents met them when they registered. Guys, this is Bethany Stillman, Mack and Elizabeth's granddaughter and our in-house RN," Cole explained.

"It's nice to meet you. And Shane, congratulations on your decision. It's the best one you'll ever make," Bethany said.

"I think I can speak for all of us, Bethany—meeting you is

our pleasure." The other men nodded their heads. "We had to come up and check on this guy here." Chancelor laid his hand on Cole's shoulder. "He's pretty special to all of us, and we had to see for ourselves how he's doing."

Mack stood and made an announcement. "To finish off the evening, Cole and Carl Beckman have graciously agreed to play a couple of numbers for us."

Cole played "Fiddlers Dream" and Carl accompanied him on the guitar. Bethany sat back and listened. They were both exceptional musicians.

When they were through playing, everyone in the room stood and applauded. Cole and Carl bowed, thanked everyone, and returned to their table.

"You two are really something. That was wonderful," Bethany exclaimed.

"Yep, you did it again. But that's no surprise." Chancelor slapped Cole on the back and brushed his hand through Carl's hair affectionately. "These two, along with their family, are hands down the best in bluegrass."

"That's for sure!" Scott, Shane, and Hunter said in unison, and everyone laughed.

"Well, Shane and I are going up to our room. It's been a long day. We'll see ya'll in the morning." Carl and Shane stood, pushed their chairs to the table, and said good night.

"Good night, guys," Bethany chorused as they walked toward the elevator.

"Well, I think I'll call it a night, too." Bethany hugged her grandparents. "Thanks for dinner. I'll see you in the morning."

She headed to the elevator, and her grandparents went to the kitchen.

"Well, bud. I can see why you're attracted to her. She's a pretty little thing. Obviously you haven't told her who you are."

"Not yet."

Chancelor looked directly at Cole. "You need to tell her before you get involved with her. You're looking to get hurt, Cole. There's a lot of animosity where her dad's concerned, and when she realizes you were the driver of the car that night, well, it's not going to be an easy thing to get past."

"You're right, but I'm hoping to get to know her before I drop that bit of news. If she knows who I am, I'll never have a chance with her. I haven't given up trying to win her over, and I'm hoping, Lord willing, that by the time I do, she'll care enough that she'll be able to forgive me." Cole watched Bethany walk to the elevator.

"I hope you're right. I'll sure be praying about it," Chancelor said.

"Thanks. I've only known her for two weeks, but I felt a connection between us the minute I met her on the plane. I feel the Lord has a future planned for us, and I think it started back ten years ago on that cold winter night. I don't know how it'll happen, but one thing I do know is that the Lord is bigger than all of this. If He plans for us to be together, He'll work it out. As frustrating as it is, I feel she's worth waiting for, so I'll be patient and pray."

"I'll be praying, too, Cole." Scott drank the rest of his coffee.

"Well, guys, we know the power of prayer. Nothing is impossible with the Lord." Hunter drank the last of his iced tea and set his glass on the table. "I don't know about the rest of you, but I'm bushed. It's been a long day."

"Yeah, I think it's time we called it a night. And, guys, thanks for the prayers and coming out here. It means a lot." Cole stood and pushed his chair under the table.

"Hey, what are friends for?" Chancelor laid his napkin on the table as he stood up.

"That's right," Scott agreed.

"You know us, bud—we always stick together. When one has a problem, we're all there. Just be careful, Cole. I'm with Chancelor. I don't want to see you get hurt. You've been through enough," Hunter stated.

Cole gave each of them a one-arm hug. "Thanks. See you in the morning."

Cole headed upstairs to his room. He was fortunate to have those three for friends. They'd been close since fourth grade. Their friendship seemed to get stronger as time went by, and he'd trust his life to any of the three. He knew they'd be praying for him and Bethany. He couldn't seem to get anywhere with her. She'd talk and cut up with him, and she seemed to enjoy his company. But when he'd ask her to spend time with him alone, she'd politely refused.

Father, You know what's best, and I ask that You would soften Bethany's heart toward me. Please work this out according to Your will. Thank You, Lord. Amen.

Cole felt better after his prayer. He knew he needed to tell Bethany who he was soon, but he wasn't looking forward to it. He was tired, so he brushed his teeth and went to bed.

Chapter 6

Bethany pulled the carton of milk from their small refrigerator, poured some into a cup, and placed it in the microwave. "Anyone want some hot chocolate?"

Stephanie lifted her cup. "I have coffee, but thanks."

"Me, too," Scarlett said.

"I'll take a cup, please," Michaela said as she sat down at the table in their small kitchen.

Bethany gave her the cup she'd just made and fixed another for herself. "Since it's Saturday, I'm going to spend the day skiing. Anyone game?"

"No, thanks," all three said in unison.

"Okay. Guess I'll go by myself." Bethany took a sip of her hot chocolate.

"Be careful and stay in a populated area if you're going alone," Scarlett cautioned. "And while you're up there in the quiet by yourself, I suggest you take time to talk to the Lord about Cole. He could be your future mate."

"I'll think about it. And I'll be careful, but it's not like I'll be totally alone. The slopes are full of skiers this time of year." Bethany finished her chocolate, rinsed the cup, and put it in the dishwasher. "I'll see you all later."

Bethany checked out a pair of skis from the lodge ski shop, told her grandparents she'd be out for the day, and headed up to the lifts. Ski lifts weren't her favorite part of skiing, but they were the only way to get to the top of the hill. She showed the man in charge her ski pass and hopped onto the next lift. Bethany didn't like the way lifts would swing back and forth as they traveled. She always felt like she was about to fall off, so she held on for dear life until the lift came to a complete stop. She hopped off of the lift and slipped her skis on. She pulled her gloves off long enough to buckle her ski boots good and tight, then tugged them back on to keep her hands warm. Then she skied over to the intermediate slopes.

Bethany breathed in the pine scent. It was so beautiful up here, truly a winter wonderland. She pushed off with her ski poles. The cold wind blew against her mask, the damp air numbing her skin. But in spite of that she loved the feel of sailing down the slopes as if she didn't have a care in the world. That became her routine for the remainder of the afternoon. Her last time up to the top, she decided to try a different run. It was one of the advanced slopes, and she was excited by the challenge.

As she pushed off, she thought about Cole. Were her friends right? Was she using her new career as an excuse not to see him? Was the real reason she wouldn't go out with Cole that she was afraid of getting hurt again? *Lord, what should I do? I have to admit I have feelings for Cole, and I'd like to get to know him, but I'm afraid. Roger just pretended to be a Christian, and he betrayed me. I know Cole isn't Roger, and I've seen Your light shine through him. Deep down I know that Cole isn't pretending. He truly loves You. Guide me, Lord. Please help me to make the right decision.*

Bethany skied for a while longer, thinking about Cole and whether she wanted to take a chance and go out with him. After a while she stopped and pulled her goggles off so she could look around; she didn't see any other skiers or hear anyone nearby as she had earlier. Her surroundings were totally quiet—eerily so. She didn't recognize the area. How long had it been since she'd seen anyone? She didn't know, and that was unnerving. What had Scarlett told her just before she left this morning? Not to get off the beaten path. And she had done just that.

Panic gripped her when she realized she was lost. Where did this run lead? If she skied to the bottom, where would she come out? Would it be somewhere familiar or would she be even more lost? *Okay, Bethany, get a hold of yourself. Panicking isn't going to help.* There weren't a lot of choices at this point—she couldn't ski up the slope, and she couldn't stay here. The only option was to go down no matter where she wound up; maybe it would be somewhere she recognized. She then noticed it was beginning to snow.

Bethany took a deep breath to calm herself and put her goggles back on before she started down the hill. She hadn't gone far when she hit loose, untracked snow. Her skis stuck fast, one knee twisting painfully, and the next thing she knew, she was falling, falling, toppling head over heels down the slope. Her last coherent thought as her head connected painfully with something solid was the realization that she was going to die out here, all alone.

"Hi, Elizabeth." Cole sat down at the table across from her in the dining room with a cup of coffee. He had just finished a Bible study and devotional with the guys. Shane, being a new Christian, had had several questions they'd tried to answer. Elizabeth glanced up at Cole, and he could see right away something wasn't right. "Elizabeth, what's wrong?"

"Well, I hope nothing, Cole. But Bethany went out skiing this morning and she hasn't returned. It isn't like her to be out this long. I'd ask Mack to go look for her but he went to town to run some errands. I'm probably worrying for nothing, but in another hour and a half it'll be dark. I just can't understand her not being back by now."

Cole set his coffee cup on the table. "I'll take one of the snowmobiles and go look for her. Don't worry. I'm sure she's fine. She probably just lost track of time. I'll find her, and we'll be back in a little while. If she comes in, call me—I'll take one of the radios and clip it to my belt."

"Thank you, Cole. I appreciate it. I'm sure you're right and she's fine, but just in case something is wrong, I'll feel better knowing you're out looking for her."

Cole tried to reassure Elizabeth, but he was worried himself. Something *must* be wrong. As Cole went out the door, he glanced around; all he could see for miles were ski slopes in the distance and snow-covered mountains. He stopped and took just a moment to bow his head and pray. *Please, Lord, lead me in the right direction. Help me find Bethany. Please let her be all right. In Jesus' name I pray, amen.*

Cole continued out to the shed where the snowmobiles were housed and chose one that would hold two passengers. He started up the hill that led to the intermediate slopes, praying that's where she'd be. Over the next hour, he covered all of the intermediate slopes and every area he could possibly imagine Bethany could be, but she was nowhere to be found. Where in the world was she? The temperature was dropping rapidly; she'd freeze to death before morning. And if he didn't find her soon, it would be dark. *Please help me to find her, Lord,* Cole prayed frantically.

Bethany slowly regained consciousness and became aware of her surroundings. Her knee was throbbing to the point of making her nauseous. She slowly sat up, trying to get her bearings. She was dizzy and her head hurt. Where was she? What had happened to her? Then all at once she remembered exactly what had happened—she'd fallen down the ski slope. Looking up the hill, she realized she was fortunate to be alive. She hurt all over; she feared she'd be bruised from head to toe. Of course, it wouldn't matter if someone didn't find her soon. It was snowing steadily, and it would be dark before long. She could freeze to death out here. Were there animals that came out at night looking for food? That wasn't a very cheerful notion. She felt she'd rather freeze than be eaten. She shuddered at the thought.

"Please, Lord, forgive me for being so foolish, and send someone to find me. I don't want to die out here." She prayed softly as tears rolled down her cheeks. Bethany didn't know when she'd ever been so scared. She was *so* cold; her body was shaking. The temperature was dropping rapidly, and she was getting sleepy. But she knew better than to go to sleep. She shook her head trying to stay awake. Her teeth were chattering, and she knew she was going to be in real trouble if someone didn't find her soon. Gradually she became aware of a distant noise. A snowmobile? She heard the engine fade away and feared it was gone. "Oh, Lord, please help them to find me. Don't let them leave without me!" She'd barely finished her prayer when she heard someone calling her name.

"I'm here! Please help me!" she yelled, and the engine started up again.

A minute later, a snowmobile came over the hill. Bethany waved her arms frantically and prayed the person would see her. The snowmobile driver pulled up as close to her as possible and shut off the engine. She realized it was Cole when he knelt down beside her. *Oh, thank You, Lord.*

"Bethany, what happened? Are you hurt?"

Through chattering teeth, she said, "I–I'm so glad to see you, Cole." She wrapped her arms around his neck. "I g–got lost, and then I hit deep powder about halfway down this slope. My skis got hung up, and the n–next thing I knew, I was falling." She started to cry.

"Take it easy, darlin'. It's going to be all right. I'll get you out of here and get you warmed up. How bad and where are you hurt?"

Bethany moved her arms from around Cole's neck. "I h—hurt everywhere, but I don't think I'm badly injured except maybe my knee. It's throbbing. I don't know what I've done to it, but I know I can't stand on it." She looked at him.

"Did you lose consciousness?"

"I must have—I don't remember actually hitting bottom."

"Does your neck or back hurt?"

"Only b—bruised I think. I can turn my head okay."

Cole took the pen light out of his pocket and shined it in her eyes. She knew he was checking for signs of a concussion. He then checked her knee. He was very gentle, but she gasped at the pain.

"I'm sorry, Bethany. I didn't mean to hurt you. I don't think it's broken, but we need to take you for X-rays to be sure. I'm going to lift you onto the snowmobile." Cole glanced at the sky. "It's snowing so hard, if we don't get out of here in the next few minutes, we aren't going to make it back. I'll be as gentle as I can when I move you."

"I know. Do what you have to, Cole. I'll m—manage."

Cole lifted Bethany, and she felt him wince as she cried out. He gently set her onto the back of the snowmobile. "I'm sorry. Are you okay?"

"Yes, it just hurt more than I thought it would to move my knee. I don't think I can bend it to put it on the peg, Cole." She was touched by his caring, gentle way of handling her.

"Let me get on and put my foot on my peg. I'll help you slide your leg inside mine, between it and the snowmobile, and then your leg can rest against mine. My leg will keep yours from bouncing too much. It's going to hurt any way we go about it, but I think this will be the best we can do."

"Okay. And thanks, Cole, for coming after me. I thought I might die out here." After the way she'd avoided him and turned down his invitations ever since she'd met him, she was surprised he'd even bothered. But she was sure glad he had.

"Sure, darlin'. I'm just glad I found you. I was getting worried after more than an hour of searching."

Bethany leaned close so she could hear Cole over the noise of the snowmobile. He radioed the lodge, and her grandfather answered. Bethany heard him tell her grandfather that he had found her; once again she appreciated Cole's kindness. She knew Gram and Papa must be frantic by now, and her girlfriends would be, too. She listened as he explained that he didn't think she was seriously injured but he was concerned about her knee. And she'd had a concussion, so she needed to be taken to the hospital to be checked.

"Your grandfather said they will have the Escalade ready to take you to the hospital as soon as we arrive."

They had gone about halfway when they got stuck in a snowbank for the second time. Cole rocked the snowmobile back and forth until it finally broke loose, and they were on their way again. But they had lost precious time. It was totally dark now, and the snow was coming down so hard, they couldn't see anything.

"We need to pray that we're heading in the right direction, Bethany."

"You drive, and I'll pray. We'll make it, Cole." Bethany knew he was concerned that they'd hit a tree. "Please, Lord, we can't see, but You can, and I ask You to send Your guardian angels to go before us and guide us safely down the mountain. And, Lord, please help my knee not to be too badly injured. Thank You, Lord, for sending Cole to find me and for protecting me. In Jesus' name I pray, amen." Bethany prayed out loud against Cole's ear, and she heard him echo her "amen."

Bethany's knee was hurting so badly, she couldn't hold back the tears. She prayed it wouldn't be much longer.

"We're almost there, darlin'. I'll get you off this thing soon, and your knee into a more comfortable position," Cole said gently.

Bethany didn't want anyone to see her cry, but she just couldn't help it. The pain in her knee was almost unbearable. She prayed Cole was right and that they were near the lodge. She didn't know how much more she could stand.

Chapter 7

"Okay, darlin'—here we are, safe and sound." Cole parked the snowmobile next to Bethany's grandfather's SUV. "Thank You, Lord," he prayed out loud and heard Bethany echo *him* this time. He lifted her carefully from the back of the snowmobile and carried her to the Escalade.

"Easy now." He placed her gently in the back so she could lay her leg on the seat, and climbed in behind her. He covered her with the blanket Elizabeth handed to him.

"Are we ever glad to see you. Your grandmother and I were so worried. We love you, sunshine." Mack turned the key in the ignition and started down the mountain toward the hospital.

"I'm sorry. I didn't mean to worry you." Bethany laid her head against the doorframe.

Cole brushed the hair out of her face that had come loose from her ponytail when she'd pulled her hat off. "Is your head hurting?"

"Yes, it's throbbing, but not as much as my knee."

"We'll be there soon, and the doc will give you something for the pain."

"Thanks again for coming after me."

"There's no need for thanks. I'm just glad I found you." He took a handkerchief from his pocket and wiped the tears as they spilled over and ran down her cheeks. "I wish there was more I could do to make it easier for you. . . ."

Cole would be glad when they got to the hospital. He couldn't stand to see her in pain and not be able to help. All his training, and there wasn't anything he could do for her. He held her hand and talked to her softly all the way down the mountain to the hospital. Mack parked, and Cole jumped out and ran inside. In a few minutes he was back with an orderly and a gurney. He opened the door of the SUV, gently lifted Bethany out, and carefully laid her on the gurney. He held her hand all the way to the examining room in the ER.

"I'll be right here when you come out. They'll take good care of you." Cole squeezed her hand gently before letting go.

Elizabeth gave the young lady at the counter enough of Bethany's information to get the paperwork started, and then went in with Bethany while Cole and Mack sat anxiously in the waiting room. An hour and a half later, Bethany was brought to them in a wheelchair with her knee bound in a heavy Ace bandage.

"What did the doc say?" Mack asked before Cole had the chance.

"After X-rays of my head and knee, he said I have a minor concussion, lots of bruises, and pulled muscles in my knee. I was fortunate. I could have been killed. He gave me an injection for pain, something for nausea, and told me never to go skiing by myself again. He told me to take it easy for a day or two, to use my crutches, and stay off of my knee for the first week. Then I can gradually put weight on the knee. He wants to see me again in two weeks." Bethany closed her eyes, and Cole knew she was exhausted on top of the meds the doc had given her. If they didn't get her out to the car, she was going to slide right out onto the floor.

Cole took hold of the handles of her wheelchair. "Let's get you home and into bed while the meds the doc gave you are still working. Hopefully you can get some rest tonight before they wear off; then you'll need to take some more. He did give you something for pain to take home for tonight, right?" Cole glanced at Elizabeth when he realized that Bethany had fallen asleep.

He saw Elizabeth take a bag of Peanut M&M's from Bethany's hand before she dropped them, and then answered for her as Mack held the door open for him to push the wheelchair through. They followed him outside.

"Yes, he did, and a prescription to fill tomorrow for pain meds and muscle relaxers."

"Thanks so much, Cole. I don't know how we can ever repay you for bringing our girl back to us safe," Mack said and choked up as they made their way out to the SUV.

Elizabeth laid her hand on her husband's arm. She looked up at Cole, and he could see the tears in her eyes as she nodded.

"You don't owe me anything. She's okay, and that's all that

matters." He lifted a very drowsy Bethany into the back of the Escalade, covered her with the blanket, and once again climbed in behind her for the trip to the ski lodge. "Okay, now I have to ask—what's with the Peanut M&M's?"

Elizabeth glanced back at Cole and smiled. "Annie, Bethany's mother, calls them Bethany's 'crutch.'"

"Her crutch?"

"Yes. Everyone has their way of dealing with uncomfortable situations. Well, ever since Bethany was a little girl, her way is to eat Peanut M&M's."

After Elizabeth's explanation, they fell silent the rest of the way up the hill. Bethany slept. When they got back to the Snowbird Lodge, Cole carried Bethany inside and followed Elizabeth and Mack up to her suite. Scarlett opened the door, and Cole carried Bethany into her room and laid her on her bed. After assuring the three young ladies that Bethany was going to be all right, he went into the living room and waited with Mack while the girls helped Elizabeth get Bethany ready for bed. A few minutes later, Elizabeth called the men in to say good night.

Cole stooped down beside Bethany's bed and took her hand. "How are you doing, darlin'?"

"I. . .wouldn't have made it without you, Cole." She could hardly keep her eyes open.

"Try not to think about that anymore. It's behind us. Just concentrate on getting well. I'm going to go, darlin', so you can rest. I'll check on you in the morning. Good night." He gently squeezed her hand before he left the room.

Mack walked Cole to the door. "Thanks again, Cole. You'll never know how much we appreciate all your help."

"No thanks needed, Mack. Call if you need me in the night."

"I will, son. Good night."

Cole left and headed up the hall to his room. He was tired and his bed would look pretty good right about now. But first he had to pray. "Thank You, Lord, for helping me find Bethany, for being with us tonight, and for watching over her. Please heal her knee and her concussion. This could have been a whole lot worse if not for Your watch-care over us. I love You, Lord. In Jesus' name I pray, amen."

The next morning, Cole went down to talk to Elizabeth. He wanted to know how Bethany had fared through the night.

Cole found Elizabeth in the kitchen baking cinnamon rolls. "Good morning. How's Bethany?"

"Good morning, Cole. I talked to her a few minutes ago, and she was sitting up on the sofa enjoying the fire. She said she slept pretty well. Scarlett gave her some crackers and milk, along with a pain pill, at about two this morning."

"It's nice to have friends." Cole accepted the warm cinnamon roll and cup of coffee Elizabeth handed to him. "Thanks. I figured they'd take good care of her."

"Yes, I knew they would. Those girls have been friends so long." She filled a plate with warm cinnamon rolls. "I told Bethany I'd send some of these up with Mack, but maybe you'd like to take them?" She smiled. "I'll see you at church. The girls are going to stay here with Bethany."

"I'll take them up right now." Cole picked up the plate and headed up to Bethany's room.

He would stay a few minutes and then head downstairs to meet the guys in time to go to church. Afterward, Shane and Carl would catch their flight back home. Cole would go with Chancelor, Scott, and Hunter to see them off, and then they planned to go into Incline Village for a while. Maybe he'd pick up some flowers for Bethany.

Cole knocked on Bethany's door, and Scarlett answered.

"Good morning, Cole. Come on in. Umm, those cinnamon rolls smell heavenly." Scarlett closed the door. "Sit down. How about a cup of coffee?"

Cole set the rolls on the table and took the chair across from Bethany. She had her leg propped up on a pillow that rested on the coffee table. "That sounds good, Scarlett. Thank you. How are you doing this morning, darlin'?"

Cole wanted to hold Bethany's hand but he resisted. She'd held his hand last night, but he wasn't sure if that was only due to the circumstances, and he didn't want to do anything to make her uncomfortable. Considering the number of times she'd brought out the Peanut M&M's when she'd been around him, he hadn't been successful in making her feel comfortable in the past. He hoped to be able to change that. He spent just a few minutes visiting with Bethany and her friends and then walked over to the small kitchen and placed his cup into the sink.

"Thanks for the coffee. I'd better go so I won't be late for church. I'm glad you feel like being up this morning, Bethany. Is there anything you want from town?"

"Not that I can think of, but thanks anyway."

"I'll check on you when I get back. If you need anything before then, call me on my cell." He handed her his business card. "Take it easy today, okay?"

"I will. Thanks for coming by, Cole. I'll see you this evening."

He nodded, opened the door, and walked out, closing it softly behind him.

Chapter 8

Cole and his friends spent the afternoon at Incline Village. Just before they left to go back to the lodge, they stopped at the florist and picked up a bouquet of long-stemmed pink roses with baby's breath that Cole had ordered for Bethany earlier in the day. As they'd wandered around in the village, he'd also purchased a vase at one of the stores they visited.

"You've got it bad, bud," Chancelor said when Cole got back into the car.

"Long-stemmed roses, huh? Bet that set you back a pretty penny." Scott grinned.

Hunter whistled. "I sure hope she's worth it."

"Trust me—she is." Cole fastened his seat belt.

The guys took Cole back to the lodge and picked up their luggage. It was time to return the rental car and catch their plane back to Springfield, Missouri.

"Have a good flight, and plan to come up again before I leave in the spring." Cole gave each of them a one-arm hug.

"Take care, buddy. I wish you the best with Bethany." Chancelor laid his hand on Cole's shoulder.

"Yeah, keep in touch and let us know what's happening." Scott playfully slapped him on the back.

"We'll expect e-mail frequently with updates," Hunter said with a grin.

"Don't worry, you'll hear from me. But all kidding aside, it means a lot that you guys came. You're the best. Take care, and have a safe trip back."

Cole picked up the flowers from the table where he'd set them to say good-bye to his friends and headed up to Bethany's room. He hoped she'd been okay. He'd thought about calling. He'd been anxious about her, but he knew he needed to take this slow, so he had waited to talk to her until this evening.

Stephanie answered the door when he knocked. "Hi, Cole. Come in."

"Hi, Stephanie. How's Bethany?"

"She's doing pretty well, as you can see for yourself." She indicated Bethany on the sofa when he walked into the room.

"Hi. You look great. These are for you." Cole handed her the vase and flowers. He loved the way her eyes lit up as she opened the box.

"Oh, Cole. . ." She smiled brightly at him. "They're beautiful. Pink roses are my favorite. Thank you!"

Stephanie helped Bethany arrange the flowers in the vase and place them on the coffee table where she could enjoy them.

"Oh, they're so pretty. I love them, Cole. This was so nice of you."

Obviously the flowers were a hit. Cole was glad he'd decided to get them. "It won't be dark for another hour or so. I thought maybe you'd like to get out for a bit. Would you feel like going into Incline Village for ice cream? Mack said we could take the SUV."

Bethany smiled. "I'd like that. But it won't be easy getting down to the car."

"I'll get you there. Your grandfather pulled a wheelchair out of the storage room, and I brought it up with me." Cole helped Bethany into the chair. He whisked her downstairs and into the car. Within minutes they were on their way to the village.

Bethany glanced out the window. "At least it isn't snowing tonight."

"It was earlier, but it was light. Not much accumulation today."

They drove in silence for the next few minutes. "Cole, I feel I owe you an explanation for turning you down so many times when you asked me to go out with you."

Cole glanced over at her. "Not unless you just want to, darlin'. You're here with me now—that's all that matters."

"You've been so patient. Not once did you get upset. You've been so gracious."

"Spending time with you was worth waiting for." He smiled.

"Thanks. It wasn't meant to be personal. I had a bad relationship two years ago, and I'm just leery of getting hurt like that again."

Cole looked over at her. "I'll never hurt you, Bethany."

She looked up at him and nodded. "I believe you mean that, Cole."

"I do mean it. I give you my word, and I don't give it lightly."

"Somehow that doesn't surprise me. I'd like to give us a chance, Cole, but I can't help but be a little afraid of getting involved again."

"Don't be afraid of me, Bethany. I promise. . .if you'll give us that chance, you won't be sorry."

He waited quietly to give her all the time she needed to think about it.

"Okay, Cole. I really like you, so I'm going to trust you."

Cole reached over and squeezed her hand gently. He smiled as he pulled into the parking lot of a local restaurant and parked the car. "Shall we go get that ice cream?"

She grinned. "Sounds good to me."

Cole came around and brought the wheelchair. He lifted Bethany from the car and sat her in the chair. "Okay, milady, your chariot is about to depart." He gave her an exaggerated bow and then pushed her into the restaurant as she chuckled.

Cole loved the sound of her laughter. He hoped to hear it more often. They ordered ice cream sundaes and ate every bite, laughing and having a good time. About an hour later Cole lifted Bethany into the SUV and stowed the wheelchair in the back. He pulled out of the parking lot and headed home.

"Cole, I don't know when I've had as much fun as I did this evening," Bethany said when they got to her suite at the lodge. "Thanks so much."

"I'm glad you enjoyed it. I had a good time, too. We'll do it again soon." Cole reached to unlock and open the door with Bethany's key. Inside, they found Scarlett, Stephanie, and Michaela at the table with Bethany's grandparents.

"Hi. We thought you'd be home soon, so we came up to see you for a few minutes before we went to bed. Did you have a good time?" Gram asked.

"Yes, we did." Bethany smiled up at Cole, and he could see the sparkle of happiness in her pretty brown eyes. "It's just what I needed."

"Well, I'll say good night and let you visit," Cole said. "Call me in the morning and let me know how you're doing, Bethany." Cole kissed Bethany on the cheek, wished the others good night, and headed down the hall to his room.

That night set the trend for the following two weeks. Bethany spent every evening and weekend day with Cole, either in town or in front of the fire in her suite. Cole had taken over her medical duties along with teaching ski lessons. Fortunately, there hadn't been many accidents, so Cole was able to handle both jobs. Now Bethany expected him any minute, and she was getting anxious for him to arrive. Her attitude had certainly undergone a change from a couple of weeks ago, she realized.

Stephanie walked into the room and interrupted her thoughts. "So are you going to tell that poor guy how you feel about him tonight and put him out of his misery?"

"What do you mean?"

"You know exactly what I mean. Cole is head over heels in love with you, Bethany, and you know it. You love him, too. It's written all over your face every time he's around. Why don't you just tell him so he can relax? Scarlett, Michaela, and I are going into town for a while, so you'll have some time to talk to Cole without us being here."

"If you must know, I plan to ask Cole to go with me to meet my parents next weekend." Bethany shifted her leg into a more comfortable position.

"Oh, that's so exciting, Bethany!" Stephanie cried.

"What's exciting?" Scarlett and Michaela said in unison as they came into the room.

"Bethany is going to ask Cole to go with her to meet her parents next weekend. Wedding bells are in the air." Stephanie laughed.

Bethany frowned. "Now don't get ahead of yourself, Stephanie. Nobody mentioned marriage."

"Well, we all know that's usually the next step." Stephanie grinned.

Before Bethany could say anything else, there was a knock at the door, and Scarlett went to answer it. Bethany heard Cole's voice, and she was thrilled to think of an evening with just the two of them sitting by the fire.

"Hi." Cole flashed that smile that set her heart soaring.

"Hi. Come on over here and sit down." She patted the sofa next to her.

"We were just leaving. Cole, there is fresh coffee made if

you want some, and Elizabeth sent up some of her cinnamon rolls a little while ago, so help yourself. We'll be back about ten." Stephanie smiled and followed the other two girls out the door.

"So how are you doing tonight?" Cole leaned over and kissed her.

"Good. I can't wait until tomorrow. I hope the doctor will release me. My knee is so much better."

"What time is your appointment?"

"It's at ten. Papa's going to take me since you have a lesson then."

"I can change my lesson time if you need me to."

"I know, and I appreciate that, but there's no need—Papa can take me."

"Let me know what the doctor says as soon as you can, okay?"

"I will." She paused before continuing. "There's something else I want to talk to you about, Cole."

"What's that?" Cole reached up and slipped her hair behind her ear, causing a shiver to run down her spine.

"On Friday I'm planning to go home for the weekend, and I'd like for you to come with me so you can meet my parents."

"Hmm." Cole turned away from her to look at the fire, and she could sense something was wrong.

"Cole, have I overstepped here? Maybe I've misread your feelings. Maybe you don't care enough for me to want to meet my parents." Tears filled her eyes at the thought, and she reached into her purse for her bag of M&M's.

"No, Bethany. You haven't. That's not it at all." Cole placed his hands on each side of her face and gently turned her toward him. "Don't ever think that."

He reached into his pocket for his handkerchief and wiped the tears that had escaped in spite of her effort to hold them back. She didn't want to cry but was losing the battle.

"I'm very much in love with you, darlin'. There's no question about that."

"Then what is it, Cole? Don't you want to meet my parents?" She popped an M&M into her mouth.

Cole sighed. "It's not that, either. I have something I need to tell you. I've put it off for too long already, but I was afraid you wouldn't want to see me again."

"Cole, what do you mean?" She swallowed the M&M she'd been chewing. "You're scaring me."

"When you introduced yourself to me that day on the plane, Bethany, I recognized your name."

"I remember thinking you looked at me strangely, and that your name sounded vaguely familiar, but I didn't think any more about it. Why would our names be familiar to each other, Cole?"

"Ten years ago, when I was sixteen—I'd only had my driver's license for two weeks—I was driving home from youth group at our church. I hit a patch of black ice and slid through a red light."

Cold chills scudded down Bethany's spine. She knew what he was going to say. "Oh, Cole. No!" Bethany sat there as Cole put his hands over his face and shook his head.

"I'm so sorry, Bethany. I'm the one who is responsible for your grandfather being in that wheelchair. I had nightmares for years after that accident. That's one of the reasons I became a paramedic. I hoped that if I could help people, maybe I could make up—at least a little—for what I took away from your grandfather."

Cole's obvious remorse deeply touched Bethany. *Oh Lord, please help me here. How can I choose between my father and the man who crippled my grandfather, even though I love him desperately?* She had no more than breathed that prayer when a scripture, Colossians 3:13, came to mind. *"Bear with each other and forgive whatever grievances you may have against one another. Forgive as the Lord forgave you."* At that moment Bethany knew the Lord was telling her she needed to forgive Cole. She loved him, and she knew the Lord would somehow work this out.

Bethany shifted her bag of M&M's to her left hand and touched Cole's shoulder. "Cole, you were sixteen years old. It was an accident. Nothing can change things. I love you, and I refuse to let this or anything else come between us. We'll get through this."

Cole looked at her. He loved her more than he'd ever thought it possible to love anyone.

"I love you, too, darlin', more than life itself. But I know how your father feels about me. I doubt he's going to want to see me anytime soon, especially not with his daughter."

"We need to pray for a miracle before we go to see my

parents, Cole. Because that's what it's going to take to change the way my father feels. But I'll take you with me if you're willing to go, and trust the Lord to deal with my dad."

"If you're sure that's what you want to do. . . . I love you, darlin'. I'm willing to do whatever it takes."

"I'm very sure. I love you, too, Cole."

He drew her into his arms and kissed her. "If you want to give me your flight information, I'll make mine to match."

Bethany retrieved her ticket, and Cole wrote down the information. "I was thinking about going home to spend an early Christmas with my family anyway. I told your grandparents I'd stay here to help, since Christmas is a busy time at the lodge. Maybe I'll spend Friday evening and Saturday with my family, and if things work out, we can spend Saturday evening with yours."

"Okay. I'll talk to my parents Friday evening. Why don't you plan to come for supper Saturday evening, and we'll just trust the Lord to work this out, Cole."

He could see the fear in her eyes. "Don't be afraid, darlin'. I believe we're meant to be together. The Lord knows I won't make you choose between me and your father, so I believe He has a plan for us." Cole held her and kissed her again. He loved the way she fit perfectly in his arms. As he held her he began to pray softly. "Lord, this seems like a mountain to us, and we need a miracle here. We know nothing is too big for You. Please help us to trust You to take care of this."

Chapter 9

Cole kissed Bethany good night and went back to his room to call his parents. He explained everything to them and asked them to pray. They assured him that they would, and he told them he'd see them Friday night.

"Tell your mom and dad hello, and we'll see them at Christmas," Elizabeth said. She and Mack kissed Bethany good-bye.

"Cole, take care of our little girl, and we'll see you both Sunday evening," Mack said.

"Oh, Papa." Bethany smiled affectionately. "I'm not a little girl anymore, and since the doctor released me, I can even walk on my own again."

"I'm glad you can walk better, but you'll always be our little girl, sunshine." Mack hugged her.

"I'll take good care of her, Mack." Cole grabbed their two bags and followed Bethany into the terminal.

Cole's parents picked them up in Springfield, Missouri.

After introductions and a short visit, they dropped Bethany off at her parents' home, promising to pray. She just loved the Beckmans; they were such warm people and they made her feel so comfortable.

Bethany dreaded talking to her father but decided she might as well get it over with first thing. No sense putting it off.

"Mom, Dad, I'm home," Bethany called as she walked in the door.

"Hi, honey." Her mother hugged her. "It's good to see you're okay. We were worried."

Her father grabbed her in a big hug. "How's my girl? It's good to see you, princess."

"I'm fine now. You don't need to worry about me."

"Annie, how about getting us some of those cookies you just took out of the oven while I take Bethany's luggage to her apartment," her dad said.

"Sounds good." Bethany smiled. "I have something I need to talk to you both about. This will be a good time to do that."

When her dad returned, her mother said, "Here are those cookies, Chuck. Why don't you pour us some milk, and we can sit and talk at the kitchen table."

When they were all seated, Bethany asked, "Dad, how's Granddad doing?"

"As well as he can in a wheelchair, I suppose."

Bethany winced at his tone. Well, this wasn't going to get any easier, so she might as well just say it. "Dad, Mom, I met a wonderful Christian man on the plane to Gram and Papa's.

He's a fireman-paramedic by profession, but he lost his partner and very close friend in a fire a couple of months ago. He's on a leave of absence for six months. Gram and Papa hired him for the winter as their ski instructor."

"Oh, honey. His partner died? That's terrible." Her mother handed her the plate of cookies.

"Yes, it's been very hard on him. I'd like you to meet him. He came home to visit his family. I'd like for him to come for supper tomorrow evening so you can get to know him, if that's okay."

"That'll be fine, honey. We'll look forward to meeting him." Annie smiled.

"What do you know about this man, Bethany?" Chuck asked.

"His family owns several hundred acres outside of town here, Dad. He works for the Springfield Fire Department. He and his family are good Christians, and he's very good to me."

"What's his name, Bethany? Do we know his family?"

Bethany hesitated. She knew he was going to explode when she told him Cole's name. She looked straight at him. "His name is Cole Beckman, Dad."

"What!" He stood so fast he knocked his chair backward. "That man will never be welcome in my house! I can't believe you'd have anything to do with him after what he did to your grandfather."

"I love him, Dad."

"Well, he's not coming here, and you might as well know now that we won't be coming to your grandparents' for

Christmas, either, if *he's* going to be there!"

"Wait a minute, Chuck. This is my parents we're talking about," Annie said.

"I'm sorry, sweetheart. You can go if you want, but I'm not going anywhere that man will be! Bethany, you are my daughter. You know how I feel about Cole Beckman and his family. I forbid you to see him again!"

Bethany stood up. "In case you haven't noticed, I am an adult, and I love Cole. He was sixteen, Dad. It was an accident. I assure you, no one has suffered more over Granddad's accident than Cole has. He can't change what happened that night, and you can't tell me I can't see him!"

"That man is not welcome in my house!" He banged his fist on the table and Bethany jumped. She'd never seen her dad so angry.

"Then I guess I won't be welcome either, Dad, because I love Cole, and one day in the future I'll marry him if he asks me to." Bethany turned away and started to walk out of the house, tears in her eyes.

"All right, stop this!" Annie stood up. "Bethany, come back here! Chuck, this has gone on long enough. Bethany is our only child and you will not alienate her over this. It's time you forgave Cole Beckman and his family. Have you forgotten what the scriptures say about forgiveness? Colossians 3:13 says, 'Bear with each other and forgive whatever grievances you may have against one another. Forgive as the Lord forgave you.' It's time, Chuck Stillman, that you get on your knees before the Lord. You know He isn't pleased with the way you're acting!"

Bethany was so shocked, she was speechless. She had never heard her mother raise her voice at anyone, especially not her father. Obviously he hadn't either, because he stopped and listened to her. Bethany realized the scripture her mother had just quoted was the same one the Lord had brought to her mind the night she and Cole talked.

Bethany's cell phone rang, and she excused herself to go to her apartment, answering it on the way. She felt she needed to give her parents some time alone.

"Hi, Cole." Bethany unlocked her door and went inside. She sat in her rocking chair with a heavy heart and put her feet up on the matching stool.

"You sound upset, darlin'. Are you all right?"

"I'm okay." She pulled a bag of M&M's from her purse. Then she proceeded to tell Cole what had taken place with her father, and how her mother had intervened. "I've never seen my father like that, and I couldn't believe my mother raised her voice. In all of my twenty-two years, I've never heard her do that. But my father stopped and listened to her. They were talking when I left the room. I pray she can get through to him."

"I'm sorry I caused a problem in your family, darlin'. I feel horrible about your grandfather being in that wheelchair and about the way your father feels about me and my family. Believe me, if I could go back and change that night, I would."

"I know that, Cole. My father is the one in the wrong here. My mother's right about him needing to forgive. He raised me in a Christian home and always taught me to be forgiving. I've even heard my grandfather try to talk to him about this, and he wouldn't listen. Granddad doesn't hold any animosity against you and your family."

"I'm glad to hear that, and I will continue to pray for your father. I know the Lord has a plan, darlin'. We just have to trust Him."

"I know you're right. It's just that I've never seen my father lose his temper like that."

"He wouldn't hurt you, would he?"

Bethany heard the concern in Cole's voice. "No, he loves us. He isn't violent, just angry."

"I can understand how he feels, Bethany."

"I can, too, Cole. But as Christians we can't hold a grudge. It hurts us more than anything else."

"You're right about that. We need to continue to pray."

"Yes, we do. Can you come for supper tomorrow evening?"

"What time?"

"How about six o'clock?"

"I'll be there. I love you, darlin'. I'll talk to you in the morning."

"I love you, too, Cole. Good night." Bethany closed her cell phone.

Chapter 10

Bethany was about to get ready for bed when there was a knock on her door. She opened it to find her mother there.

"Would you please come downstairs, honey? Your father wants to talk to you."

Bethany followed her mother downstairs. She took a seat at the table across from her father—where she'd been sitting earlier. *Please, Lord. Work this out. You know how much I love Cole.*

"You can ask your young man to dinner tomorrow night. I'll be polite—that's as far as I can go right now." Her father got up and walked out of the room.

"Give him some time, honey. I believe with prayer, he'll come around." Her mother hugged her.

"Thanks, Mom. I appreciate your help in this. I love Cole so much, but I love Dad, too, and Cole is adamant that I won't be made to choose between them."

"Well, that says a lot about your young man, honey. He obviously loves you."

"Yes he does, Mom, and I know you're going to love him. Dad would, too, if he'd just give him a chance. Cole and his family are wonderful people. His parents and brother picked us up at the airport earlier, and I immediately felt comfortable with them. The Lord just shines through them."

"Why don't you ask them to come tomorrow evening with Cole. Maybe he'll feel more comfortable having his parents and his brother along for support, and we can get to know them, too."

"I think that's a great idea, Mom." Bethany hugged her mother. "I love you."

"I love you, too, honey. Now you'd better go to bed—you look tired. And stop worrying. Everything is going to be all right."

"Okay. Good night." Bethany kissed her mother and went up to her apartment to get ready for bed.

The next evening when Cole and his family arrived, Bethany introduced them. "Mom, Dad, this is Cole Beckman, his father, Bruce; mother, Jenny; and his younger brother, Carl. This is my mother and father, Annie and Chuck Stillman, and my granddad, Charles Stillman."

They all made the appropriate responses. If her father's weren't the warmest, no one made any comment about it.

"Come in, please, and sit down." Annie smiled. "Supper will be ready in just a few minutes."

"I hear you play the fiddle, Cole," Charles said. "I've always enjoyed bluegrass music, especially gospel bluegrass."

That broke the ice, and the conversation went well as they

gathered around the table. Bethany noticed her father was polite as he'd said he would be, but he didn't go out of his way to hold a conversation with Cole and his family.

They had just about finished supper, when suddenly her granddad began choking. Her dad patted him on the back in an attempt to dislodge the food from his throat, but it didn't work. Bethany was sitting next to her grandfather and she jumped up. He couldn't get any air. He was turning blue.

"Granddad!" Bethany cried.

Cole rushed over to him, and her dad helped him lift her grandfather out of the wheelchair. Cole quickly and efficiently performed the Heimlich maneuver, dislodging the food from his throat. Her grandfather began to cough, and Cole set him gently back into his chair.

"Are you okay, Mr. Stillman?" Cole stooped down and handed the older gentleman his glass from the table, helping him to take a few swallows. Bethany was shaking so badly, she had to sit down. She felt Cole take hold of her hand and squeeze gently.

"I'm okay now, thanks to you, young man. You just saved my life. If you hadn't been here, I believe I'd have met my maker." Bethany realized her granddad was trying to instill a little humor into the situation to lighten the mood and ease some of the fear they'd just faced.

Bethany's dad sat back down in the chair on the other side of her grandfather and took hold of his hand. "Dad, are you sure you're okay? You gave us a scare."

"I'm fine now. No need to fuss."

Bethany was surprised when her father got up, laid his hand on Cole's shoulder, and said, "Thank you. I appreciate what you just did for my father. He's right—you saved his life."

"No thanks are necessary, sir. I'm glad I was able to help him."

That changed her father's demeanor toward Cole and his family, and the rest of the evening went very well.

Bethany's father and mother walked out to the car with Bethany and Cole as they were leaving for the airport the next afternoon. Bethany hugged her mother as her father shook Cole's hand. Her father hugged her and said, "We'll see you in Lake Tahoe for Christmas."

"I'm so glad, Daddy. I'll look forward to it. I love you."

"I love you, too, princess. Have a good flight."

Cole and Bethany napped on the flight, and in just a few hours, they arrived back at the lodge safely.

The next morning, Bethany and Cole went to Incline Village with her grandparents, Scarlett, Stephanie, and Michaela to Christmas shop and to buy a Christmas tree for their suite. Bethany thought her feet would fall off before they were through, but finally they made it home. Cole and her grandfather brought the six-foot tree up to their suite and set it in the stand.

"Oh, I love it! It looks great in front of the window," Bethany said. She, Cole, and her three friends spent the evening decorating the tree and wrapping the gifts they had bought while in town. Bethany hoped Cole would like the gift she had bought for him. It was a dark brown suede jacket. It had a fiddle and a banjo with their necks crossed on the back. Music notes were scattered here and there, with BLUEGRASS MUSIC embroidered across it in royal blue letters.

"Where is everyone? It's Christmas Eve. I can't believe we're the only ones here." Bethany set her hot chocolate on the coffee table. She and Cole were in the main room downstairs, enjoying a blazing fire in the fireplace.

"Last minute errands, I imagine." Cole glanced at his watch.

"Papa and Gram went to the airport to pick up my parents and Granddad. But I would have thought some of the guests would have been in here. Scarlett is up in her room. Stephanie and Michaela went to do some last-minute shopping. I hope they all make it back okay."

"I'm sure they will, darlin'. They'll be back before you know it." Cole nuzzled her neck playfully. "Now stop worrying and enjoy the fire."

On Christmas morning, Cole knocked on Bethany's door and waited for her to open it.

"Hi! Come on in. And Merry Christmas!" She smiled and gave him a kiss.

"Merry Christmas to you. I have something for you before we go down to your grandparents." Cole followed her into the living room and sat on the sofa beside her. "The tree looks nice. We did a pretty good job on it, I'd say."

"I think so, too. We've really been enjoying it. It just didn't seem like Christmas without a tree in here."

He handed her a small box, and as she unwrapped it, she kept glancing up at him as if she suspected what might be inside.

Cole loved the way her eyes lit up as she opened the box and saw the emerald ring encircled in diamonds inside. She looked up at him with a big smile.

"Bethany, I love you. Would you do me the honor of becoming my wife? Will you marry me, darlin'?"

"Yes, yes! Oh, Cole! Nothing would make me happier than to be your wife." She gave him a big hug.

Cole took the ring out of the box and slid it onto her finger, placing a kiss where it rested. "I love you, darlin'. You are my whole world."

"And you are mine, Cole. I love you so much."

Cole kissed her and held her in his arms.

"How did you know I love emeralds?"

"Your grandmother told me. And speaking of her, I guess we had better go on down, or your family will wonder where we are."

Bethany grabbed her purse, and they went down to her grandparents' suite and knocked on the door.

When they walked in, Bethany and Cole wished everyone Merry Christmas, and then Bethany showed off her ring. She was pleased that everyone congratulated them, even her father.

Cole loved his jacket, and Bethany couldn't remember ever having a happier Christmas. Later, sitting in the dining room with all of the lodge guests, her father stood and made the announcement that his daughter was marrying Cole Beckman. Everyone cheered and congratulated her and Cole.

The seven weeks since Christmas had gone by quickly, with all the preparation for their wedding. Bethany and Cole had enjoyed the rehearsal dinner the night before, and she was relieved it had gone well. Now here it was, their wedding day, and she was so nervous, she'd already been through two bags of Peanut M&M's. "Gram, where is Mom?"

"She'll be here any minute. That was her on the phone. They had a flat tire but they're on their way." Bethany sat on a stool in the restroom at the church with her grandmother, Scarlett, Stephanie, and Michaela waiting for her mother to arrive.

"Bethany, you've got to relax. You're not going to make it through this day," Stephanie said, helping her into her wedding gown. "Your mother will be here. She wouldn't miss your wedding."

"Stephanie's right, Bethany. You're a nervous wreck, and you aren't going to enjoy your own wedding if you don't relax," Scarlett said.

Before Bethany could say anything more, her mother rushed in the door. "I'm sorry, honey."

"It's okay, Mom. You're here now. I'm so nervous."

"Honey, it's natural for you to be nervous on your wedding day, but as soon as you start down that aisle and see Cole, you'll be fine."

Stephanie and her mother helped Bethany put on her veil and fasten it securely.

"Oh, my—you look so beautiful." Annie hugged her.

"Bethany, this has your birth date on it, honey. It's a penny to put in your shoe—for something old." Gram hugged her.

Scarlett hugged Bethany and handed her a small box. "Cole asked me to give these to you." When she opened it, inside was a beautiful string of pearls. "He said they're for something new."

"These are mine for you to wear for something borrowed." Michaela hugged Bethany and handed her a pair of white pearl earrings.

"And last but not least as the saying goes, this garter is for something blue." Stephanie hugged Bethany and handed her a small bag.

"Oh, thank you all. I love each of you." Tears welled up in Bethany's eyes. She blinked to try to keep them from falling. All she needed was to mess up her makeup.

"Don't you dare!" Stephanie warned. "You'll have us all crying, and that will never do." She laughed and handed Bethany her bouquet just as the organ began to play. "I have to go. You'll be fine—just think of that wonderful man out there waiting to spend the rest of his life with you."

Bethany smiled at Stephanie as she did one last check of Bethany's dress and veil. "I'll see you up front." Stephanie gave her a quick hug.

Bethany nodded as her three best friends walked down the aisle. Michaela and Scarlett in red velvet dresses with a white sash tied in a bow at the back, and Stephanie, as her maid of honor, dressed in Christmas green with a white sash.

"Are you ready, princess?" Her father offered his arm as the organ sounded the first chords of the "Bridal March."

"Yes. But, Daddy, please don't let me step on my dress and trip. I wouldn't want to embarrass Cole."

"I won't, sweetheart. I promise we'll make it just fine. But I don't imagine anything you could do would embarrass Cole. That young man is crazy about you."

"I'm crazy about him, too, Daddy." Bethany smiled up at her father.

"Well, I'm glad to hear it since he's going to be your life-long mate, my darling girl. Before he thinks you've changed your mind, we'd better go, don't you think?" Her father grinned at her and winked, making Bethany laugh, which eased some of her nervousness.

"Yes, I think so."

Bethany's mother had been right; the minute she saw Cole and he smiled, she knew everything would be all right.

Cole couldn't believe the stunning bride walking toward him was truly his. *Thank You, Lord, for this wonderful blessing. Help me be the husband You'd have me to be.*

Bethany's father placed her hand in Cole's when the minister asked, "Who gives this woman to this man?"

"Take good care of my baby," Chuck whispered, and Cole could see the tears in Chuck's eyes.

"You can count on it, sir," Cole whispered back.

"Her mother and I do," Chuck said aloud. He lifted Bethany's veil just enough to kiss her cheek before he took the seat next to Annie.

Cole held Bethany's hand and helped her up onto the platform.

Once Cole and Bethany had exchanged their vows, the minister said, "I now pronounce you husband and wife. Cole, you may now kiss your bride."

Cole lifted Bethany's veil and kissed her for the first time as his bride, then placed her hand on his arm and turned toward the guests so the minister could announce: "Ladies and gentlemen, I now present to you Mr. and Mrs. Cole Beckman."

Cole led Bethany back up the aisle and out to the Escalade. They rode to the reception, which was being held at the ski lodge.

After the cake was served and the gifts were opened, the photographer took the last of the pictures.

The wedding and reception had been very nice, but Cole was glad it was over, and Mack was taking them to the airport. Bethany was exhausted, and they would arrive just in time to catch their plane to Orlando, Florida, where they would spend the next two weeks for their honeymoon. Bethany had always wanted to see Disney World, and Cole was determined to make that dream come true.

When Bethany's grandfather pulled up in front of the airport, Bethany took hold of Cole's hands and asked, "Cole, would you please pray?"

"Sure, darlin'. Lord, we thank You so much for the miracle you gave us through Bethany's mother, in allowing her father's blessing on our marriage. Please watch over us and our families. Bring us back home safely to them. And, Lord, please guide us in all that we do and help us to always put You first in our lives. In Jesus' name we pray, amen."

"Thank you, Papa, for everything." Bethany hugged her grandfather.

"You're welcome, sunshine. Have a good time, and we'll see you soon."

After saying their good-byes to her grandfather, Cole helped Bethany out of the car, and she wondered if life could get any better than this. She silently thanked the Lord once again for the Christmas miracle that mended the breach between their families and made it possible for her and Cole to spend the rest of their lives together. She smiled up at her new husband and placed her hand in his as they walked into the airport.

JEANIE SMITH CASH lives in the country in southwest Missouri, in the heart of the Ozarks, with her husband, Andy. They were high school sweethearts and have been blessed with two children, a son-in-law, three grandchildren, and one great-granddaughter. Jeanie feels very fortunate to have her children, grandchildren, father, sister, and two sisters-in-law living close by. She and her family are members of New Site Baptist Church, where they attend regularly. When she's not writing, she loves to spend time with her husband and family, spoil her grandchildren, read, collect dolls, crochet, and travel. Jeanie is a member of American Christian Fiction Writers, Monett Christian Writers Guild, and Mid South Writers Group. She has had two other novellas published. "A Christmas Wish" is included in the anthology *Christmas in the Country*, and "Dr. St. Nick" in *Wyoming Christmas Heroes*. She also has had two short stories published in local magazines. Jeanie loves to write Christian romance and believes a salvation message tucked inside of a good story could possibly touch someone who wouldn't be reached in any other way.

Jeanie loves to hear from her readers. You may contact her through her Web site: www.jeaniesmithcash.com or her e-mail: jeaniesmithcash@yahoo.com. You may join her newsletter at: http://groups.yahoo.com/group/JeanieSmithCashsNewsletter.

No Thank You

by Lena Nelson Dooley

This book is dedicated to my partners in writing *Christmas Love at Lake Tahoe*. Thank you Jeanie Smith Cash, Jean Kincaid, and Jeri Odell.

And thank you, Rebecca Germany, for allowing us the opportunity to create Snowbird Lodge.

Special thanks to Zach Neece for giving me permission to use the words to "The More I Seek You." The songs you write speak what my heart feels.

The book is also dedicated to two of my grandson Austin Waldron's best friends, P. J. Mayher and Big John Cunningham. I borrowed your names for two young men in my book, who, like you, love the Lord and enjoy activities like skiing and Bible study.

And every word I write is dedicated to James Allan Dooley, who loved me in 1964 and loves me more in 2009. You are the kind of marriage partner I wish every woman could share her life with. You encourage me, you sustain me, you cherish me, and you're always there when I need you. . .in any way.

"Now therefore, if you will indeed obey My voice and keep My covenant, then you shall be a special treasure to Me above all people; for all the earth is Mine."
EXODUS 19:5 NKJV

Chapter 1

"What was I thinking?"

Scarlett McKaye's first job in resort management, and she had to get one so far away. A thousand miles away in Nevada, to be exact.

"Did you say something to me?" Her mother must have heard from downstairs.

"No, Mom." She raised her voice to be sure the words were understood. "I'm just trying to decide how much to pack." Five months was a long time.

Footsteps sounded on the stairs, and then her mother appeared in the doorway. "We can always ship a trunk to you."

Scarlett placed her hands on her hips and surveyed the mess sprawled across her room. *It was the only way.* "Good idea. I really wanted to take some of my books."

Her mother shook her head. "Scarlett Ann, you're going to be in one of the most beautiful places in the world. Why would you want to waste your time reading?"

She and her mother would never agree on this. Scarlett

loved to read and didn't consider it a waste of time. Besides, other people spend most of their time on the slopes. Planning activities wouldn't take all day, and she'd have time off.

After surveying her bookshelves, she started pulling volumes and plopping them on the overcrowded bed. "How long do you think it will take for the trunk to get there?"

Mother crossed her arms. "Probably not long." She studied Scarlett a moment. "Are you sure you're doing the right thing in going so far away?"

Did she sense Scarlett's ambiguous thoughts?

"Of course I'm sure." She gave herself a mental shake to firm up her resolve. "It'll be an adventure, and five months isn't all that long."

Working at a ski resort would be a good place to start her career. Besides, she loved snow—to look at and maybe to play in. But not skiing. A person had to be crazy to zip down steep slopes, weaving between trees on thin, slick boards. That was asking to be injured.

The Dallas-Fort Worth International Airport buzzed with activity. Scarlett attached the connecting straps to each of her three bags, then pulled them behind her like a train. She made her way to the end of the long line, wondering where everyone was headed. Wishing she'd bought her ticket online so she could check in at a kiosk, she inched slower than a turtle toward the ticket counter.

"How many bags to check?" The America Airlines agent

didn't even glance up.

"Two."

The soft answer caused the distracted woman to look at her. "What did you say?"

Scarlett gave her brightest smile. "I'm checking two bags."

"You do realize there are charges for checked bags." Still no smile from the agent. "Please place them on the scale."

Scarlett wrestled the bags one at a time onto the flat metal surface and held her breath. *Please don't let them be overweight.* Thankfully, they weren't.

"That'll be one hundred and twenty-five dollars." The agent's fingers did the cha-cha over the keyboard.

"Wow!" She didn't realize the bag fees would be so high. Her first paycheck needed to come soon to cover this. She should have sent more of her things in the trunk. Scarlett handed her the brand-new credit card. Her first charge.

While waiting near the departure gate, she tapped her fingers on the arm of the gray chair. She didn't like flying. She'd have driven her Malibu to Nevada, but her father had convinced her not to drive that far alone. He was an old worry-wart, but Scarlett was glad he cared. Some of her friends' parents didn't.

Thoughts flitted through her mind at a dizzying pace. *What if. . . ? What if. . . ? What if. . . ?*

She had to stop thinking about serious possibilities and dwell on what she knew. She enumerated them using her fingers. She had graduated with honors. A degree in hotel management made her capable of filling this position. After she left Lake Tahoe, the job would look good on her résumé. Five months wasn't all that long. Once again that phrase raced through her mind. Who was she trying to convince? Herself?

The long flight and waiting for her luggage on the other end took an eternity, but finally she was on her way to Snowbird Lodge on the outskirts of Incline Village. Trying not to look too much like a tourist, she studied the landscape, marveling at God's creative wonders. Steep mountains, deep valleys, and acres of snow punctuated with evergreens. Buildings that looked like Swiss chalets. Every scene looked like a picture on a Christmas card. Being here would be a blessing and her new job a gift from God. Wasn't it? Of course it was.

When the shuttle stopped, Scarlett climbed off and went to the back to retrieve her luggage. While she walked, she dug into her jumbled shoulder bag, trying to find enough change to make three dollars to tip the driver.

"Did you lose something?" Husky masculine tones penetrated her concentration.

She looked up at the smiling face of the driver. Sean, from his name tag. "I'm digging for your tip." Her nervous giggle followed.

He held up one hand, palm out. "Not from you. You're an employee."

"How do you know that?"

He nodded toward the two young women right inside the door of the lodge. "They've been waiting for you—Scarlett, isn't it?"

"Yes."

The front door burst open. Bethany and Stephanie ran toward her, screaming her name. They joined in a dancing group hug.

Sean was halfway to the entrance before Scarlett realized he had taken her luggage. She pulled away and hurried after him, with her two friends following right behind. She didn't catch him until he stopped by the reception desk.

"You didn't have to do that."

"My pleasure." He tipped his hat and returned to the shuttle van.

She whirled around to face Bethany and Stephanie. "Do we get treated like this all the time?"

Bethany shook her head. "No, just this weekend. Monday is a workday, and we'll become staff. Come on." She headed toward the elevator. "We'll help you unpack."

When Bethany opened the door to the suite, Scarlett almost whistled. But she remembered Grammy's admonition that ladies didn't whistle. This wasn't a tiny room in the attic, as Scarlett had imagined. The spacious area would quickly become a home to them. That great bookcase had room for her books and already contained some she hadn't read.

"This is beautiful." Scarlett twirled around in the middle of the large room. "Just like home."

Bethany smiled. "I told Gram we'd all really love it."

Scarlett went down the hallway and poked her head into the bedrooms. "These are great, too. Can I have the one with the purple flowers? You know how much I love purple."

The rest of the day went by in a blur. Exploring the lodge,

Michaela's arrival, eating dinner together, then settling before the fireplace in their suite to catch up—which didn't take long, since they'd only been apart a short while.

Now Scarlett sat cross-legged on her bed, writing in her journal, her anxieties about coming here a dim memory. Of course accepting the job had been the right thing to do.

The ambience in the dining room resembled that of a fine restaurant. Actually, everything about Snowbird Lodge excelled her every expectation. What a joy to be able to plan activities for the guests. The job would be a breeze, and she couldn't imagine any complications.

"What are you doing for the next week?" The familiar voice came through his cell phone.

Derrick Greene took that question as a prelude for a request of some kind. "Nothing's going on."

He could almost hear Pastor Bob's smile widen. "Good."

"So what do you have in mind?" Derrick saved and closed the Internet page he'd been working on and leaned back in his desk chair.

"A group of the college guys want to go skiing. Although it's not a regular church trip, they wanted someone going with them who could lead a Bible study each night. I thought of you."

Skiing? "Do you know where they're going?"

"They were talking about Lake Tahoe, but they're having a bit of trouble finding any place that's not booked up."

Derrick stood and studied the bulletin board on the wall

above his desk. "I've been meaning to try a new facility there." He pulled the tack from a slip of paper and pushed it into a vacant spot on the cork. The note floated to the top of his desk. He picked it up. "Snowbird Lodge. If they want me to, I can try to get reservations. How many are going?"

"Eight or ten."

"I'll check on this and get back to you."

"Thanks."

The phone call to the lodge didn't take long. The three rooms they needed were available. Pastor Bob said they could use the church van, and the young men decided to leave early the next morning. Even with the wintery weather, the drive shouldn't take too long.

Derrick decided to take his own Xterra. They'd need the extra space to carry all the luggage and equipment, even though the guys would pack light.

A month after completing his last wilderness trek, he felt the need to get out and do something physical. His muscles tingled in anticipation.

Get in some intense skiing. Spend time with guys who looked up to him. An unexpected chance to spend special time with the Lord. Life couldn't get any better.

Chapter 2

Derrick shifted into all-wheel drive several times on the way into Incline Village. With this much new snow, the skiing should be fantastic. Driving behind the van, which didn't have the same versatility, had been an adventure in this weather. All but one of the men got out at least twice to push the bulky vehicle back on the road after it had slid off.

He huffed out a relieved breath when they finally pulled up in front of Snowbird Lodge. The last time he'd been in Incline Village, they'd just started working on this project. The building sat nestled among a few tall pines, a mix of rustic and modern, built of logs with lots of large windows glowing with welcoming light—a true showcase for the builder. Before long, this lodge would be so popular, he'd have to reserve quite awhile in advance.

"Wow, man. That was some ride." P. J. was the only one of the guys who rode with him. "I'm glad we finally made it."

Derrick shifted into Park and cut the engine. "Me, too."

He got out of the SUV and stretched his cramped muscles. Driving this distance without a break wasn't one of his favorite activities. An exhilarating ski run down a black-diamond slope would be wonderful right now, but first they had to unload the vehicles and check in.

"What are we gonna do first?" P. J. started releasing the tie-downs holding the skis to the top of the Xterra.

Derrick grabbed his duffel and shut the door. "How about if you guys start unloading? I'll check on our rooms."

P. J. mumbled something that sounded like, "All right," and continued with his task.

When Derrick stepped into the lobby, the view out the floor-to-ceiling windows on the opposite side of the large area was a billboard urging him to ski. Snow on the slopes had only a few trees showing, the evergreens dark against the field of blinding white. His kind of place.

"Snowbird Lodge, how may I help you?"

He turned toward the registration desk to see who spoke. His eyes widened, and he forgot to breathe. The most beautiful woman he'd ever seen held the telephone to one ear while she used the keyboard on the computer with the other hand.

Dressed in something deep red and velvety, she had abundant curls falling around her shoulders. Her hair shone deep black with dark blue highlights like a raven's wing in sunlight.

Derrick took a deep breath and huffed it out. *Get a grip.* He felt embarrassingly like a teenager unable to control his hormones. He couldn't take his eyes off her. Smooth skin, a clear pale ivory, with just a touch of pink in her cheeks. He wondered if it was as soft as it looked. From here he couldn't tell what color her eyes were. Like metal shavings to a magnet, he was drawn closer to the desk while she finished accepting a reservation and entering it in the computer. He leaned his forearm on the front edge of the high desk.

This close, he caught a sweet scent that wafted from her when she moved. Kinda like his grandmother's kitchen when she was baking his favorite cinnamon rolls. His duffel thudded to the floor beside him.

She turned bright hazel eyes toward him. "May I help you?"

He cleared his throat. "Yes, I. . .we have a reservation."

Her glance searched the lobby beyond his left shoulder. "We?"

"Yes. I called. . .made the reservation." He glanced toward the door. *Where are those guys?* "We're with Harvest Fellowship Church."

Her hands danced across the keys. "Oh, here it is. How many of you are there? The space has a question mark."

He crossed both arms on the counter and leaned closer. "I didn't know for sure how many we'd have, but we did reserve three rooms."

"That's right. We'll need to know how many are in your party and list the names, in case of an emergency." She kept her eyes trained on the screen, long eyelashes framing them.

"There are nine of us. Eight college guys and me." He listed all the names, pausing as she typed them into the file.

The front door opened and the guys scuffled inside. Sometimes they acted like such boys.

"Hey, Derrick." P. J. stopped beside him while the others dropped what they were carrying near his bag. "We decided to give you a break."

"What kind of break?" He never knew what to expect from this group. They were all godly young men who loved the Lord and lived out their faith, but they could get some harebrained ideas sometimes.

"Hey, lady." P. J. turned his attention toward the receptionist. "The rooms sleep four, don't they?"

Her thousand-watt smile was for P. J. "Yes. Most of our rooms have two queen-sized beds."

"So, Derrick, we decided we'd all bunk in two of the rooms. Let you have one all to yourself." A twinkle lit P. J.'s eyes, and he clapped Derrick on the shoulder. "Then if the old man wants to go to sleep sooner than we do, he can."

"Thanks a lot, man. But we'll see who's old when I beat you down the slopes tomorrow." When he looked back toward the woman, disappointed that she wasn't wearing a name tag, he found her attention was once more on the computer file.

"If you want to do that, I can give you a room with only one bed, and it'll save you some money." This time her smile was for him, once again sucking the breath from his lungs.

He gave a quick laugh. "These guys will be occupied during the day, so I'll be alone a lot of the time. How about joining me on the ski slopes sometime?"

Her smile vanished, and her features hardened into a mask. "No, thank you." Her firm tone held a note of finality. "We provide ski lift tickets for each person registered here. Is there anything else I can help you with?"

What's up with her? He'd never been shot down so quickly. "We need a map of the slopes. I want to find the black diamonds and the double black diamonds."

Big John pushed through the door and dumped his bag with the others. "Hey, Derrick. Better be careful this time. My dad's not here to put you back together." He laughed at his own joke.

For an instant, something flickered in the woman's eyes, then she whirled away. After grabbing several maps from a display behind her, she turned toward them. "Sorry I forgot to get these for you." She had finished passing them out when the phone rang again, and she answered with her shoulder shielding her from his gaze.

Derrick wanted to get to know this fascinating woman. He had to get her to ski with him this week. Two trips to the rooms with their equipment, and he headed back to the registration area. Instead of the gorgeous woman he'd flirted with earlier, a short blond worked on the computer. She wore a name tag.

"Sarah, can you tell me who the other woman is?" He felt a little awkward asking.

The woman looked up at him. "What other woman?"

"The one who was working behind the desk when we checked in."

A bright smile lit her face. "You must mean Mrs. Langston. She and her husband own this place. She's the one who gave me my lunch break today."

Mrs.? He was way off base here. No wonder she was so

prickly when he made his move. "Thank you." How could he have missed the fact she was married? He hadn't even glanced at her ring finger. He wished he had.

He headed back up to his room, which was across the hall from where the guys were staying. But he didn't want to see any of them right now. He hoped they wouldn't knock on his door anytime soon.

Dropping to sit on the side of his bed, he held his head in his hands. Why was he so off kilter? He'd decided long ago not to date just to be dating. He was waiting for the woman God had for him. *I shouldn't have flirted with that beauty.* But more than her looks had drawn him. Something deeper, maybe even spiritual; but she wasn't the woman for him.

Lord, clear my spiritual vision. Keep me focused on You.

Glad he'd been able to spend a couple of hours skiing, Derrick headed back to the lodge. He wanted a long, hot shower and maybe a short nap before dinner. Tonight they'd eat in the dining room at the lodge. Later, they might try out some of the other places in the village.

A sharp rap on his door broke into his dreamless sleep. Derrick sat up and shook his head to clear it. He'd pay a price for thinking so much about that married woman. She'd invaded his dreams. He was going to have to concentrate on the guys and giving them thought-provoking devotions. They often asked hard questions, and he'd have to be prepared to handle them.

The knock sounded again. "Hey, Derrick—you asleep or something?" He hoped P. J.'s voice hadn't disturbed any of the other guests.

He opened the door a crack. "Yeah, I took a short nap."

"We're going to the dining room."

"Meet you there in a few." He threw on his clothes and was out the door in less than five minutes.

After all nine of them had their food, they bowed their heads and Jack offered the blessing. Derrick had just put his first forkful into his mouth when an older lady with red hair and brown eyes stopped by their table.

"Did you want to see me, Mr. Greene?" Her eyes twinkled when she spoke.

He stood, grabbing his napkin to keep it from falling out of his lap, and quickly chewed and swallowed his food. "I don't think so, ma'am."

She tilted her head and peered up at him. "That's funny. Sarah told me you came by the desk and asked about me."

His bewilderment must have shown on his face.

The woman thrust out her hand. "I'm Elizabeth Langston."

He grasped her fingers and gave them a shake. "You're *Mrs.* Langston?"

"Why, yes. Who did you think I was?"

"Good question!" He stifled a laugh. "I'm glad to meet you, ma'am." A chuckle crept out. "I was actually looking for the other woman—the one with the long black curls."

"Oh, you mean Scarlett McKaye. Mack, my husband, needed my help for a few minutes, so she took my place." Interest sparkled in her eyes. "You men enjoy your stay with us."

Derrick stared after the woman, his thoughts in turmoil. He apparently hadn't flirted with a married woman. *Whew!* And it should be all right to get to know her. But first he'd have to pass it by the Lord.

"What was that all about?" Big John stared pointedly at him.

"Nothing." He took another bite. *Nothing at all!*

Chapter 3

Scarlett eagerly helped when Mrs. Langston needed to leave for a few minutes during Sarah's late lunch break. Little did she know how much this event would affect her. When she first caught a glimpse of Derrick Greene, her heart jumped into her throat. Sure he was handsome, in a clean-cut way, but something else drew her. Something indefinable. And he'd felt it, too, if his flirting was any indication. But she could never, ever, get involved with him.

Why did men think they had to prove their masculinity by taking foolish and often disastrous chances with the life God gave them? She'd given her heart to a man her freshman year in college. Their love had grown until they pledged to be married after graduation. He chose to take chances. Irresponsible chances. One too many. She stood by his grave and promised herself she would never fall for another man who wasn't careful. So Derrick Greene was totally off limits. She'd just have to stay out of his way.

The next morning, Scarlett took a shower early. She wanted

to dry her hair by the fireplace while she spent quiet time with the Lord. Today's reading was from John 14. Sections of this chapter troubled her soul. In verse 27, Jesus said, "Peace I leave with you; my peace I give you. I do not give to you as the world gives. Do not let your hearts be troubled and do not be afraid."

The verse reminded her that although she trusted the Lord, somehow she didn't feel peace. She didn't feel really afraid, but no sense in taking chances, right? Being cautious was part of her nature, wasn't it? Then why did she have this lack of inner peace?

She closed her Bible and picked up her hairbrush. Since her hair was almost dry, she'd try brushing it. With the strands a tiny bit damp, maybe some of the tight curls would relax. She leaned her head toward the heat and hummed "Majesty" while she spread out the veil of her hair. Choruses were her favorite music, and she liked so many of the newer ones, but this older song resonated within her heart this morning. She could worship His majesty, even if her heart wasn't exactly settled.

The light snapped on. Scarlett squinted at the brightness. Bethany stood in the doorway.

"What are you doing in the dark?"

"It's not really dark. I had the light from the fireplace." She raised her head and swept curls from her face. "I was drying my hair and having quiet time."

"Oh. Sorry I bothered you." Bethany turned to go.

"That's okay. I'm finished with both." Scarlett stood and let her curls fall where they pleased. "Did you want something?"

Bethany came farther into the room. "Stephanie, Michaela,

and I are going shopping this morning. We want to check out a few shops in Incline Village. Want to go with us? We really haven't spent a lot of time together in the last couple of days."

"Which stores?"

"Redbeard's Book Den, Tahoe Store Emporium, and we can't miss Incline Wine and Chocolate. I have to have some gourmet chocolates."

"I thought your chocolate of choice was Peanut M&M's."

"I like other chocolate, too."

The desire to go with them tugged at Scarlett. If she didn't have so many books on hand, she'd love to go to the bookstore. "Bookaholic" is what her mother called her.

She pulled the belt of her terrycloth robe a little tighter. "I miss us spending time together, but I'm working on activities for Thanksgiving Day. I plan on surfing the Internet this morning."

"You really like your job, don't you?" A smile brightened Bethany's tone and face. "I'm glad. I would have hated if you got up here and were unhappy."

Scarlett dropped onto the sofa and pulled her feet under her. "I would have, too, but I'm learning a lot, and I love meeting the people." A handsome face flashed across her mind, and she felt heat make its way into her cheeks. She hoped Bethany would think it came from being so close to the flames.

Scarlett hunched over the computer in her office, clicking through several Web sites, looking for ideas. Since so many people would be here over Thanksgiving, she wanted holiday activities that a variety of ages would enjoy. *Bingo!* What a goldmine of information on this site. After copying and pasting two games onto a page to print, she stretched her back.

The elevator opened, and she heard her three best friends chatting as they came into the lobby. Laughter preceded them.

She jumped up and rushed to the door. "Hey! Is it too late to change my mind?"

Bethany stopped by the reservation desk. "You want to go into town with us?"

Scarlett leaned both arms on the top of the high cabinet. "Yeah, I found a couple of fun games, and I need to buy supplies for them."

Michaela and Stephanie joined them.

Stephanie peered at Scarlett. "Good. Maybe we can do lunch while we're out."

"I've been wanting to try Hacienda De La Sierra." Scarlett pulled on her coat and wrapped a long, green plaid wool scarf around her neck. "I'm already missing Mexican food. You know how it is with Texans."

When Sean stopped the van and let them out at Raley's Shopping Center, he told them he would be back to pick them up in a couple of hours. They rushed inside then outside, shopping from store to store until they ended up in Incline Wine & Chocolate.

Bethany and Scarlett headed toward the chocolate section, with Michaela and Stephanie dragging behind.

"Hey, guys, we're not going to a fire," Stephanie called out to Bethany and Scarlett.

"No, but there's a lot of chocolate to see." Bethany already had a couple of bags of gourmet chocolates in hand.

Scarlett picked up a basket with a large assortment of the delicious treats. "This would make a good grand prize, wouldn't it?"

"If I could be the winner"—Bethany's gaze searched through the colored cellophane surrounding the basket—"I could really go for some of those items."

"That would last you for a whole week, wouldn't it?" Stephanie laughed at her own joke.

Scarlett started toward the register, struggling to hold on to her other packages while carrying the large prize.

"Let me help you with some of your things." Michaela hadn't bought much. She relieved Scarlett of three bags.

After Bethany and Scarlett finished checking out, the four of them headed across Tahoe Boulevard to the Mexican restaurant, which looked more like a ski lodge than any of the Mexican restaurants back in Texas. Too bad they couldn't see Lake Tahoe from here. The hostess seated them at the only empty spot, a table for six. After going in and out so much, Scarlett welcomed the warmth, and they had a couple of chairs to pile all their packages in. The friends studied the menus and decided to each order a different foot item and share, so they could try a variety of dishes.

The waitress left with their order, and Scarlett turned to Bethany. "So tell me about the new ski instructor. I see him eyeing you a lot. Do you know him?"

Scarlett watched pink tinge her friend's cheeks. Maybe her comment touched a nerve. *Very interesting.*

"We flew out on the same plane. I told you about helping the man with the heart attack. Cole's a fireman and a paramedic. That's all I know." Bethany started searching through her packages. "Did you see what I bought?" She pulled out a pair of sky-blue kid gloves lined with white rabbit fur. "These will be really warm."

Scarlett put her hand on Bethany's arm. "We saw the gloves when you paid for them. Don't change the subject. Do you have some kind of connection with the fireman who teaches skiing? And what's going on? Why is he giving lessons when he has other, more valuable, skills?"

"He's good at skiing, too. Maybe he just wants a break from his usual work routine. There's nothing wrong with that." Bethany shoved the gloves back into the sack.

Michaela leaned forward. "I've noticed the chaperone with the church youth group looking at you, Scarlett."

Now Scarlett felt a blush on her own face. "He's not my type."

"How do you know he's not?" Stephanie trained her attention on Scarlett, too.

Actually, three pairs of eyes bored into her, and more heat trickled into her cheeks. They were probably fire-engine red by now. "He asked for the map to the black-diamond and double-black-diamond slopes first thing. I knew right then I needed to steer clear of him." She tried to swallow the lump forming in her throat.

Bethany patted Scarlett's hand. "And we all understand why."

Michaela leaned back. "Maybe he's an expert skier and can handle the black-diamond slopes."

"Maybe he can," Scarlett agreed. "But what if he can't? I will not become involved with a man who risks his life on such a silly pursuit."

Stephanie sighed. "We're not talking about you getting involved. He's just a real hunk, and when he's looking at you, he doesn't have a chance to notice any of the rest of us."

"I'm not interested. I just try to ignore him." Scarlett picked up her fork and turned it over and over. "He actually asked me to go skiing with him when I checked them in."

"He did?" Three voices chorused, and six eyes widened.

"And you didn't tell us?" Bethany quirked one eyebrow, almost making Scarlett laugh. "Wonder why?"

Scarlett heaved a sigh of relief when the waitress arrived with their food. The tantalizing aromas made her stomach growl. Maybe, just maybe, everyone would forget what they were talking about while they ate. She didn't want to continue this discussion now—or ever.

Back at the lodge, Scarlett went to her office to store her treasures. Everything she bought, except one large gourmet chocolate bar, would be used for the activities. She sat at the computer and opened the design software the Langstons had purchased for her to use to make flyers. She had other things to do today, but first she had to get the flyers together.

In half an hour she had created a sheet with a turkey border. Inside, she announced a special game night after dinner on Thanksgiving. Prizes would be provided for one of the games. For the other, anyone who wanted to participate had to bring a wrapped gift. They'd play a game to exchange them. Paper, ribbon, and tape were available at the front desk.

Excitement thrummed through her veins while she hung the flyers on the bulletin boards beside each elevator door. Then she taped two on the front entrance. Thursday evening would be the first test of her skills as an activities director.

On Monday, Derrick had skied the black-diamond slopes alone. Most of the guys didn't have the experience he did, so he'd spent much of Wednesday with them. They'd asked probing questions when he led the Bible study late last night. Between trips on the ski lift and swooshing down the trails, they'd all shared deeper things in their hearts. God spoke to him about giving himself to these guys. Derrick praised God for allowing him to be a part of what He was doing in these young men's lives.

They arrived back at the lodge, and Derrick led them through the front entrance. The horseplay along the way died a quick death inside. These guys could act really childish, but they had a well-developed sense of respect when it counted.

"Did you see this?" P. J. pointed toward a colored flyer taped to the door.

Derrick backtracked. "Nope. What is it?"

"The activities director's been busy. We're going to have a special game night after the football games tomorrow."

Big John stopped beside P. J. and Derrick while the other guys headed toward the elevator. "Says here we need to wrap a present. Let's do it. Might be a good way to get acquainted with some of the girls."

"Yeah." P. J. ran his finger along a line on the paper. "The gifts don't have to be new. Just stuff we brought with us." He laughed. "I didn't carry anything extra."

Big John looked over at the ski shop opposite the registration desk. "I see stuff marked on sale in there. Bet we could find something interesting to girls."

Derrick watched the two friends head toward the store. Adults, but still boys at heart. Maybe he was, too. He looked forward to the activities tomorrow evening, but for a different reason. Scarlett would be there. Maybe this time he could make up for his gaff, and maybe she'd agree to go skiing with him before their week ran out. After he cleaned up, he would go to Incline Village and look for something nice for the game—just in case Scarlett played, too.

Chapter 4

Scarlett moved the ladder a few feet, then hung the end of the Thanksgiving garland on the top rung. She climbed almost to the top. Being so far from the floor made her stomach muscles tighten like an overblown balloon. Why hadn't she asked for help in hanging the decorations in the lobby?

She picked up the garland and held it as high as she could reach. *Oh, rats!* Up one more rung, her breathing accelerated. *Don't look down.* Blood rushed from her head, leaving her light-headed. She took a deep breath and exhaled slowly. Stretching as far as she possibly could, she taped the string of autumn leaves in place.

Without hesitating a second, she clambered down the ladder. Not until both feet connected with the solid floor did she breathe freely. That was the last of the decorations, and not a second too soon.

Leaning the ladder against the wall behind the counter, she finally felt safe. The outside door opened, and she turned.

Derrick Greene entered with a shopping bag from Tahoe Store and Emporium. His gaze found her, and his long strides brought them almost face-to-face. She'd never been so thankful for the counter. Being perched on a rickety ladder had nearly taken her breath. She didn't need some giant hunk coming too close and using up her much-needed oxygen.

"You've been busy while I was gone."

She picked at the nail polish on her thumb and avoided his gaze. "Why do you say that?"

"These decorations weren't up when I left." He leaned one elbow on the counter, with the package dangling from his fingers. "Besides, what else would you be doing with that ladder?"

She had to laugh. "You got me there. So how do you like it?" Her wave encompassed the whole lobby, where autumn arrangements sat on every table in addition to the swag garlands.

"Nice." He didn't take his eyes from her. "And festive. . .real festive."

His intense gaze kept her off balance. "Thank you. That's the effect I wanted. . .for everyone to feel festive. . .for Thanksgiving."

He straightened to his full height and smiled down at her. "You don't have to work all day tomorrow, do you?"

She shook her head. With him looming over her, she would have backed up if the ladder wasn't behind her. "No. I'm just working in the evening. I found some fun things to do."

"So I noticed." He held up the dusky blue bag. "That's why I went to the village. I wanted a nice gift."

She leaned her arms on the counter. "Looks like something special."

"Maybe." He studied her for a moment. "We'll have to wait and see."

When he didn't turn to go, she suddenly couldn't think of anything to say. How awkward. "So—"

"Have—"

They spoke in unison. He stopped and gave her a jaunty wave. "After you."

"No, that's okay. What were you going to say?"

His smile brought fireworks to his green eyes. "Have you thought any more about going skiing with me?"

"No, thanks." His question caused an ache in her heart. She'd stepped right into that one. When would she learn?

She whirled and without glancing back, hurried around the ladder and through the door to her office. She needed to check on the job she'd left printing when she started decorating the lobby. She wasn't really running away from the man, no matter what he thought.

Derrick watched Scarlett's back until she disappeared from sight. That didn't go very well. Why would a simple question turn her from a friendly woman into one frigid and unbending? There had to be more to it than just him. Someone had hurt her. Was it a skier? Or someone else? He wished he could read her thoughts better than he had been reading her body language. She'd been enjoying their banter before he asked the question—he was sure of it.

Sarah, the desk clerk, came across the lobby and went behind the counter. "Can I help you with something, Mr. Greene?"

"Yes." He focused on her. "I need some of the wrapping stuff you have. For my package for tomorrow night."

She pulled out several different colors of gift bags, wrapping paper, tissue paper, and tape. "Take what you need."

He studied the assortment. One bag made him think of Scarlett and the bright colors she wore, so he chose that one. Of course, the last two days, she hadn't left his thoughts for more than a moment.

"This tissue would look good in that bag." Sarah picked up a contrasting shade.

"Great." He put both items in the bag with his purchase. "Is it hard to make this look pretty?"

She laughed. "You've never used a gift bag?"

Sheepishly, he shook his head. "I usually have all my gifts wrapped at the stores where I buy them."

"You're missing all the fun." She opened one of the other bags and stood it on the counter. "You put the item in there. You can either wrap the gift with some tissue first, or just put it in. Then you take a sheet like this." She deftly twisted the paper into a flowerlike shape. "Then you put the twisted end into the bag and fluff the top. You might have to use two or three pieces of tissue for the size bag you have."

"Thanks for the lesson, Sarah."

She smiled and nodded.

He whistled as he went to the elevator. Just like God to have someone there to teach him what he needed to know. This package had to look inviting. He hoped Scarlett would choose his bag. *God, do You think You can make that happen for me?*

Most of the people staying in the lodge attended Thanksgiving dinner at 1:00 p.m. With the meal served family style, Scarlett almost felt as if she were home. Turkey and all the trimmings, followed by pumpkin pie and pecan pie with heaping mounds of real whipped cream.

Stephanie, Michaela, and Scarlett sat at the table with Bethany and her grandparents. Scarlett enjoyed the family atmosphere. It helped her keep her homesickness at bay while they shared the meal. Most of the men left quickly to watch football either in their rooms or on the big-screen TV in the lobby, but Bethany's grandpa lingered with them, enjoying large slices of the pies.

Scarlett excused herself first and went to her room to call her parents. Even though her eyes brimmed with tears, she convinced them she was having a wonderful time. And she was, but she'd never before been away from home on a major holiday. Standing by the large window beside the fireplace, she watched people in colorful clothing going up or down the slopes. Closer to the lodge, several of the younger children played in the snow.

The boys had built two forts and pelted each other with stockpiled snowballs. The girls lay on their backs making snow angels. For just a moment, she thought about joining them. Hers could be a giant guardian angel. Over to one side, a lone child worked on a snowman. Because this kid was so bundled up, she couldn't tell if it was a boy or a girl. If she wanted tonight to be successful, she'd better finish the prep work for the games.

When she stepped from the elevator, she caught a glimpse of Derrick heading out the front door, probably on his way to the black-diamond slopes. Gloom darkened her day. Why did that man have to take so many risks?

With the ski mask pulled down over his face and goggles protecting his eyes, Derrick pushed off. He made himself thrust thoughts of Scarlett aside and concentrate on the slope. Every undulation of the snow. Each bordering tree, rock, and shrub. Taking his mind from what lay before him could mean disaster.

He hadn't ever wiped out on a black-diamond slope. Knowing the danger, he hadn't allowed himself to ski on one until his skill level met the challenge. But the exhilaration. The breathless wonder. The feeling of being at the top of the world and flying down the winter wonderland. These thrills lured him back to the tops of the slopes. And each time, he praised God for His awesome creation.

The guys he'd come with lounged in the lobby in front of the big screen, rooting for their team. Derrick chose to work off some of the massive amount of food he'd consumed. He loved the food at Thanksgiving. Maybe too much.

On the ride back up on the ski lift, his mind wandered to Scarlett. He could see her smile like she had before he asked her to ski with him. He wanted to get to know her, find out what was wrong. Maybe help her get over it.

At the top of the slope, he shoved those thoughts away, determined to concentrate on skiing and enjoying the thrill of the ride. Instead, he felt like a hamster running the wheel in its cage. Finally, he gave up and headed back to the lodge. Maybe he'd catch a glimpse of Scarlett on his way in.

Scarlett stopped in the dining room and put together a turkey sandwich. She returned to her office to finish laminating the last of the items for the games. The closer it got to the time for the party, the more doubts flitted into her thoughts. She rebuked them. Finally, she gathered up her supplies and headed out the door.

Why hadn't she noticed all the chatter? Guests milled around in front of the fire, getting acquainted with one another. The table that usually had coffee and hot water for an assortment of tea bags now sported hot chocolate and hot apple cider. Plenty of the people had already visited that corner, indicated by the number of mugs they held. She knew that later Mrs. Langston would serve more pie down here.

Her gaze collided with Derrick's. She hadn't even noticed him. She wondered how long he'd been studying her. Quickly, she shot her gaze to the floor before she dropped something as she made her way toward the welcoming fireplace. Flames danced in rhythm to the soft music and gave a romantic feeling to the atmosphere.

"Can I carry something, Scarlett?"

She looked up into intense green eyes that were far too close for comfort. Derrick must have moved fast to reach her so soon. She started to refuse, but she really could use the help.

"Thanks." She quickly off-loaded about half of what she carried. "I'm taking it to that table beside the window."

A quick glance showed the moon showering the winter wonderland with a luminescent glow. *How romantic.* Startled at her mind's turn toward romance, she hoped Derrick wouldn't stand close to her.

She arranged the items she carried, then reached for his. Their hands brushed, and a strange awareness sent heat pulsing up her arm. She was afraid to look at him to see if he'd felt it, too.

When everything was just the way she wanted it, she turned toward the crowd. "Everyone ready for game time?"

Conversations shut down all around, and finally, Derrick moved over to lean against a log column. She took a deep breath and smiled.

Derrick crossed his arms and watched Scarlett. He got the feeling she'd relaxed when he moved away from her.

"What are we going to do?" A preteen named Sherry squirmed in her seat, and her mother shushed her.

"I have two Thanksgiving games." Scarlett picked up a stack of laminated cards. "First, we'll play Thanksgiving Bingo."

"What's Thanksgiving Bingo?" Sherry's younger brother stood up. "I don't know how to play."

Scarlett smiled at him. "I'll teach you." She held up a card. "I've made bingo cards, but instead of numbers under the letters, we have information or items that have to do with Thanksgiving in the squares. As you can see, the turkey is in the middle square, and that is a free space. I'll call out the items, and you'll mark your cards with these dry-erase markers, so we can use the same cards for more games. We have enough prizes for several."

She held up a few of the prizes and grinned at the oohs and aahs from the crowd.

"Each winner gets to pick one of these prizes." She turned and lifted something that had been hidden below the tablecloth. "The last bingo game will be for this grand prize."

Derrick laughed when most of the women drooled over that one. Whoever won could really suffer a sugar overload if they weren't careful. That much chocolate could also create a caffeine high.

"Now let's get started."

He enjoyed watching Scarlett take charge of the room. In addition to being beautiful, she was poised and gracious. A very desirable woman on many levels. Only one thing bothered him—he wasn't sure if she was a Christian.

The bingo games took on a frenzy, with everyone trying to win. Along the way, Derrick learned a few things about the history of Thanksgiving. He was sure others had, too, so the game served more of a purpose than just having fun. A good strategy for Scarlett to use.

When Sherry's mother won the grand prize, other people moaned about their bad luck. The smiling winner opened the basket and started sharing her bounty. Along the way, more of the guests became friends.

Derrick didn't know if that was part of Scarlett's plan. If so, she was entirely successful.

"All right, everyone." Scarlett had to raise her voice to get everyone's attention. "We have one more game."

The din receded.

"How many people brought a gift for the next game?"

Every hand went up, and the smile that brightened Scarlett's face lit the whole room.

"Please set your gifts in the middle of the floor."

Soon, colorful packages made a haphazard circle in the center of the room.

When everyone was seated, either in chairs or on couches or the floor, Scarlett continued, "This is probably different from most of the gift exchanges you've done before. It was for me, but it looked like fun. We'll start closest to the fireplace on this side." She pointed toward Sherry. "You'll roll these dice. If you roll numbers that add up to six, you get to choose a wrapped surprise. If you roll anything else, the game rotates clockwise to the next player. As each person rolls a total of six, they get to choose a mystery gift. They can take a gift from another person instead of the pile if they so choose. But the catch is, no one can open a gift until everyone has one. You have to do all your choosing from looking at the outside of the package. In other words, you have to judge the gift by the cover, not the contents. After everyone has a prize in hand, we'll take turns opening the mystery gifts."

She paused a moment, looking around the room. "Does everyone understand?"

A cacophony of assents filled the room.

Scarlett held up the dice until everyone settled down. "No fair peeking into any of the bags."

The first three people threw numbers that didn't add up to six. Each of them groaned. The fourth person got to pick a package.

"Miss Scarlett." Sherry held up her hand as if she were in school.

"Yes."

"What happens if someone takes your gift from you?"

"I guess I forgot to tell you that. Then you'll get to take another gift, either from the middle of the floor or from someone else. But you still can't open it until the game is over." Scarlett sat on the floor near her friend Bethany, the nurse who worked at the lodge.

After Bethany took a turn, Scarlett rolled the dice and threw a five and a one. "Yea! I get to pick a package."

She stood and walked around the gifts left in the middle of the floor. Finally she picked the one Derrick had bagged. He was sure the colors drew her. Now he had to wait to see if she got to keep it.

During the course of the game, someone took it from her, but when her second gift was also stolen from her, she went back to the one he had bought. Waiting to see if she would finish with his gift was almost as exciting as playing the game.

At the end, she still held it. She asked the person on her left to start by opening her package. Each person in turn did the same, the process continuing around the room.

When it was Derrick's turn to open his, he took out a ski mask. He wished he knew who had brought it, so he could thank them.

Finally, Scarlett opened her bag. When she lifted the scarlet—that's what the saleswoman called the red color—cashmere scarf, Scarlett held it up. Then she fingered the softness and rubbed it against her cheek before placing it around her neck, letting the ends hang long on the front of her green velour jogging suit. With her black curls surrounding her beautiful face and the sparkle in her eyes, she looked like a Christmas angel.

An invisible medicine ball slammed into Derrick's chest, forcing the air from his lungs. Tonight would be a long night on his knees. He had to know what the Lord thought about him seeking a relationship with Scarlett. And he wouldn't stop praying until he had an answer.

Chapter 5

After breakfast, Scarlett went to her office. She opened her calendar program and made a schedule for the rest of the week—just two days, but she felt a need for structure in her life right now. Last night, P. J., one of the young men in the church group, complimented her on how good the red scarf looked on her. P. J.'s words had surprised her: "Derrick hoped you'd end up with it."

"How do you know?" Her heart had beat erratically while she waited for his response.

"I went to his room when he was wrapping it."

As she'd watched P. J. walk away, questions scrambled her thoughts. Why had Derrick bought the scarf with her in mind? She remembered him stopping by the front desk with the sack in his hand. The thought of him shopping and thinking about her sent heat surging through her, not just into her cheeks. No man had ever done anything like that. Not even her former fiancé. When Gordon wanted to give her a present, he took her with him to pick it out. Said he wasn't good at choosing the right thing. Derrick had paid attention to her and discerned what she would like. And the scarf did look smoking on her.

Making a schedule would help get her mind back on business.

Friday: Take down the Thanksgiving decorations.

Saturday: Put up the Christmas decorations.

She would work this Saturday, even though Elizabeth told her that since she had worked on Thanksgiving, she should be off. Putting up the Christmas decorations would keep her too busy to think about that man risking his neck out on the black-diamond slopes. Who knew? He might even be on a double black diamond. She shuddered.

Scarlett headed out of her office. Sarah's fingers clicked a staccato on the keyboard of the computer behind the counter.

"I'm going to take down the Thanksgiving decorations today. If anyone needs me, I should be easy to find."

Sarah jumped off of her stool. "I could help you."

"You don't have to do that."

"There's no one scheduled to arrive today, unless we get a walk-in."

"Then come on." Scarlett headed toward the closet where they kept the ladder. "I didn't have any help putting them up, and it took awhile."

Sarah took the ladder from her. "Who held this for you?"

"No one."

"It's dangerous to climb without having someone hold it. You should've asked for help."

Scarlett nodded. "I learned that the hard way."

With Sarah's assistance, Scarlett cleared away the decorations and stored them before noon. And Scarlett hadn't had to climb the ladder. However, all the effort, and even their conversations, didn't chase Derrick from her mind. At least the group of men would only be here two more nights. Then she'd never see Derrick again. That thought dimmed the brightness of her day. She'd just have to forget the handsome man. Besides, she wasn't at Lake Tahoe looking for a relationship.

While Derrick rode the ski lift to the top of the mountain, he studied the map to the slopes. He'd wanted to ski all the black diamonds, but now completing the task didn't seem as important. During the week, he'd skied Thunder, Lightning, Diamond Back, Battle Born, and Powder. Today, he'd already done Chute. On this run, he'd do Corkscrew, then he'd return to the lodge. With any luck, he'd get a chance to talk to Scarlett.

After all his prayers last night, he didn't feel a check in his spirit about getting to know her better. Maybe if they talked today, he could find out if she was a Christian.

Near the bottom of Corkscrew, he wiped out. He hit a patch of ice and his skis slid out from under him. He tumbled and landed on his right shoulder. Then he slid quite a long ways on the hard-packed surface. Fortunately, both skis released, so his injuries were more black-and-blue pride than anything else. At least nothing was sprained or broken. By the time he climbed partway up the slope to retrieve his skis and poles, it was time to return to the lodge.

He opened the door and cringed. In the hope of catching sight of Scarlett, he'd forgotten and used the sore arm. Sarah sat behind the front desk.

"Have you seen Scarlett?" He leaned on the counter, welcoming the chance to rest a bit. He was already starting to feel the soreness that would probably be screaming in the morning.

She nodded. "I've been helping her take down the Thanksgiving decorations."

He glanced around the lobby, noticing the difference for the first time. "Is she working in her office?" He stared at the closed door.

"No. She went through the Christmas decorations that had already been purchased." Sarah fluffed her short blond curls with one hand. "Then she left to buy some more things, to give everything just the look she's wanting."

"Should I go pick up a tree?" He could carry one easily on the Xterra.

"She said something about having one delivered in the morning. I think she plans to put up the Christmas decorations tomorrow."

Derrick straightened up. "Thanks for the info." He needed to stretch his muscles before they cramped too much.

He would just have to make himself available to her tomorrow. Maybe she'd relax and tell him about herself.

In the dining room that evening, Scarlett sat with her three friends and Mack and Elizabeth. "I have everything I need to decorate the lobby just right for Christmas."

"Did we give you enough money?" Mack reached for his billfold.

She held a palm toward him. "One thing I know is how to stretch money to cover what I need."

Elizabeth smiled. "Do you want us to help?"

"I've set tomorrow aside for decorating. I think I'll be okay."

Conversation continued to ebb and flow until Derrick Greene stopped by their table. "I was wondering if it would be all right for my group to have a worship time in front of the fireplace in the lounge area tonight." He'd directed his request toward the Langstons.

"I think so." Mack turned toward his wife. "What do you think?"

"Some of our guests left late today, and many others are checking out early in the morning. I don't expect them to linger in the lounge much this evening. So, sure."

After a little more small talk, Derrick left with his friends. Scarlett's eyes followed him until he was out of the room. When she turned back, Bethany, Stephanie, and Michaela cut their eyes toward her and all three smirked. *Smirked!*

"What?" Scarlett calmly picked up a piece of fried chicken and took a bite before chewing it slowly, trying to show her friends she was not interested in the man.

The others returned to their meals, too, but they couldn't hide their smiles. She hoped Mack and Elizabeth wouldn't notice the silent exchange.

Scarlett finished eating and stood. "I'm going to my office and Skype my folks. It's great to talk to them face-to-face."

First she went to her room and checked her hair and makeup. She wanted to look really good during the visit.

Her mom and dad were waiting when she connected with them on her computer.

"Scarlett." Her mom stared at their computer screen instead of looking into the video cam. "You're looking really good."

"It's only been about a week since I left home." She tried not to laugh. "I shouldn't have changed *much* in that amount of time."

"But you have." Once again, her mother studied her. "There's something different about you. What is it?"

"Probably just the new sense of responsibility because I have a job." Scarlett didn't want to tell her parents how silly she'd been about a crazy man who took too many chances.

"How was your Thanksgiving?" Dad scooted closer to where Mom sat at the computer.

They shared about their holiday, and Scarlett told them about her Thanksgiving dinner and her success that evening. When she mentioned game night, a flush crept into her face. She hoped Mom didn't notice.

After several minutes, they signed off. Scarlett sat in front of the computer, thinking about her holiday. Through the closed door she could hear singing. Probably the church group. The haunting melody tugged at her heart, but she couldn't understand the words. After she caught on to the complete melody, she hummed along and felt her spirit lift toward heaven. She wondered if it was a new chorus the men were singing. By the time she got up and opened the door, the song had ended. She didn't want to interrupt their Bible study, so she quietly headed up to the suite she shared with her best friends. Somehow, she dreaded having to answer the questions she knew they would have ready for her.

Last night, Derrick had noticed Scarlett slip quietly from her office to the elevators. Something about her seemed different, but he wasn't close enough to tell what it was. He hurried to get dressed and eat breakfast so he could be in the lobby when she started putting up the decorations.

As he left the elevator, he was the only person in the cavernous lobby. He stepped down into the lounge area where they had played Thanksgiving games, remembering how Scarlett looked with the scarf around her neck. Wood was stacked in the fireplace, ready for a flame to light the kindling. He took the lighter from its hidden hook on the side of the wooden mantel and flicked it against several pieces of the wood shavings. Each one grabbed the flame, and a pleasant woodsy fragrance accompanied the warmth on its trek across the area.

He turned but kept his hands behind him toward the fire. He scanned between the front door and the lounge area and decided that closer to the edge of the step-down would be a good place for a tall fir tree—like the one being hauled through the doorway by two large men. What a coincidence they would arrive at the precise moment he had that thought.

Scarlett stepped off the elevator. Her eyes were trained on the deliverymen. "I thought I'd get down here before you arrived. You're here bright and early."

One turned toward her. "We have several of these to deliver this morning, miss. Had to get an early start."

"Where do you want us to put the tree stand?" The other man came forward, carrying a metal contraption with a large, deep pot that should hold plenty of water, so the tree wouldn't dry out too quickly.

Scarlett stood with her hands on her hips and surveyed the area. She chose a spot about where Derrick had figured the tree should go.

He hurried over and offered to help. With him and one of the men holding the tree in place, the other man tightened the stand until the fir stood on its own.

"So how does it look?" the deliveryman asked Scarlett.

She put one finger on her cheek and walked around the tree, studying it. "I believe it's straight, and all sides appear even." She turned toward one of the workmen. "This tree is perfect. Did you bring an invoice?"

"No. I'll send a bill t' Mack like I do fer the wood." The man pulled off his heavy suede gloves and tucked them under his arm. "Ernie 'n' his boy 'r' unloadin' the firewood."

While Scarlett accompanied the man out the side door to the woodpile, Derrick craned his neck to see the top of the tree. Must be well over ten feet tall. It would take a lot to get decorations way up there. Surely she would welcome his help.

"Mr. Greene." Scarlett stopped beside him. "I thought

you'd be skiing today. Are you going later?" She sounded almost hopeful.

Did she really want him out of her way? "I thought I'd hang out here in the lodge."

She turned and stared hard at him. "On your last day? Aren't you leaving in the morning?"

"Yeah, we'll head out early, but I decided you might need some help with the decorations. I'd like to give you a hand." Did that sound lame? He couldn't just blurt out the real reason he wanted to get to know her.

"I wouldn't want to take you away from what you love to do." She turned and headed toward the front desk.

He followed her. "Actually, I really want to help with the decorations. That tree is too tall for you to reach the top without a ladder, and if you hang things from the ceiling like you did for Thanksgiving, I can climb up for you." He gave her his most beguiling smile.

After studying him for a moment, she finally grinned. "Okay. I was really dreading the ladder."

When she laughed, he joined her. That broke the ice. From that moment on, they worked together as a team. He helped her bring out all the boxes of decorations from the closet in her office. They set about putting multicolored lights and garlands on the tree.

Scarlett lifted an angel in a white dress with gold trim and golden wings and halo from a smaller box. "I want her to be on the very top." She lifted the skirt. "See? She has bulbs inside. We'll have to plug her into the end of the top string of lights."

Derrick opened the ladder and scooted it as close to the tree as he could without pushing it over. "I'll climb, and you can hold the ladder."

The smile that lit her face rivaled the sunlight against the dazzling white snow. "I'd like that."

He took the angel and set it on top of the ladder, then started up. "Who helped you with the Thanksgiving decorations?"

"No one." Chagrin tinged her words. "That's why I quickly accepted your offer. Climbing that ladder with no one to help steady it was not fun."

He stopped on the middle rung and looked back down at her. "I'm glad you didn't fall."

"So am I." A welcoming smile accompanied her words.

Mission accomplished, he looked around. "Do we need to put ornaments near the top?"

"Now how would the tree look with no ornaments up there?" Her tone teased him.

"Not very balanced." He studied all the things spread across the floor. "Which ones now?"

She handed him red shiny balls, and he tried to space them evenly. When he needed to, he climbed down and moved the ladder. People came and went through the lobby, but he concentrated on Scarlett and getting the tree decorated.

He took the last step to the solid floor and turned. "Want to start decorating the rest of the tree?"

She shook her head and picked up a box of multicolored shiny balls. "I thought it would be fun to let everyone who comes to the lodge pick a ball and hang it where they want.

138

Give the tree some personality."

"Good idea. I'll start." He picked up a bright blue ball and hung it on a limb that pointed toward the front door.

Scarlett set the box down on the front desk. "Want to take a short break and grab some coffee?"

"Sure." He'd like a little break before he started hanging the garlands around the lobby.

She went to the coffee bar and poured a cup. "What do you take in yours?"

"Actually, I like it black."

"I do, too." She handed him a steaming mug. "Unless I get a mocha latte at a coffee shop." She laughed at the face he made.

"Want to sit down?" He led the way to the sofa.

She set her mug on the low coffee table then dropped onto the cushy leather sofa.

He sat beside her. "What did you do before you came to work here?"

She picked up her coffee and took a tiny sip. "Are you trying to find out about my life?"

"I'd hoped we could be friends."

"I'd like that." She finally smiled. "I graduated from college and spent the summer and early autumn at home in Hurst, Texas, with my family. Do you know where that is?"

"Oddly enough, I do." He relaxed into the comfort of the sofa. "I've had business dealings with some people from near there."

He could see a spark of interest in her eyes. "So what do you do?"

"I own my own company."

"Must be nice." Scarlett set her mug back on the table. "I hate to call a halt to our break, but these decorations won't climb out of their boxes and put themselves up."

After they'd strung garlands around all sides of the room and decorated both ends of each swag with wreaths, they put arrangements on several small tables around the area. All of them had either tiny deer or elk in addition to the red and green florals.

Derrick glanced over at the larger table that contained the coffee bar. "You want to put anything on that table?"

Scarlett went to the counter and picked up another box. "I bought a nativity set for over there."

"So you like to celebrate the real reason for the season." He took a deep breath and awaited her answer.

"It wouldn't be Christmas without Jesus, would it?"

Of course, she had known he and the guys were Christians. Now he was sure she shared his faith. "Want to go get some lunch?" He almost felt like he was asking for a date. Maybe he should take her into town. "We could go into Incline Village."

She agreed, and they headed for his truck. As corny as it sounded, he was almost walking on air.

Chapter 6

Derrick Greene had been gone two days, and still Scarlett couldn't get him out of her mind. He wanted to be friends, and they'd had a good time the last day and evening, but that's all he wanted. Why did she miss him so much? He was just another guest at Snowbird Lodge, right?

When they went to Incline Village that last night, he took her to Lone Eagle Grill in the Hyatt Regency resort. Seated between one of the massive rock fireplaces and the wall of windows, they watched the lights of Incline Village and the moon reflecting off Lake Tahoe. The upscale ambience made the evening feel more like a date, but she felt sure Derrick didn't consider it one.

She'd ordered the duck, and Derrick had a steak. Good food, romantic location, interesting conversation. No wonder the man was always front and center in her thoughts. The sooner she could push him out, the better. Life was too full to let futile thoughts keep her anchored in the past.

The printer started cranking out the schedule of activities, jolting Scarlett back to the present. While she waited, she hummed the melody that had been playing in her mind since the weekend. She didn't even know the words to the song. She wished she'd gone out of her office sooner, so she could have heard Derrick's group singing it. Another thing that invited the man back into her thoughts. She shook her head, picked up the brightly colored papers, and headed out of her office.

"Here are the activity schedules for this week and next, Sarah." Scarlett slipped the papers into the clear plastic holder she'd purchased to keep them accessible but out of the way on the check-in counter.

Sarah hung up the lodge phone and gave her a huge grin. "You'll never guess who just booked two weeks, starting this Friday."

Scarlett heaved a sigh. "I'm not good at guessing games, but I'm sure you'll tell me. Has some celebrity chosen Snowbird Lodge for a winter vacation?"

Sarah stared at her a moment with a gleam in her eye. "Not exactly a celebrity, but someone I'm sure we'll all enjoy having back." She dragged out the word *all*, giving it a strong emphasis.

"Have back?" Scarlett scrunched up her face, trying to figure out who Sarah was talking about. The lodge hadn't been open long enough to have many returnees.

"Yes, a certain very handsome man is returning." Sarah turned toward the computer and started clacking the keys.

Scarlett moved behind her and read over her shoulder. *D-e-r-r...*

She didn't need to continue. Only one man with a name starting with those letters had been here, and he'd just left...*two days ago*. Why was Derrick coming back? And so soon?

For a moment her heart wanted to believe it had something to do with her, but what a foolish wish. "Friends" didn't do things like that.

He spent a lot of time with the young men in the church group. She'd heard them discuss their activities. Maybe he hadn't been able to ski on all the black-diamond and double-black-diamond slopes. That thought brought her mind back to square one.

Why did the man want to take such chances? With his bent toward the dangerous, they could never be anything but friends. The realization dampened her spirits. In any other circumstance, she could see their friendship developing into something more substantial. More permanent, maybe...

Derrick threw his duffel and another suitcase into the truck. He'd packed more this time because he wanted to be prepared for what he hoped would develop.

After he turned onto the interstate, his thoughts raced before him toward Snowbird Lodge. *Wonder what Scarlett will think when I show up?*

That last night had been superb. Going out as friends turned into something else for him. When he chose the Lone Eagle Grill, he'd not allowed himself to think about anything but the wonderful food choices. But once they sat at the table, the night felt like a date to him. He'd wished it had to Scarlett, too.

He'd eaten one of the best steaks he'd ever had, but he didn't realize it until he was mulling over the evening later. His attention had been completely captured by the woman sitting across from him.

While they talked and enjoyed the food, he'd watched the candlelight shimmer in her eyes. Scarlett was beyond beautiful inside and out. Her intelligence shone through the lively conversation, and her love of the Lord sprinkled throughout her words, snippets that sounded like the natural flow of her vocabulary.

She studied the moonlight on the lake and talked about God's creative force. The same thing he often felt. They'd connected on so many levels.

That's why he spent much of the last five days in prayer. Would God approve of a relationship between them? God didn't close the door, even when he asked Him to if He didn't want Derrick to pursue Scarlett.

Derrick didn't casually date, but this woman drew him in a way he'd never experienced before. He wanted to explore the possibilities. To do that, he had to return to Snowbird Lodge. Never had a drive seemed so long.

The lodge front door opened, and the bell Scarlett had placed above it rang. She stilled her fingers on the keyboard in her office and listened for voices. A group this time, with both men and women. She assumed Derrick would be alone. She'd looked at the reservation to see if anyone was coming with him. The other people checking in today were couples or families from other far-flung places.

Ding, ding, ding. Someone else.

With all the interruptions, she wasn't accomplishing anything in her office. She needed a break. And a cup of dark hot chocolate.

She headed out of her office, and the bell rang again. Since Sarah was waiting on the family that just came in, Scarlett glanced toward the entry.

Derrick stopped right beyond the threshold, dropped his bags, and stared at her.

He looks good. Too good for her peace of mind. She moved up behind the counter.

"May I help you?"

Finally, his gaze disconnected from hers. He reached down and picked up the two pieces of luggage. He quickly approached and put the bags down again. "You look wonderful, Scarlett."

The words poured over her like warm honey. Soothing and sweet. "Thank you." *You do, too.* How she wished she had the right to speak the thought.

"When you left, you didn't say anything about coming back." She kept her tone from sounding accusatory. "I had no idea."

He propped one strong forearm on the tall counter. "Neither did I. One of the perks of owning my own company."

"What is?"

"Being able to take off whenever you want." He grinned. "That didn't come out right. If you take off every time you want to, you soon won't have a company. . . . Anyway, are you going to check me in?"

"I can." She went to the auxiliary computer and started inputting data. "Let's see. You plan to be here two weeks. Is that right, Mr. Greene?"

"Come on, Scarlett. We're beyond the Mr. Greene stage, aren't we?"

Heat filled her cheeks before she glanced up. "Derrick," she whispered.

His smile pierced her heart, chipping away a chink in the wall around her heart. Part of her fear escaped.

A smile split his face when Scarlett looked at him. Her pink cheeks complemented the flecks of green in her hazel eyes. No, they were hazel like his father's. The velvety green jogging suit helped, too. He loved the bright colors she wore. And her coal black hair—oh, man! She really knew how to dress to look her best.

"Yes."

Surprise widened her eyes. "What?"

"Yes." His heart lifted. She was as affected by him as he was by her. "I'm going to stay two weeks."

She glanced down, and her fingers danced across the keys before she looked up again. "You're all set." She continued to stand there, smiling at him.

He would love to stay here all day, but he wanted to unpack, and she was on duty. "Are you going to give me a key card and tell me what room I'm in?"

The pink in her cheeks darkened. She ran a key card through the machine, then held the card toward him. "Room 211."

He closed his hand around her fingers, holding them just a little longer than necessary. They were icy. *Cold hands, warm heart.* He wouldn't go any further with the rhyme. "Thank you, Scarlett." He didn't let go, and she didn't pull away. "What time do you get off today?"

Feeling a slight tug from her, he let go.

She shoved her hand in her pocket. "I finish at five."

"Would you like to go out and play in the snow before it gets too dark?"

His question must have surprised her. Her eyebrows raised, and she glanced across the lobby. She reached behind her and put a small box of ornaments on the counter. "Would you like to put an ornament on the tree?"

"Only if you come over and help me choose a place." He picked up a shiny green ball that matched her clothing.

"Of course, Mr. . . .Derrick." She went around Sarah and came out from behind the counter.

As they walked toward the tree, he thought about taking her hand, but he held back. He didn't want to rush her. Something still stood between them. He wanted to find out what it was before he left. But he'd have to take his time and not push her too hard. She had to want to tell him. That's what he would be working toward.

147

"So. . .want to play in the snow?" He glanced at the ornaments that had been added since he left. Noticing a bare spot, he hung the ball in the middle of it. "Does it look okay right here?"

"Yes."

He turned toward her. "Yes, what?"

"Yes, the ball looks fine there." A smile teased at her lips. "And yes, I'd like to play in the snow. . .if it doesn't include skiing."

"I was thinking more like building a snowman or making snow angels or even just taking a walk in the crisp, cold air."

"Sounds like fun."

Making a little headway—he hoped.

Scarlett tried to settle down to work out the next schedules, but her mind wandered upstairs. The hours crept by on sloth's feet while she watched the hands of the clock laze around the face. Had she ever experienced a longer afternoon? Not even as a small child waiting for Christmas or her birthday.

That's how she felt. She was waiting for a wonderful present to unfold before her.

Chapter 7

Derrick stepped in front of Scarlett and held the door open for her. *What a gentleman!* She could get used to this.

"So what do you want to do first?" He leaned close and his warm breath brushed her cheek.

Breathe. I want to breathe. The strong man beside her, not the frigid air, stole her breath. His athletic body exhibited his physical strength, but she hadn't understood his spiritual strength until she got to know him better that last night he was here.

"You said something about snow angels." She glanced up into his eyes that had darkened to the shade of the evergreens surrounding the lodge. "Did you mean it?" She felt sure he didn't. What man wanted to lie down in the snow like a child?

A grin broke out on his face. "I don't say things I don't mean." His words sounded like a promise.

They walked around the side of the building and found a pristine area of snow.

Derrick studied the layout with an analytical expression. *Just like a man.* She hoped he didn't overanalyze everything.

"How do we want to arrange our angels?" He looked so serious.

"Don't you just lie down and move your arms and legs? They fall where they fall." She hoped her smile took the bite out of the question.

"What ya doin'?" a child's voice interrupted.

Scarlett turned to see Lynzie, an elementary aged neighbor girl, standing with her arms folded over her chest. "We're going to make snow angels."

The girl's brown eyes widened with her grin. "Can I do it, too?"

Scarlett glanced at her companion, and he gave a slight nod. "I don't know why not. Does your dad and grandma know you're out here?"

Lynzie gave a vigorous nod that bounced her dark hair around her face. "My dad does."

Scarlett hoped she was telling them the truth. "So I guess we'll just flop down and make the angels."

The girl squinted her eyes and stared at the ground. "We could make a family of snow angels." She smiled up at Derrick. "You could be the daddy, and you can go right there." She pointed to a spot before looking at Scarlett. "You can be the mommy, right there." Her gesture indicated a place about three feet from Derrick. "And I'll be the kid, and I'll be in between, like we were taking a walk together."

She plopped down between the spaces she'd pointed out

for Derrick and Scarlett. Her arms and legs pumped until the snow angel appeared. Then she got up.

"You go ahead, mister. You're next."

Scarlett gave a quick cough to keep from laughing. Derrick dropped into the snow and soon finished his angel.

"Now you." Little Miss Dictator jabbed her red-striped mitten toward Scarlett.

Obediently, she lay down in the snow and completed her angel.

When she got up, a huge smile bloomed on the little girl's face. "That looks good."

Unmindful of the snow, Derrick knelt beside the girl. "What's your name?"

"Lynzie Brooks. It's spelled L-y-n-z-i-e." She stuck out her hand. "Pleased to meet you, mister. What's your name, so I can tell my dad?"

"I'm Derrick Greene." He clasped the mittened hand and gave it a firm shake. Then he stood. "This is my friend Scarlett McKaye. She works at Snowbird Lodge."

Lynzie's gaze traveled up toward her face. "I know. I've met her before, but I didn't know her last name."

After Lynzie walked away, Scarlett glanced at Derrick. His eyes followed the little girl until she went around a clump of bushes. "She's cute, isn't she?"

"Yes." Knowing that Derrick interacted well with children warmed her heart.

Too bad she couldn't really trust him with her affections. If only he didn't take so many chances with his life. When she was with him, she kept forgetting that important detail.

A siren's wail came closer and closer to the lodge. The personnel from the first-aid station hurried out with a wheeled stretcher between them, reminding Scarlett of Bethany's recent skiing accident. An injured skier moaned as they moved him over the uneven terrain toward the place where the ambulance had stopped beside the curb. Cole Beckman, the ski instructor for Snowbird Lodge, ran along beside, trying to calm the patient. Paramedics leaped from the back of the emergency vehicle and fired off a volley of questions.

As Scarlett and Derrick moved closer, she only caught a few of the words: ". . .broken. . .punctured. . .bleeding. . . surgery. . .serious." Not the kind of words anyone wanted to hear. When Cole mentioned Corkscrew, Scarlett shivered. Then resolve stiffened her spine. She couldn't fall for anyone who put himself in that kind of danger, and the man who walked beside her was just such a man. How could she have relaxed her vigilance as she had? Just because she liked everything else about Derrick didn't mean he could possibly be the man for her.

A red danger sign flashed in her mind. He put himself in harm's way, but he was also dangerous to her heart. How could she get out of her predicament without either of them getting hurt? She didn't know the answer, but she had to start easing away from this man.

Derrick enjoyed their little interlude with Lynzie, but after she left, something had changed with Scarlett. Something subtle, and he couldn't figure for the life of him what had caused it. She'd been more open and connected, but after the snow angels, she drew away from him once again.

"Want to build a snowman?" Maybe that would get her back into her playful mood.

"Sure. Why not?" He puzzled over her lack of enthusiasm.

Together they rolled a large snowball through the drifts, stopping when it was about three feet across. The next one was slightly smaller, and while he picked it up and placed it on the base, Scarlett formed the head. They returned to the lodge to scavenge items to finish their man. As she set about to decorate the snow tower, Derrick hunted for sticks to use as arms. Too bad someone kept the grounds so clean. It took him quite awhile.

Soon Mr. Snow, as Scarlett called it, sported a jaunty hat, a row of pom-pom buttons, pieces of burned wood from the fireplace for eyes, a carrot nose, and a green plaid scarf around his neck. Derrick punched the arms into the sides of the body, and they laughed together about their creation. But his laughter was more genuine than hers. He'd heard her laugh with abandon. This definitely was different.

Their boots crunched over the frozen ground. Despite the moonlight glinting off the snow, their former camaraderie never returned.

Scarlett stood under a hot shower and replayed the evening in her mind. Derrick was a lot of fun to be around. She enjoyed talking to him, and the more she learned about his strong faith and convictions, the more she respected him as a man. Her one sticking point was his penchant for taking risks. When she thought about him out on the double-diamond slopes, fear wrapped her heart in its icy grip. She could not become involved with another man who flirted with danger all the time. Once in a lifetime was more than enough.

She toweled off and wrapped herself in her long terrycloth robe. Leaning close to the mirror, she studied herself. What was there about her that drew dangerous men like a magnet? She couldn't tell. Her curly hair was hard to tame sometimes, and her features may be a little sharp. Couldn't they see the woman underneath? A woman who only wanted to be loved by a man she didn't have to worry about. One who would come home to her every day, cherish her, and take care of her and their children.

Lord, is that too much to ask?

The next two weeks would be hard for her. Derrick would be around all the time. He might want to spend time with her, though he didn't mention it when they parted earlier.

So many things about the man drew her—his walk with the Lord, his fun side, the man deeper inside who she caught a glimpse of that night in the Lone Eagle Grill. Maybe it wasn't that she drew dangerous men. Instead, she was drawn to them. Well, she could control that, couldn't she? Keep their time together to a minimum. Just be friendly on a surface level. Then, when he left again, she would be heart-whole. For some reason, that thought spread a gloomy pall over her.

For the next few days, Derrick followed his original plan. He sought Scarlett out in the dining room at mealtime. When he asked to join her and whomever she sat with, she agreed. They all talked and seemed to enjoy each other's company, but Scarlett kept herself more aloof than before.

The first time he asked her when she would get off work, she told him she had plans. He didn't really want to spy on her, but when she left her office, he noticed she went up to her room and didn't come down the rest of the evening.

He prayed a lot that night and still didn't get the sense that the Lord wanted him to back off from a relationship with Scarlett. He also poured out his heart to the Lord, praying for her and the Lord's will in her life. Somehow he felt that he would have a part in her future. He just wasn't quite sure what his part would be.

The evenings that she had planned activities in the lounge area were the easiest for him to spend time with her. Of course, they weren't alone, but just watching her as she interacted with everyone warmed his heart. Sometimes he was the recipient of her undivided attention during the activities. Those times were a premium.

After a week, he was tired of playing this game. He waited near the front desk on Friday afternoon. There weren't any group activities, so he asked if she would like to go into Incline Village for dinner.

She almost declined. He could see it in her eyes—eyes that

held a sadness in their depths. He had to know why.

"I need to pick up a few things. Maybe I can find what I need at Raley's Shopping Center. Then we could get something to eat."

She wavered. "I need some things, too."

"So go with me. Friends do that kind of thing." He gave what he hoped was a winning smile as he held out his hand.

"All right. . .friends." She laughed and gave his hand a good shake but quickly broke the connection. "Just let me go up to my room and grab my purse."

Scarlett must have done more than that, because he waited almost half an hour. When she exited the elevator, she looked terrific. Maybe there was hope. She'd taken time to let her hair down and add more color to her face. Not too much, but enough that he could tell.

He hurried to open the front door, then led her to his truck. After helping her in, he rounded the cab and climbed into the leather driver's seat.

"You like driving an Xterra?" Her gaze wandered all over the inside.

"Yeah." He shifted into Reverse and backed out of his parking spot. "It's really handy in my business."

"I don't think you've ever mentioned what kind of business you own." She smiled at him.

"I own a wilderness trekking company."

Her eyes widened. "What does that mean?"

"I take groups into the wilderness for retreats or just to camp."

Her smile faded a little. "Isn't that dangerous?"

"Not if you know what you're doing." Something about this appeared to bother her. Maybe it was tied in with what else was going on. "I'm very good at what I do. I haven't lost a single trekker yet."

Her smile went into total eclipse. What he meant as a joke didn't make her laugh.

He needed a diversion. "Would you like to listen to Christian music on the way?"

"Sure."

Derrick slid in a CD by his favorite Christian group—the worship team from a church he often visited in Texas. He'd even become friends with a couple of the guys who wrote some of their music.

As the melody filled the cab, he watched Scarlett slowly relax. She leaned deeper into the seat, and her hands rested quietly in her lap.

Maybe his business was too close to her problem. He didn't want to ruin their time together in town, but they *were* going to discuss it later.

Chapter 8

When Scarlett and Derrick arrived back at Snowbird Lodge, she hurried from the truck to the front door. Icy air swirled and bit at her face. She drew the warm red scarf—the one she had received from Derrick the night of the gift exchange—up around her mouth and nose and clutched the items she'd bought close to her chest.

Woodsy warm air met them as they stepped into the lobby. A welcoming fire blazed in the lounge area. She hurried toward the warmth. After dropping her packages, she tugged off her gloves and unwound the scarf from her neck. She huddled with her hands extended toward the flames.

Derrick dropped his coat and gloves and joined her. "Feels good, doesn't it?"

She glanced up into his face. He studied her, his gaze tender. Not exactly what she wanted to see. Every time she was with this man, her emotions pulled her into an arena she wasn't ready to face. "Maybe my fingers will thaw soon. They feel like icicles."

He turned his back to the fire and clasped his hands behind him. "Hot chocolate would hit the spot. Holding the mug could warm our hands."

She nodded.

"You like the really dark kind, right?"

How did he remember so much about her? "Yes, but with marshmallows on top."

His eyebrows lifted. "Doesn't that defeat the purpose of the dark chocolate?"

"Not really." She turned her back to the fire, too. "At home I also shave extra dark chocolate into the cup and let it melt into the drink. Heavenly. You should try it."

He shook his head. "I like my coffee black but my hot chocolate more milky."

Scarlett glanced over at the coffee bar. All the makings for the drinks were still out. "Want to make some? We could sit and talk, since no one else is around."

"I'll help." Derrick trailed after her as she went to the table.

While she worked, she hummed that tune that had been going over and over in her head ever since she first heard it. *Wish I knew the words.*

Derrick glanced at her. "You like 'The More I Seek You'?"

She stopped stirring. "What?"

"You're humming 'The More I Seek You.' One of my favorite choruses." He picked up his mug and followed her to the leather love seat near the fireplace.

She slid onto the cushion and set her mug on the table

beside her. "I didn't know the name of the tune. I heard it when you and the young men from your church had your worship time here in the lounge. I was in my office Skypeing my parents. I could hear the melody but not the words. I haven't been able to get the tune out of my head." She pushed a throw pillow behind her back and leaned against it.

Derrick sat at the other end of the short couch. "When I go to north Texas, I attend a church there. The man who wrote this song is on the worship team. I talked to him. Told him how much the song means to me." He took a sip of his hot drink and set it down then turned toward her with his arm resting along the back of the sofa.

"That must have been interesting." She'd never met a songwriter.

"It was."

"So what are the words to the song?"

He grinned. "I'll sing it for you, if you promise not to laugh."

She held up her right fist with two fingers extended. "Scout's honor."

"You were a Girl Scout?" Interest gleamed in his eyes.

"No, a Boy Scout." She laughed. "I know, that's corny, but I just couldn't resist. So go ahead and sing it for me. I'll lean back, close my eyes, and just listen."

Soon his pleasant tenor voice enclosed them in a cocoon of music. "The more I seek You, the more I find You. The more I find You, the more I love You. I want to sit at Your feet, drink from the cup in Your hand, lay back against You and breathe, feel Your heartbeat. This love is so deep, it's more than I can stand. I melt in Your peace, it's overwhelming."

His voice faded, but the peace didn't. It blanketed her, and Scarlett felt more settled than she ever had in her life. She didn't want to break the silence.

After a few moments, Derrick spoke softly. "What do you think about it now?"

She opened her eyes and studied his face. "I don't know what to say. . . . I feel the overwhelming peace, too. That's a powerful song. Do you know what gave him the idea for it?"

"Yeah." Derrick gazed at the fire. "He said the idea came from John at the Last Supper with Jesus. It's about communing with God."

She pondered that for a moment. "I've been a Christian a long time, but I don't know if I've experienced what the song describes."

Derrick turned back, and his gaze roamed over her face, ending on her eyes. "Can you imagine sitting at the feet of Jesus? And He offers you a drink from His own cup. You wouldn't refuse. If you leaned back against Him, your breath would mingle with His. Like when God breathed into Adam. Jesus breathes into us while we commune with Him. Leaning against Him and feeling His heartbeat, our heart syncs with His. We're able to see ourselves through His eyes. Feel His love for us and His love for others—wanting to see people come to know Him the way we do."

Wow! Scarlett had never considered that. So much to mull over. She closed her eyes. "Please sing it again."

While he sang, she remembered all he'd said, and she understood Jesus in a deeper way. She allowed His peace to overwhelm her.

When Derrick was finished singing, he spoke again. "One of the reasons I started the trekking business was to help other people get away from their fast-paced lives and take time to really communicate with God. Not just pray, but also sit and listen to Him. He'll talk to you if you let Him."

Derrick's words pricked at the ball of fear still lodged in her heart.

Derrick watched Scarlett. She opened her eyes and sat forward.

"How can you take such dangerous risks with your life? I know you've been on the double-black-diamond slopes. We saw that man who was seriously injured on Corkscrew last week, and right after Thanksgiving, Bethany had a skiing accident. I'm sure there are other things you do that I would believe were dangerous. What if you die doing one of those risky things?"

Finally, he caught a hint of what had caused her to pull away from him before. "I don't do anything that I've not prepared for."

She gave him a hard stare. "You can't prepare for every eventuality."

"You're right, Scarlett, but I don't live in fear."

She jumped up and went to stand with her back to the fireplace. "Taking chances like you do, you could be *killed*."

The last word showed her pain as it escaped. And it stabbed at his heart.

He followed and stood in front of her. "I could be killed in an automobile accident, just driving around town. Or in any number of ways that I have no control over. I'm not afraid to die. I'll go to heaven."

She pulled back as if he'd slapped her and whirled away from the fire. "But you shouldn't tempt fate." She paced across the floor, the rug silencing each step.

"I don't believe in fate. I trust God, who numbered the days of my life."

"I knew a man who. . .took unnecessary risks, and I—I helped bury him."

Is that what this is all about? Sympathy stirred him when he saw her grab her upper arms and grip so tightly her knuckles whitened. She'd have bruises tomorrow. "Who was he, Scarlett?"

She stopped and glared at him from across the room. "My fiancé."

Concerned that she was about to burst into tears or run from the room, Derrick hurried toward her. "I am so sorry." He coaxed her into his arms and pressed her head against his chest. "I didn't mean to bring up sad memories."

He kissed the top of her head and led her back to the love seat. "Scarlett, when I'm at the top of a double-black-diamond slope, it's indescribable—an awesome sight to see God's majestic creation spread out before me. Every time I'm up there, I feel closer to Him. We commune together." He shook his head. "I won't ski the difficult slopes unless I'm in tip-top physical shape." Reaching for her hand, he cradled her soft fingers between his callused ones and looked deep into her eyes. "And I wouldn't go up there if I hadn't trained for it. I'm not really taking that much of a chance."

"How can you say that?" The words whooshed out of her. She released her arms and clasped her hands in her lap.

"Actually, I wiped out on one of them the other day. But I didn't get hurt, except for some bruises, because I knew what to do. Most of the skiers who are hurt seriously, like the man they took away in the ambulance, go up without the proper training."

She stared at her clasped hands for a moment. "When I stood at the edge of Gordon's grave, I promised myself that I wouldn't get involved with another man who took unnecessary chances."

That could change things. "Remember the song I sang." He waited for her to nod. "I live for God's overwhelming peace. There is a scripture that says His peace can guard us if we allow it. I do. I spend time communicating with God. When I plan to do anything, I talk to Him about it. If I don't feel that overwhelming peace, I don't continue with my plan. Only when His peace is present do I set out."

A tiny spark of understanding entered her eyes. "Okay. You don't do anything dangerous unless God gives you peace about it. Right?"

"Right." He hoped she really did understand.

"I think I can accept that." Finally, a smile broke through. "I'll try it myself, if you'll teach me the words to the song."

For the next half hour, they drank their hot chocolate, talked, and sang the song together. Derrick felt the barriers between them coming down. He'd use the rest of his time here to remove them completely.

"Scarlett, would you allow me to pray with you?"

With her consent, he took both her hands in his and lifted her heart to the Lord.

Scarlett rose early the next morning. She'd slept better than she had in a long time. After reading her Bible and praying, she sang the song Derrick had taught her, then waited and listened. God's words to her were special and private—words that affirmed how much He loved her.

By the time she arrived at the dining room, Derrick was seated, drinking his coffee. He asked her to join him, and she did. When they finished breakfast, she couldn't remember what she ate, but she did remember all she'd told Derrick about her morning devotions.

"Do you have to work today?" He leaned his elbows on the table as if he were anxiously awaiting her answer.

"I did plan an activity for tonight. Many people are leaving today, and others are checking in. I like to have something special when a new group arrives."

His smile drooped a little.

"But everything is ready, so I'm free for the day."

"Have you had a chance to see much of the Lake Tahoe area?"

"I've only been to Incline Village."

He stood and helped her up from her chair. "I could drive you around the lake, and we could do some sightseeing."

"I'd like that."

He didn't let go of her hand, and she didn't try to pull away. The connection felt right.

Derrick's last week at Snowbird Lodge went better than he'd hoped. He and Scarlett spent most of her off time together. They played together, laughed together, worshipped together, and grew closer in more ways than he'd anticipated when he returned to the lodge.

While he prepared to spend the evening with her, he took stock of where their relationship stood. Today was his last day. He had to leave at sunup tomorrow. Although he needed to get back and take care of business, he didn't want to leave. Every moment he'd spent with Scarlett brought them closer together.

He took one last look in the mirror, adjusted his collar, then went to the lounge area to wait for her. When she stepped off the elevator, his heart leaped. That was either a very good thing or a very bad thing. If their relationship wasn't going anywhere, he needed to know soon.

When he started toward her, she met him halfway. He surveyed her from head to toe. "You look. . .gorgeous."

A pleased smile brought warmth to her eyes. "You did tell me to dress up. This is as good as it gets."

"Who could ask for anything more?" Even though he was flirting with her, he meant every word. He didn't idly compliment women, especially not Scarlett.

"I thought you'd like this red dress." A blush stained her cheeks. "I mean, after all, you got the red scarf for me."

He gulped. "How did you know?"

"One of the young men told me."

"Had to be P. J." He laughed. "Never tell him anything you don't want the world to know. Shall we go?" He stretched his hand toward the exit.

When he pulled up close to the door of Lone Eagle Grill, Scarlett turned to him. "I wondered if you might bring me here. I loved it when we came before."

He got out and opened her door without turning off the engine. He walked her to the entrance. "Wait inside where it's warm while I find a place to park."

She put her gloved hand on his cheek and stared deep into his eyes. "You are so thoughtful."

Her tender touch made the cold walk from the parking place to the restaurant unimportant. Like before, they were seated where they could view Lake Tahoe but still enjoy the rock fireplace nearby.

"What do you want to eat tonight?" He closed his menu and waited to hear her choice.

"I loved the duck, and I don't get to have it very often."

"Then duck it is."

The waiter came to take their order.

"The lady will have the duck, and I'll have a porterhouse."

Scarlett laughed after the waiter left. "You ordered the same thing, too."

"I want to remember both evenings we've spent here. This will make it easier." He reached across the table and took her hand. "We need to have a serious discussion."

"Okay?" An agreement, but a question, too.

"I enjoy being with you."

She nodded and placed her other hand on their joined ones. "Me, too. . .I mean, I enjoy being with you, too."

"Since I'm a Christian, I don't date casually." He reached his other hand toward her, and she slipped her hand into his.

"I don't date much either."

"There's a reason." He cleared his throat. "I promised the Lord that I would wait for Him to bring the woman He had for me."

She shifted but didn't withdraw her hands.

"I want to be very sure what His will is, so when I leave Snowbird Lodge, I'm going to go home and pray about whether the Lord plans for us to be together. Would you do that, too?"

She turned her gaze toward the moonlit vista outside the cozy room. When she turned back, her eyes held an affirmation. "I'd like that."

In the last week, he'd explored so many things with her. He knew she was just as beautiful on the inside as on the outside. Her strong faith matched his. He hoped it wasn't just his own desires overshadowing what the Lord wanted for them.

Scarlett hung up her cell phone, overwhelmed with loneliness. Derrick had been gone for a couple of weeks, and she missed him so much. She had prayed and sang and listened, and God hadn't said no to her. But Derrick must have forgotten what he had asked her before he left.

He'd called almost every day, and they talked about so many things—except for the most important one. He never mentioned the pledge they made to seek God's will for their lives. Maybe he'd forgotten, but maybe he'd changed his mind.

When she spent time with God, her heart felt at peace about her and Derrick being together. But after hanging up from a call without Derrick saying anything about their relationship, she felt troubled. Had she set herself up to be hurt again? She knew better than to open the inner part of her heart to a man, but Derrick was different. He had slipped by her defenses when she wasn't looking. She brushed away a tear that escaped.

Today was Christmas Eve. Probably the reason she felt so sad. This would be her first one away from home. She'd planned activities for the guests staying over the holiday, but she didn't feel like celebrating. If only she could just stay in her room and read. Participating in the lodge's activities didn't appeal to her, even though she was in charge of them.

The phone in the suite rang. She picked it up. "Hello."

"Scarlett"—Sarah's voice droned a monotone—"can you come down to the front desk, please?"

"I'll be right there."

She went to her room to touch up her hair and put on some powder to try to disguise the gloom.

When she stepped off the elevator, all she could see was a giant bouquet of flowers. Then Derrick peeked around the blossoms. "Hello, beautiful."

Her breathing accelerated so much, she thought she was going to hyperventilate. "Derrick? But I just finished talking to you. . . . You're not here—but you are here." She almost burst into tears.

Bethany stepped up beside him. Scarlett hadn't even noticed her.

"I'll take these upstairs and put them in the suite for you."

Scarlett managed a flustered nod.

When the bouquet was no longer between her and Derrick, he dropped to one knee. She glanced around to see who might be watching. Actually, a lot of people were, but who cared? She didn't.

She trained all her attention on the man who had taken up residence in her heart.

"Scarlett, I've prayed and sought the Lord, and I believe He means for us to be together." He reached into his pocket and withdrew a tiny velvet box.

Feeling light-headed, she took a deep breath and let it out slowly. *He's not really going to propose, is he?*

He flipped the lid open, and a gorgeous ring with a giant ruby surrounded by diamonds glittered and danced before her eyes. "Will you marry me?"

Like tinkling golden bells, those precious words hung in the air surrounding them, connecting them as never before. For a moment, she was speechless. Then she reached for him. This was one question she wouldn't answer with "No thank you."

"Yes. Oh, yes!"

He put one arm around her. "Don't you want to put this on?"

She held out her hand. Derrick's hands were busy holding her and the jewelry box, so she took the ring and slipped it on her own finger. Perfect. She studied it a moment, then threw her arms around Derrick's neck.

He pulled her even closer. She fit so well against him. . .like they were made for each other. With the first gentle touch of his lips, everything around them faded away. Love sealed their first kiss. She melted completely into his embrace. The most wonderful kiss she'd ever experienced went on for what seemed an eternity. . .but it ended far too soon.

When they eased apart, she realized that everyone around them was applauding. She didn't care. She would be married to the one she sought God about—the love of her life.

Derrick wondered how long it would take Scarlett to notice that her parents had been standing there watching during the proposal.

"How did you know I would love a ruby ring?"

He smiled down at his fiancée. "God told me."

"What happens now?" Her adoring gaze bathed him in warmth.

"I believe introductions are in order." At her scrunched brow, he motioned for his parents to step forward. Scarlett McKaye, I'd like for you to meet my parents, Mr. and Mrs. Greene."

He watched the shock appear on her face, then she offered her hand in greeting. Her father cleared his throat from the other side of the group. Scarlett glanced that way then did a double take before her parents enfolded her in a three-way hug.

After they broke apart, Derrick claimed Scarlett's arm. "We're taking our parents to the Lone Eagle Grill. We have lots of plans to make."

He pulled her into his arms once again and tasted the sweetness that he planned to enjoy every day for the rest of his life.

LENA NELSON DOOLEY is an author, editor, and speaker. *Christmas Love at Lake Tahoe* is her twenty-second book release. A full-time writer, she is the president of DFW Ready Writers, the local Dallas-Fort Worth chapter of American Christian Fiction Writers. She also has hosted a critique group in her home for over twenty years. Several of the writers she's mentored have become published authors, too.

Lena lives with the love of her life in north Texas. They love to travel and spend time with family and friends. They're active church members, where Lena serves in the bookstore, on the Altar Ministry team, and as a volunteer for the Care ministry and Global Ministries.

The Dooley family includes two daughters, their spouses, two granddaughters, two grandsons, and a great-grandson.

You can find Lena at several places on the Internet: www.lenanelsondooley.com, http://lenanelsondooley.blogspot.com, and her monthly newsletter is at http://lenanelsondooleynewsletter.blogspot.com. You can also visit her on Shoutlife, Facebook, and Twitter.

Tinsel, Tidings, and Time-share

by Jean Kincaid

To my son, who is the light of my life. Firstborn and beloved. I imagined you and my precious daughter-in-law while writing this story. I wonder why?

To my heavenly Father, who is my strength and shield.

And of course to Dale, whom I'll love forever.

Thanks to the novella team for all your help, and a special thanks to Becky Germany, our editor.

*Wherefore he is able also to save them
to the uttermost that come unto God by him,
seeing he ever liveth to make intercession for them.*
HEBREWS 7:25 KJV

Chapter 1

"All is calm!" A full moon, round and silver, provided a swath of light that caused the freshly made snow crystals to shimmer. The words from the Christmas song that she'd heard sung last Sunday for the first time this season appropriately fit the scenario in front of her. It was night, two o'clock in the morning to be exact, and not a skier was in sight. Silence reigned. Even that inner voice that incessantly prodded her to do more, work harder, so she would be as good as her friends, was quiet. No, tonight God's glory manifested itself in the sheer beauty of His creation.

Stephanie St. John sat cross-legged on the carpeted floor of her bedroom, her back propped against the cedar chest at the foot of her bed, content to stare out over the twenty-four-hundred-acre ski resort. Her lot had been the last room of the suite, sharing the same wall as the fireplace in the living room, and as luck would have it, a matching picture window. Every clear morning, the sun bounced off of Lake Tahoe and stole through the long vertical blinds, beckoning and tempting her spirit of adventure in this magnificent spot. Children's laughter, as they began early-morning ski lessons, mingled with greetings called out by staff and visitors alike. But tonight all was calm, all was bright; it definitely was a "silent night."

She heard the whisper of her door opening and knew it was Bethany. Whether Bethany's vocation as a nurse caused her to be more sensitive to others' needs, Stephanie didn't know. She just knew that since early on in college, Bethany seemed to possess a sixth sense concerning the moods of the people around her. She had that healing touch, those words of comfort, the encouraging spirit that Stephanie had so often needed during the long study hours of college finals. How had Bethany known, with all that transpired in her own life the last few weeks, that tonight Stephanie needed to unwind, to scrutinize every aspect of the day, to weigh the good against the bad?

"I knew you'd be up." Bethany lowered herself to the floor beside Stephanie, hooking her arms around her legs and resting her chin on her knees. They wore the same style of pajama pants with a long-sleeved T-shirt top.

"And I knew you'd come talk to me," Stephanie replied. They sat in silence, kindred spirits, conversation unnecessary for the moment.

The girls and the newly hired ski instructor were the only staff, other than Bethany's grandparents, who lived at the lodge. Life couldn't get much better—living in the beautiful Lake Tahoe area in a huge log resort with ten log cabins of various sizes dotting the hill above and below them. Stephanie's job was to sell a week's stay to fifty-two people in each of the log cabins. A daunting task, but one she planned to enjoy to the fullest.

Jerked from her thoughts by Bethany's firm grip on her arm, Stephanie turned to see her friend's mouth formed a perfect O, her eyes alight as she stared at something beyond the glass. Stephanie glanced back at the window. Large snow-flakes drifted down in a spiral and settled on the already-white ground. What could be more perfect?

"It's beautiful," Bethany whispered, as if speaking aloud might cause the snow to vanish.

"A winter wonderland," Stephanie responded. "I feel like a princess looking out over my kingdom."

"I know, I know." Bethany released Stephanie's arm and joined their hands the same way they'd done the first year of college, when both girls had been so homesick. "Oh, Stephanie, I hope we're all successful here, so we'll always have a place to call home."

"Yeah, me, too. And we will, girlfriend." Stephanie snapped her fingers and cut them through the air in a Z shape. "I feel it in my bones."

Bethany laughed. "Your bones. You're twenty-two. You've got a few years before your bones feel anything."

"Speaking of feelings"—Stephanie paused for effect—"why are you trying so hard to avoid Cole?" Stephanie knew the cause of friction between the new ski instructor and her friend, but had picked up on an undercurrent of a different nature each time the two were near each other.

Bethany stood and walked to the window. "I don't have time right now for romance. My job requires that I be on call twenty-four/seven, and to tell you the truth, I feel like the world is my oyster. I can do anything. No more papers to write, classes to rush to. So why should I tie myself down in a relationship when I finally have the freedom to do anything I want?"

Stephanie looked at her friend, the exact opposite of herself in every way. Bethany had enough confidence for the both of them, and Stephanie had borrowed from her often enough in that area. Stephanie's short blond hair lay on her shoulders, while Bethany's dark auburn hung almost to her waist, her light brown eyes often seeing the confusion and hurt in Stephanie's green ones, brought on by parents that lacked sensitivity where their only child was concerned.

"Yep, I know. I feel the same way. We have a mountain to conquer." Stephanie watched for Bethany's response and wasn't disappointed as her friend smiled.

"And what a mountain it is!" Bethany continued to stare out over the valley from her mountaintop perch.

Stephanie felt the bed bounce behind her. "Well, if you two don't get your tails into bed, the sleep fairy's gonna clobber you tomorrow about two o'clock." Michaela landed on her stomach, feet up in the air, her face near Stephanie's shoulder.

"We saw it snowing and wanted to wake you to watch with us." Scarlett joined Bethany at the window. "We were too excited to sleep. Besides, we forgot to pray."

Stephanie never had figured out what the prayer thing was

all about, but the other three depended on those nightly sessions to keep them on track. She felt so included by these three friends that a few words to God seemed a small debt to pay. And she believed in God. She'd been assured many times that believing was all it took. She just didn't understand how one needed to pray daily in order to manage their lives.

The girls piled on her bed and began the nightly ritual started four years ago on their first day of college. They held hands and Bethany prayed earnestly that God would be honored by their lives. Michaela asked Him to forgive their sins, and Scarlett prayed that He would guide their steps according to His will. Routinely it fell to Stephanie to ask His blessing on their families and those less fortunate, and she did so with eloquent words. A resounding "amen" signaled the end to their session. She wondered when they'd stop this childish practice, as often that feeling of something missing plagued her for days until she squashed it by singing a special at the church or helping at the senior citizens' home.

"Are you guys still happy we came to work for my grandparents?" Bethany, ever the healer, believed that happiness went hand in hand with good health, and she constantly examined their frames of mind.

For the next fifteen minutes they discussed the events of their day and plans for tomorrow. Scarlett yawned. "Nine o'clock will be here before you know it, so I'm outta here."

"Me, too." Michaela crawled off the bed and Bethany joined her, calling good night over her shoulder.

Stephanie lay against the pillows, silence once again settling around her, the excitement of the first day at work gradually seeping from her mind and body. Tomorrow she again would face one Darrin Hart, and she'd ignore him like the fly on the wall he was. She'd overheard him firing questions at Papa Langston, questions that undermined the time-share program. For instance, was he aware that a failing economy didn't bode well for such a venture? And did he know that many buyers reneged on their contracts? But the thing that troubled her all evening, which she could never discuss, was Bethany's grandpa's reply. "We're not sure the program will be a success." Up until this very day, Papa Langston had expressed excitement over her plan. He'd supported her 100 percent. But after Darrin's negative tirade, Papa grew uncertain. Stephanie rolled to her side and curved her body around the extra pillow. And the worst thing of all? Another person in her life doubted she would succeed.

Chapter 2

Stephanie pulled the last set of credit applications from the bubble wrap, resisting the childish urge to squeeze until a resounding *pop* could be heard. Instead she lifted the paper to her nose and sniffed the ink, a picture forming in her mind of prospective clients filling in the information required by the bank to purchase time-shares in the resort. She carefully placed them in the appropriately marked black tray on her desk.

Satisfaction in her job thus far could not be squelched, even with hurt from the recent betrayal of Papa Langston and handsome Darrin Hart. Stephanie felt a feather-light awareness tickle the back of her neck. *Great day.* Surely just the *thought* of someone wouldn't make it seem like they were in the room. Besides, resentment, mistrust, and anger were feelings, not mere musings about a man she once was interested in.

"Earth to Stephanie."

She swiveled quickly to face the doorway. The knuckles still in contact with the door spoke of the knock she hadn't heard, but the cause for the tickle of awareness stood before her with a question in his eyes.

"Where were you? I knocked, cleared my throat, and called your name. You were totally zoned out. You're not worried about tomorrow, are you?"

The first of Stephanie's guests began to arrive earlier this morning. Tomorrow morning at 8:00, they would be served a free breakfast and then the tour would begin, followed by at least two hours of tag-team sales pitches.

"Not worried at all, Darrin." Stephanie narrowed her eyes, intently searching his features for an expression of gloating at her insecurities, but found only concern. "Everything is in place. I've assembled an excellent team and they're anxious to get started, so no worries here." Except for the numerous things that could go wrong, but she wasn't about to give him any more information. Like the naive girl she was, she'd taken him into her confidence when he'd shown interest in the time-share program, explaining every step, and her plans to make it a success.

Tilting her head, she allowed her pride to conceal her inner turmoil. She wanted to hurt him like he'd hurt her. Yet she never wanted to see him hurt. A tumble of confused thoughts and feelings assailed her.

"Then what's the matter?"

"Nothing." Stephanie struggled to keep the chill out of her tone.

"Are you mad at me?"

"Why do you ask?" Her mind working overtime, Stephanie wondered if she should confront him with the conversation she'd overheard last night between him and Papa Langston.

"You seem withdrawn, not quite yourself." He reached to take her hand, but Stephanie wrapped her arms around herself and sat in the chair behind her desk. She pretended not to understand his question. Why should he get by with what he'd done to her?

"Oh? How so?"

"Well. . ." He shrugged and cleared his throat.

As their eyes met, she barely controlled her gasp of surprise. How could she be feeling sorry for this man's discomfort? To her annoyance, she found herself anxious to set him at ease. Well, that would *not* be happening. She took a deep breath. Girding herself with resolve, she said matter-of-factly, "You don't know me, so how would you know if I'm acting like myself or not?"

"Stephanie, what's going on? Call me crazy, but I thought we were becoming more than just friends. We've gone out together several times. And we've attended church services together."

"And all those times were group outings with my friends. We were never a couple."

Stephanie felt an unwelcome blush creep into her cheeks, but the embarrassment quickly turned into annoyance when she saw understanding relax his features and an expression of satisfaction in his eyes.

"So that's what this is about. Why didn't you say something sooner? I thought you might not date alone, so I was happy to be with you in a crowd. I wanted to spend time with you no matter how it came about."

"You did?"

"Yes. How could you not know? I always sat beside you, held the songbook with you, rode only in the shuttle bus you were in. I even saved you a seat when I didn't know if you were coming or not. Surely one of your friends told you."

"Yes, they did, but—"

"And whose office did I help set up? Was it Bethany's or Scarlett's? No, it was the pretty blond's, the girl who stole my breath away the first moment I laid eyes on her." As he talked, he walked slowly around the desk, causing Stephanie to swivel her chair to face him. He stopped in front of her and she looked up into eyes as dark as chinquapins.

"Really? At first sight?" Stephanie could hardly lift her voice above a whisper.

Darrin leaned and placed a hand on each arm of her chair, cocooning her in warmth, his breath feathering her face.

"It's the truth," he said with quiet emphasis.

"Uh-oh. This looks cozy."

At Michaela's voice, Stephanie jumped guiltily. Darrin straightened slowly but kept his eyes locked on hers until she broke contact, turning to address her friend.

"What's up, Mikey?" Pleased at how nonchalant she sounded, she didn't miss the obvious examination and approval on Michaela's face. One more thing she'd have to straighten out.

"Sorry for interrupting, but I need your W-4 forms for your new employees if you have them ready."

Stephanie opened her desk drawer and extracted a folder, handing it to Michaela.

"Thanks, Stephanie."

"So this is where everybody's hiding out."

As Scarlett plopped into one of the empty seats in front of her desk, Stephanie didn't know whether to strangle her two friends or hug them really hard. Until she straightened out the turmoil roiling through her, she'd accept her friends' interruptions as God-sent. Whatever that meant.

"No hiding here. I'm working." Stephanie placed her empty folder back in the drawer.

Michaela waved the tax forms she'd removed from Stephanie's folder. "Me, too."

"Well, as activities director, it's my job to ensure that you guys be at the meet-and-greet tonight for Stephanie's time-share group. So I'm working, too."

All three girls turned to look at Darrin, who stood motionless, staring out the window. At the cessation of conversation, he turned, and the expression on his face was priceless. He hadn't a clue what they had said. He shrugged his shoulders in mock resignation. "What'd I miss?"

"You're all going to miss lunch if you don't hurry." Bethany stepped into the room, her nurse uniform starched and white. Her eyes perused the little group, looking for signs of who knew what. Ever the nurse, she zeroed in on anything out of the ordinary.

Her gaze landed on Stephanie, and not quite ready to share her feelings with anyone at the moment, Stephanie pasted a smile on her face and jumped to her feet. "Never let it be said that I held up lunch." She stepped from behind her desk and held the door open until everyone had passed through, then closed and locked the door behind her, dropping the keys into her pocket. The chatter from the others as they took the wide stairs down to the foyer concealed the fact that Stephanie remained quiet—right on through the meal. Or so she thought.

As she stashed her tray and refilled her sweet tea to go, Darrin spoke from over her shoulder. "Can we sit in the lounge area for a bit? You still have about ten minutes before your lunch hour is over."

The girls, and apparently Darrin, too, had learned early on that Papa Langston, though he very obviously loved the girls, ran a tight ship and expected rules to be obeyed. They were to report each morning at nine, take the allotted time for breaks and lunch, and leave only when the eight- or nine-hour workday ended.

Stephanie headed toward a chair near the fireplace, but Darrin, with a light touch on her arm, guided her to the sofa. A quick glance as he sat down proved Darrin was staring at her intently, so she clasped her hands together in her lap. She was by no means blind to the attraction she felt for him, which caused a sense of inadequacy to sweep over her. How could she be attracted to a man who would try to undermine her job to her boss? Something flickered in the back of her mind. What was it he'd said earlier?

"Stephanie?"

Her thoughts halted at the sound of his voice, a voice that affected her deeply. It wrapped around her like a warm blanket.

She looked up and her heart lurched. His countenance was somber yet tender. Her reaction seemed to amuse him, and his mouth quirked with humor.

"You zoned out on me again. What can I do about that?"

He was teasing her affectionately, perhaps aware of her unease.

"I'm sorry. I have a lot on my mind."

"I know you do, and I'm here for you." He took her hand, maintaining the distance between them on the sofa. She liked that he observed the Christian principles Bethany, Scarlett, and Michaela held dear to their hearts. While in college, the girls had talked incessantly about the "rules" for dating, and so far Darrin had toed the line.

"Stephanie, I'd like for us to date each other exclusively. I want to get to know you better. There's this thing between us that I've never felt for anyone else. Ever. Do you feel it, too?"

Stephanie could only nod. Her voice seemed to have permanently lodged in her throat. An illusive thought flittered around the edges of her mind. She felt it warning her, cautioning her that all was not exactly as it should be. But what was it?

Her attention focused on Bethany at the end of the corridor off the lobby, arms laden with white packages bearing the insignia of a red cross. She entered a room with one of the maids on her heels, carrying the same type of bundles. The inventory for the infirmary had arrived, and Bethany would finally get to set up her office. Her inventory had been the last to arrive. And the puzzle pieces all fit.

"Whose office did I help set up? Was it Bethany's or Scarlett's?

No, it was the pretty blond's, the girl who stole my breath away the first moment I laid eyes on her." That's what he'd said earlier, when he'd tried to convince her of his interest. But he wasn't interested in her; it was her job that he wanted. He'd repeatedly asked questions, and she'd eagerly answered every one. Why, she'd practically trained him herself to take over her job. He'd tried to convince Papa Langston of all the things that could go wrong with the time-share program, creating doubt that a woman could handle such a job.

Swallowing the sob that rose in her throat, she stood. She felt like an old woman with the one spark of hope in life suddenly extinguished. When she spoke, her voice held the note of finality she hoped it would.

"I can't date you, Darrin. Not now, not ever."

Chapter 3

What just happened? Darrin watched as Stephanie walked away, and a pulsing knot within him demanded that he go after her. Searching his mind for a plausible explanation for Stephanie's reaction, he felt ill equipped to understand the workings of the female brain. She'd just walked away without a backward glance. It had been a long time since he'd felt so humiliated, so deflated. He stiffened, embarrassment quickly turning to annoyance.

He had not misinterpreted the signs. Her smiles when they met had been genuine, and she had sat beside him when they went into town for group activities on a couple of occasions. And before the girls had entered Stephanie's office earlier, he'd been physically very close to her, and he'd felt no resistance. When she'd explained the time-share program as they'd worked late one evening, her voice had been warm with affection, and her eyes had flirted, compelling and magnetic. So why the sudden deep freeze? She didn't seem the type of girl to lead a man on; or maybe he'd lost his ability to discern such things.

He shrugged his shoulders in resignation. As a child, he couldn't wait until he became an adult so he wouldn't have to put up with spite, jealousy, and deceit. But as he grew up, he found adults acting worse than children. They didn't explain why they were upset; you had to guess. And more lies were told than you could shake a stick at. What happened to honesty, integrity, and the desire to share God's love? Was it all hype? Half in anticipation, half in dread, he started after Stephanie. Why should he stand here and agonize over what had gone wrong? The Bible said, "Ye have not, because ye ask not." Well, he needed answers, so he'd ask for them. If this was a game, she'd quickly learn that he did not play games.

Four years ago, he'd given his heart to the Lord and had begun to pray for a wife. He'd made a decision to wait for someone special—someone God sent his way—specifically asking God to create an interest in him for the one woman meant for him. Stephanie had been the first girl to ignite that interest. He clenched his jaw, deep frustration causing a muscle there to tic. Now she'd walked away, leaving him with an inexplicable feeling of emptiness.

"Son, you seem to be contemplating something pretty serious. Two things come to mind when I see a man in such deep concentration." Darrin snapped out of his reverie to find Mr. Langston folding his arms across his chest and widening his stance as if in preparation for a good long chat.

"Oh? And what two things would that be?" Might as well see if any good advice was in the offing. After all, the man had lived a lifetime; he should know the ways of the world. Darrin took the same pose and gave the man his undivided attention.

"The first relates to accomplishing a goal. You know—a man dreams of doing something big. Makes a how-to list and sets out to get the job done. A smart man will think it through, measure the pros and cons before he ever heads to the bank to borrow money. Pretty much like the scripture, Luke 14:28, that says, 'For which of you, intending to build a tower, sitteth not down first, and counteth the cost, whether he have sufficient to finish it?' Never known a man to amount to much who wouldn't consider the outcome before beginning something."

Darrin waited a moment for Mr. Langston to continue, but the man seemed to be pondering his own words. Maybe he was thinking about the lodge and whether he'd reached his goals. Or perhaps the Lord had given Mr. Langston the scripture he'd just quoted during the building phase of Snowbird Lodge. Darrin didn't know, but he was interested in hearing the rest of what Mr. Langston had to say, so he gently prompted the man.

"And the second thing that came to mind?"

"Hmm? Oh yes." Mr. Langston smiled and said, "A woman." He turned and began walking away.

"Sir, wait." Darrin hurried after him. Didn't the man know he couldn't just walk away after a comment like that? They left the lounge area and crossed the lobby side by side. Darrin noticed the look of happiness that settled upon Mr. Langston's features as he surveyed the scene before him. He understood the satisfied feeling of a job well done that the man must feel when he looked at the beautiful business he had created.

Darrin hoped to feel the same sense of accomplishment

at his own estate. The remodeling was almost finished. If he could just get the time-share program up and running, he'd be well on his way to seeing his dream realized.

One thing was for certain: If he had entertained even for a moment the thought that Stephanie might implement the program at Green Mountain Manor, he needed his head examined. She'd shut that door good and tight. Apparently he'd misread the signals big time.

They entered the kitchen, now busy with staff cleaning tables and the sound of dishes being stacked somewhere in the background. Mr. Langston sat at one of the tables near the tall windows that overlooked the slopes. The view was breathtaking, and Darrin never grew tired of watching skiers whiz down the hill, snow billowing up from their skis. But, oh, how he wanted to be home staring out over his land, listening to the sounds of staff—many of whom he'd grown up with, who'd taken over jobs their parents had held before them—laughing and chatting as they worked.

"So. . .what's she done that's got your gut turned inside out and your head spinning?"

"Who?" For a moment the question confused Darrin, then all too sudden, Stephanie's rejection cut into his heart again. "Oh, her."

At Mr. Langston's chuckle, Darrin ducked his head, a wry smile turning up the corners of his lips. He'd walked right into that one.

"That would be the lovely Stephanie." Darrin felt exhausted, and it was barely past noon.

"Ah. I thought it might be her. I've seen the two of you together quite a bit. I wondered if there might be something brewing."

Darrin's mouth twitched with amusement. Mr. Langston's simple way of saying things and his facial expressions when he placed one finger across his lips, reminded him of the colonel on *I Dream of Jeannie*, an old sitcom he'd seen in reruns when he was a kid.

"Well, I, too, thought there might be something developing between us, but I was wrong."

"Um-hm." Mr. Langston nodded his head, his gaze focused in the distance as if waiting for inspiration, his finger still across his mouth. "Misread the signals, did you?"

If he hadn't been so tormented by mixed emotions, Darrin would have laughed out loud.

"I didn't just misread them, sir. I destroyed any chance I might have had for forgiveness."

"What'd you do that you need forgiveness for?" Mr. Langston stared at him as if concerned that he might have hurt one of his girls.

"I don't know what I did, sir."

"Aah." Mr. Langston drew out the word and nodded again as if the meaning were suddenly clear to him, but he turned to look out the window, leaving Darrin sadly lacking in understanding.

Darrin waited for a moment, then asked, "Mr. Langston, do you ever offer advice? I sure would appreciate any help you could give me."

"I actually do have some counsel for you, young man." Darrin sat up straighter, a ray of hope entering the sad places in his heart. "Hmm, yep. . .that's what I'd do if I were you." The older man rubbed the side of his face as if feeling for stubble growth. Impatience clawed at Darrin like talons.

"What would you do, sir?"

"Go skiing."

"I'm sorry?" Darrin's mind floundered. Weren't older people supposed to be full of sage guidance?

"Skiing, son. You heard me. And don't just go on any slope; ski one of the black diamonds or double black diamonds. It'll give you a good workout. You'll come back worn out and ready for a good long nap."

Darrin was caught off guard by his suggestion. He stared, tongue-tied, at the older man.

"Well go on. Don't hang around here all gloomy. By the time you get back, she'll have changed her mind and you'll be the new best thing since sliced bread. When womenfolk get all wound up about a matter, it's better to just get out of their hair for a while. The absence of your presence gives them time to think things through, and then, when they see ya again, you don't look so lacking in possibilities."

Darrin saw the pale blue lighting of amusement in the other man's eyes, and a chuckle floated up from Darrin's throat, bursting into peals of laughter that caused several of the waiters to grin, even though they knew nothing of the conversation.

He stood and shook Mr. Langston's outstretched hand.

"Now doesn't that feel better, son? The Bible says, 'A merry heart doeth good like a medicine.' When you're crying the blues, always look for something to laugh about and you'll feel your spirits lifting."

"Thank you, sir. I do feel better."

Darrin walked into the foyer and took the stairs to the second floor. He took the elevator from there to his room. He stepped onto the thick carpet to find Stephanie coming toward him, reading something she held in her hand. She looked up, straight into his eyes, then turned and walked in the opposite direction.

Darrin sighed in exasperation. Girding himself with resolve, he lifted his chin and punched the UP button on the elevator a little too hard. He'd straighten out this mess later. Right now he had an appointment with one of the most difficult double-black-diamond ski slopes in the west—the Corkscrew.

Chapter 4

Stephanie's legs trembled as she walked away from Darrin. Bethany's office was just across the foyer and at the end of the hall. A hall that at the moment looked longer than a football field. She felt bereft, as if someone had died. Maybe something *had* died. Her chance for a relationship with Darrin. But who wanted a relationship with someone who undermined you to get their own way?

She rushed into Bethany's office, out of breath and almost in tears.

"Hey, what's up with you? You look like you've run a marathon." A frown furrowed Bethany's brow and she advanced toward Stephanie with a hand raised to test her forehead for fever, but Stephanie ducked in the opposite direction.

"There's nothing wrong with me, Bethany. I'm not sick. At least not that kind of sick. Although I do feel a bit queasy."

"I knew it. You were quiet at lunch. I should have checked you out then. Do you have a sore throat?"

"No, Bethany. I told you, I'm not sick."

"I'll be the judge of that." She felt Stephanie's wrist. "Your pulse is erratic and you have a cold sweat. Your body's fighting something."

"Now *there* you might have hit on something."

"Do you feel tired?"

"Well, yes, but—"

"How long has it been since your last bowel movement?"

"Bethany, for Pete's sake! There is nothing wrong with me."

"So you're light-headed, tired, sweating, pulse racing, stomach upset, bowels regular, and nothing's wrong. Is that what you're telling me?"

"Exactly!"

"Then I'm ready to give you my diagnosis."

"Oh?" This should be good. She'd always been amazed at Bethany's desire to treat anyone with any kind of ailment, whether it be physical, mental, or spiritual. She'd been right on with a couple of her conclusions in the past. However, Stephanie was not sick, so Bethany's diagnosis could only stem from the fact that she was eager to start her job.

"It's a man."

Stephanie sank into the only chair not crammed with white boxes and rolls of lethal-looking stainless-steel things.

"How do you do that?"

"Do what?" Bethany bent to scoop a package from the floor, and when she raised her head, they were eyeball to eyeball, and Stephanie could see the satisfaction in Bethany's expression. The smirk on her face said it all.

"Girl, you are too much."

"Thank you. Now tell me what Darrin has done that has your pulse racing and your body sweating."

"You are so evil. But you know what? I feel better, so I think I'll get back to work." Stephanie stood to leave.

"Oh no you don't. You sit right back down there. You were quiet all through lunch—evidently without the symptoms that sent you scurrying into my office—so what was going on in that head of yours then? We'll discuss the man-eating disease next."

"But my lunch hour is over and your grandfather will fire me."

"No he won't, because I'm doing my job, taking care of an employee. Now stop with the excuses and give." She swept packages from the desk chair and sat down, pulling a legal pad from under boxes of bandages. She picked up a pen and then looked at Stephanie.

Stephanie stared at her, then burst out laughing. "You're gonna take notes?"

"Of course I'm going to take notes. This is important, and I don't want to miss anything when I'm mulling it over later. Plus, I need the practice. Now shoot."

"I overheard Darrin trashing my time-share program to Papa Langston."

"No way."

"Yes, I did. And I feel so stupid, because I'm the one who gave him the ammunition. If I hadn't been so eager to share everything I knew about the program, he would never have been the wiser, but he seemed so interested. I pretty much told him everything I knew."

"Tell me how he trashed the program. He seems like such a nice guy."

"I thought so, too. I overheard him tell Papa that the economy was uncertain, and that no time-share was financially sound at the moment. He said people would renege on their contracts. And he claimed giving away free nights and meals to prospective buyers was not good business management."

"Oh no."

"Yes. And if you promise not to mention this to anyone, I will tell you the worst thing of all."

"I promise."

"He made Papa Langston doubt that I could do the job."

"No way."

If things had not been so serious, Stephanie would have laughed. "Oh yes way."

"Well, he's just a dirt. . ."—Stephanie watched in fascination as Bethany searched her mind for something unkind to call a man who would dare hurt her friend—"clod."

"Bag."

"What?" Bethany stood and began to pace the small area left uncluttered with boxes.

"It's *dirtbag*, not *clod*."

"Whatever." She returned to the desk and tapped her pen against the legal pad she'd forgotten to write on. "I just can't believe he'd do something like that. And he used us, too. Always asking Michaela, Scarlett, and me to make sure you came with us to the Lone Eagle Grill or to Incline Village to shop. The clod-head."

"Bag. Clod-bag." Stephanie shook her head to dislodge the confusion rattling around in her brain. "Dirtbag."

"Whatever."

"So now I will just have to work harder to prove to Papa Langston and everyone else that I can do the job and that it is a financially viable program for Snowbird Lodge."

"No, Stephanie, you don't have to prove anything. You can stop with that right now. No more proving. You proved to your parents that you could finish college and you proved them wrong when they said you couldn't be happy in one place for more than six months. Those of us who love you do not require proof of any kind. We love you as you are, and Papa does, too. I wish I had overheard the conversation, because Papa has nothing but good things to say about you. He knows the time-share program is a risk, but it's one he's willing to take." She paused as if deep in thought, so Stephanie waited for what she would say next, certain that whatever it was, she would feel better once Bethany had said it. That's how Bethany operated. She fixed the brokenhearted as well as the physically wounded. "What makes you think that Papa doubts you can do the job?"

"He told Darrin that he wasn't sure I could pull it off."

"Oh, Stephanie. I'm so sorry."

"No reason to be. I will just work harder and make it a success."

"You're working hard enough now. It will be a success. We trust the Lord to help us, right?"

"Um—yeah, I guess."

"Why do you do that, Stephanie?"

"Do what?"

"Always avoid talking about the Lord. You know the right vocabulary to use at the right times, but you never personalize your words or even include the Lord in any of your conversations. You do believe in God, right?"

"Yes, I believe there is a God. I just don't feel He's as interested in me as you, Michaela, and Scarlett seem to feel He is in you."

"Have you ever invited Him into your heart, Stephanie?"

Bethany spoke in an odd yet gentle tone that disturbed Stephanie even more than Darrin had earlier in the lounge.

"No. Is that what I'm missing that you guys have?"

"Yes, I'm certain it is."

"Then I'll do it tonight, although I don't see what good it will do."

"Stephanie, why don't you listen for that gentle coaxing by the Holy Spirit before you do the inviting? It's not our heavenly Father's plan that any should be lost, so He prepares the heart first. When the time is right, there will be no doubt. Then you can accept His wonderful free gift of salvation."

"Whatever you think is best, Bethany." Thoughts of salvation and the Holy Spirit and free gifts made Stephanie uncomfortable, so she sought a topic of discussion that would bring the conversation back to safer ground. "So, do you want to know why I was queasy and sweating?"

Bethany seemed lost in her own thoughts, almost sad even, and Stephanie began to worry that her friend might have problems with that ski instructor that she wasn't talking about. She made a mental note to pay more attention to Cole and Bethany in upcoming days.

"Oh yes. Please. Tell me what brought on the episode of anxiety."

"Darrin asked me to date him exclusively. You know, not date anyone else but him."

"I know what *exclusively* means, Stephanie." Bethany rolled her eyes as she spoke. "So what did you say to him?"

"I told him it wasn't going to happen."

"Oh, Stephanie. I'm so sorry. I could see that you were happy with him. You opened up more in the last two weeks than I've ever seen you do. I hate that he destroyed your trust in him."

"Me, too. He made me feel good about myself, and it felt great to have him show such interest in little ole' me. What a bunch of boloney, right?"

"No, that part of it was good, which makes me think you should wait a bit before you close the door on a relationship with him completely. There could be a major misunderstanding here." Bethany began to pull wrappers off the boxes nearest her, her thoughts obviously turning to her work. Or so Stephanie thought. But Bethany's next question proved her wrong. "Why would God allow such feelings for him to grow in your heart if he wasn't Mr. Right?"

"Who knows?" *And what would the Lord have to do with any of this?* Stephanie found it difficult to keep from rolling her eyes. "But I didn't say I had feelings for Darrin."

"You didn't have to." Bethany tossed a box of latex gloves to Stephanie. "Put these with the others on that shelf behind you."

"Then what makes you think my feelings for him have grown?" Stephanie stacked the box with the others and wondered briefly why a nurse would need ten boxes of latex gloves at a ski resort.

"Remember the cold sweat and racing pulse?"

"Oh." Stephanie nodded.

"A dead giveaway."

Stephanie watched as Bethany began to count the boxes of guaze she'd just unwrapped, comparing the numbers with a list in her hand. "I need to let you get back to work. Thanks for the support, Bethany. You're the best."

"My door's always open, Stephanie. You know I love you, right?"

Stephanie looked into the eyes staring back at her, eyes that were gentle and contemplative. Of the three of them, Stephanie knew Bethany understood her best. "Yeah, I know, Bethany. The feeling's mutual." She reached for a hug, then waved over her shoulder as she left the infirmary.

"Stephanie. Glad I found you." Michaela hurried up to her, holding one of the 1099 forms Stephanie had painstakingly filled out the day before. "One of your employees marked the wrong box, so this one needs to be corrected. We don't withhold taxes—they are all contract labor, since they're part-time. So will you explain that to..."—she looked at the name on the form— "Jonathan Hart, and get this back to me pronto?"

Stephanie took the paper and looked at the error. "I'll do it right now."

"Thanks, Stephanie. Is Bethany in there?" Michaela asked, pointing at the infirmary door.

"Yes, she is."

Michaela entered and Stephanie heard the murmur of voices as she pushed the UP button on the elevator. She exited on the second floor and walked toward her office that sat just left of the huge staircase leading down to the foyer. She never went to her office without first looking out over the foyer; the beauty of the gleaming wood and huge floor-to-ceiling windows never failed to take her breath away.

She looked up from the paper Michaela had given her and her heart forgot to beat. Darrin had just reached the top step, and his eyes were filled with a curious longing. The very air around her seemed to be electrified, and she felt an odd pull at her heart. How she wanted to love this man. The thought barely crossed her mind before another followed. He wasn't trustworthy, just like her parents. She'd wasted too much emotion on people who didn't see her for the person she was. She swiveled quickly, turning her back on Darrin and the attraction that drew her like a magnet.

Chapter 5

Darrin felt the wind rush against his face as he cut to the left, his skis slicing the snow and throwing a soft spray of powder into the air. His first time on the Corkscrew, and he felt the exhilaration coursing through his body as he whizzed down the snow-covered slope. The sun glistened off the snow with the brilliance of diamonds. The few scattered trees in his path wore the burden of a recent heavy snowfall. He reached the bottom of the slope and slid sideways, the steel edges of his skis cutting into the frozen surface.

He pushed and slid his way to the ski lift and knelt to unfasten his skis. The next chair arrived, and he moved into position next to another skier waiting for the lift. The chair wobbled up behind them, and then the attendant closed the bar down over them. Mr. Langston had been right. Darrin's mind was now free of worries, released for a time from thoughts of Stephanie and the affection he felt for her.

Soaring down the mountain, he'd caught glimpses of Lake

Tahoe, and its magnificence reminded him of what an awesome God he worshipped. This morning his devotional time had been in Psalms 33:6 and 9—"By the word of the Lord were the heavens made; and all the host of them by the breath of his mouth. For he spake, and it was done; he commanded, and it stood fast." *That He would make something so beautiful for man to enjoy is such a blessing. I will praise Him, and I will forget about the lovely Stephanie if she is not the one He plans for my life. The Lord wants the best for me, and I desire to have only those things He plans for my life. Father, please take my life and use it for Your glory. Make something beautiful of me like You did that spectacular mountain.*

The ski lift arrived as he finished praying, and he waited, poised and ready to jump, for the person beside him to exit first. He hit the ground and hopped to the right to dodge the chair as it moved forward again. He fastened his skis securely, again donned his mask, and made another exhilarating run down the slope. The last run of the day was the best of all.

The skier who had ridden the lift with him launched away from the top before Darrin did, reaching the lodge ahead of him. The skier held the door for him to pass through, his skis now strapped together and carried over a shoulder. He caught a glimpse of green under the fleece ski hat and did a double take.

"Stephanie?"

"Hi, Darrin." She ducked her head, and brown lashes shielded her beautiful green eyes from his view.

"I had no idea that was you sitting beside me." His mind

raced through possible scenarios of chaos he'd likely triggered by not speaking to her.

"Really?"

Darrin studied her face as she looked up at him. Her voice sounded eager to take him at his word, but he'd been wrong before and had no desire to step in front of a steamroller that kept mowing him down. Or at least that's how it felt.

"Of course not. Had I known, I would have spoken to you or offered to carry your skis."

"I thought you might be mad at me. You know. . .for. . ." Her voice faded into an embarrassed silence. She let the door close behind him, then headed down the hall toward the closet behind the gift shop.

"You mean mad because you zapped the last bit of hope I had to spend time with the most beautiful girl on the planet? Or for sending me out in the cold, placing my life in imminent danger as I hurtled sixty miles an hour down the Corkscrew?"

"You skied the Corkscrew?"

They stashed their skis against the hooks that kept each pair separated from the others, and then he felt, rather than saw, her shocked movement as she lightly smacked his arm.

"Why would you do something so harebrained? You could've been killed." Her voice had risen with concern.

"Careful, Stephanie, I might think you care." His dark eyes never left hers, anxious to capture any signs of rejection. Instead, a probing query stunned him.

"Do you want me to care?"

"With all my heart," Darrin answered, his voice hoarse

with hope and frustration.

The truth surged through him; he forgot to breathe. He loved her. When it had happened, or even how, he didn't know. He just knew that he felt for her something he'd never felt before. He imposed an iron control on himself to keep from blurting it out. In that same instant a painful realization overwhelmed Darrin; she held his very happiness in the palm of her pretty hand. She could heal him or destroy him. He prayed it would be the former.

He stared at her, hardly daring to breathe, until a tiny smile trembled over her lips.

Stephanie studied the tall man before her. There was no rhyme or reason to her actions. She just knew the light had gone out of her day when she'd rejected him. On the chair lift, she thought he'd known it was her beside him, and sorrow had burdened her heart because he appeared to be unwilling to speak with her. She'd felt like she had a stomach virus.

He wanted her to care. *"With all my heart"*; that's what he'd said. And for whatever reason, she *did* care. She shouldn't, and she'd probably regret it, but at the moment it felt good to have his interest again. Maybe tomorrow she'd be stronger and she could tell him it wouldn't work out, but today, she just wanted him near.

A group of tourists exited the gift shop, their hands holding ski masks, hats, and goggles, forcing her and Darrin to move out of the way. By tacit consent, they both turned and walked toward the stairs in the foyer.

"Tonight I'm hosting a small do that Scarlett is putting together for the time-share guests. All have been invited, but most likely, not all will attend. Would you like to be my cohost?"

They stopped at the foot of the stairs as she waited for his answer. Flakes of melting snow still clung to his shoulders, and she lifted a hand to brush them off. He caught her hand in his, leaned forward, and whispered into her hair, "I don't think Mrs. Langston would appreciate us making puddles on her gleaming wood floor." His breath fanned the side of her face and sent a warming shiver through her.

"No, I guess not."

"In fact"—he entwined their fingers and pulled her toward him—"let's stand behind the stairs on the rug, so we don't make a mess." He turned, pulling her along behind him, an indefinable feeling of rightness flowing through her.

"About the hosting tonight. . .you don't have to—"

"I want to. Anything that keeps me close to you. Do you understand what I'm saying, Stephanie?"

Her heart sang with delight, and her defenses began to crumble. A part of her reveled in his open admiration of her. Her confidence spiraled upward and she felt like singing and dancing.

"I think so, but if I get it wrong, you have all evening to correct me, right?" Was that *her* flirting? She didn't know how to flirt. "I have to help Scarlett set up for the party. I'll see you at six?"

Reluctantly she pulled her hand from his, and, taking a deep, unsteady breath, she stepped back. The gleam of interest still smoldered in his dark eyes, creating an unfamiliar sense of power in Stephanie. She liked the feeling.

"I'll be there. Dress up?"

"No, it's casual. We want them to feel at home."

"Sounds good. Oh, and Stephanie?"

"Yes?"

"I will correct you if you get it wrong. Okay?"

"Classic." At his questioning look, she explained, "That's what the gang and I call something good."

He touched his forehead with two fingers in a mock salute, his smile broadening in approval. "I like it. And I like you." He disappeared on the opposite side of the stairs.

Chapter 6

Stephanie rode the elevator to her floor. "Anyone home?" she yelled as she entered their suite. No one answered, so she flew to the shower, tossing clothes left and right. *I'm so late. Scarlett's going to kill me.* She turned the water to warm, wound her hair tight, and placed a shower cap over her head. No time for a shampoo. Despite her rush, she found herself humming a praise song that had been sung during Sunday morning's service. The words of the song encouraged her to worship, to bow down before God. Somehow, that seemed the right thing to do.

She dressed quickly and then had a thought that left her hands suspended in midair; they'd been about to release her hair. *"Have you invited Jesus into your heart?"* Bethany's question from this morning tore through her. Tonight she was supposed to ask Jesus into her heart, but she'd promised Bethany she would listen for God's voice inviting her to come to Him. Today things had happened that made her happy, and she had instinctively sung praise songs. Did that mean God was preparing her heart? Something fluttered in her chest. Could she really belong to the King? She felt for the edge of the bathtub and sat down, the wonder of such a thought making her legs tremble.

She felt closer to Bethany, Michaela, and Scarlett than she had to anyone in her life. They made her feel she belonged. She'd always been on the outs with her family. She'd never understood them, and judging by their actions, they felt the same about her. When she turned eleven, they left her with an aging grandparent, and Stephanie wound up being the caregiver, rather than the other way around.

When she met the girls in college and they accepted her into their lives, she'd become whatever they needed her to be, always fearful she'd do something that would destroy the friendship. She'd been ever vigilant to copy their practices, always praying when called upon, reading Scarlett's inspirational romances, sending scripture notes of encouragement—along with a bag of Peanut M&M's if sent to Bethany—and posing hours on end till Michaela learned each new feature of whichever new camera she had at the moment. She loved them all dearly—even *they* probably didn't know how much—but she'd always been afraid of losing them.

The pastor had said Jesus would not force you to accept His gift of salvation, that He gave us all free will, to accept it or not. If this salvation thing was what she'd been lacking all this time—the glue that held her beloved friends together—then she wanted it more than anything in the world. But how did a person invite Jesus into her heart? Were there certain words you needed to say? She'd have to ask Bethany.

She removed the shower cap and bent over almost to the floor, allowing her hair to swing freely as she shook it, fluffing it with her hands. A touch of eyeliner, a bit of lip gloss, a spritz of perfume, and she raced from the suite to the elevator. On the second floor she hurried past her office to the conference room at the end of the hall. She entered with an apology on her lips, only to let it die as she surveyed her surroundings.

A long white linen-covered table sat in the middle of the room with a huge chocolate fountain dominating the center. Trays of every fruit imaginable, and cheeses. Turkey- and ham-filled croissants. Greenery with red holly berries and glass globes holding red candles served as centerpieces on the surrounding tables, and Christmas ornaments hanging from the ceiling created a festive holiday spirit.

A commotion in the corner drew her attention, and she turned to find Scarlett almost upended, rummaging around in a bag on the floor. She heard a muffled "Ah-ha!" and then Scarlett stood upright, clutching something red in her hand.

"Scarlett, I'm so—"

A shriek rent the air and Stephanie jumped. Scarlett placed a hand over her heart in an exaggerated show. "You scared a year's growth out of me, Stephanie. Don't sneak up on me like that." She dropped her hand and placed the red thing behind her back as if hiding it. "What are you doing here anyway? You're early."

"Early? Scarlett, have you checked the time?" Stephanie glanced at her watch to make sure she wasn't mistaken. "It's almost five. I should have been here an hour ago to help you."

"No, I wanted to surprise you. . .make your first event a special one."

"You must have worked in here all day. It's beautiful." Stephanie fingered the holly berries, uncertain if they were real.

"They're fake." Scarlett answered the unspoken question. "But it's hard to tell, isn't it?" Scarlett's features became animated. "And what do you think of the chocolate fountain? Isn't it great?" She clapped her hands like a child, happiness radiating from her eyes.

"Scarlett, you shouldn't have done all this." She turned to find her friend staring at her, hands on hips.

"You don't like it?"

"Are you kidding? I love it. I never dreamed the room could look this good." Her gaze perused the room again. "Won't this damage your December budget?"

"Oh, let me tell you how I worked that out. The Rotary Club met this morning in the first-floor conference room and some food was left over, so I had Maggie wrap it up and put it in the fridge. All I had to do was buy the chocolate. The fountain and decorations belong to the lodge. Isn't that great?"

"How will I ever repay such a wonderful gesture?" Stephanie felt an unfamiliar tightness fill her throat.

"Will you listen to yourself? This is me, doing something nice for my friend—that would be you. Your response should be, 'Thank you, your royal highness.'" Scarlett giggled infectiously. "Come sit down and I'll tell you the bad news." She grabbed Stephanie's hand and pulled her to a chair.

"It must be really bad if I have to sit down for it."

"Silly girl. Sit so I can do *this*." Scarlett pulled the red thing from her back pocket, and Stephanie finally saw it was a Santa hat.

"I have to wear that?"

"Yes, but not just you. All the lodge employees I invited to help win over your prospective customers have to wear one."

"What a great idea, Scarlett. Wait, who all did you invite? I don't want to scare people away."

"Just the four of us and the Langstons. Plus the lodge ski instructor, Cole—I can't remember his last name. And little Lynzie, who's always hanging around Michaela. She's dressing up as an elf. Won't that be cute?"

"Won't you guys be bored?"

"No, we will mix and mingle and answer any questions they might have. We'll eat and then when the guests leave, we'll all pitch in and clean the place up. We'll still have time for a leisurely night of girl talk and possibly a chick flick with popcorn. What do you think?"

"I think you're one fantastic friend. I was dreading this evening, and you've turned it into something special. You have that talent, you know—making the way for others a bit smoother."

"I do what I can." Scarlett exaggerated a long sigh then secured the Santa cap by pinning it to Stephanie's head.

The Langstons entered and Mrs. Langston exclaimed over the decorations while Mr. Langston plugged the fountain into the floor outlet underneath the table. Michaela and the elf strolled in next, then Cole. Bethany entered with Darrin on her heels. He made a beeline to Stephanie's side.

When the first customers arrived, Stephanie almost laughed out loud at the eagerness of the workers to make the lodge a happy, fun place to vacation. Only three couples of the ten registered attended, but there was such camaraderie in the group, they lingered long after the hour scheduled for the event.

"Thanks so much for coming, Mrs. Baker. We'll see you tomorrow morning." Stephanie patted the elderly woman on the shoulder. "It was lovely meeting you." She held the door open, feeling in her bones that the Bakers would be purchasing a time-share. Although she'd tried to steer clear of any business talk, Mr. and Mrs. Baker had asked pointed questions, garnering much of the information that would be shared tomorrow in the meetings.

"You did a fantastic job entertaining your prospective clients, dear. Papa and I were very impressed." Stephanie turned to find Mrs. Langston preparing to go. "We're going into town to have dinner with the Bakers and show them a little of the Tahoe area. We're leaving the cleanup to you young people."

Mr. Langston opened the door for his wife and remarked, "Your little meeting was a surprising success, Stephanie. It seemed to make a big impression on your clients."

"Thanks to the both of you. You put everyone at ease with your kindness, and any success is due to you."

"Not at all." Mr. Langston brushed away the compliment without a thought. "Don't let these big guys get out of here till they've helped you clear things away."

"I won't. 'Bye now."

Stephanie walked to the chocolate fountain, Mr. Langston's words gnawing away at her confidence. *Your little meeting was a surprising success.*

A chocolate-covered strawberry appeared before her eyes. She stepped backward, a hand automatically lifting to take the tempting morsel Darrin held out to her.

"Why the frown? All the clients had a fantastic time. Did you see Mr. Hart corner me for twenty minutes or so? He was determined to prove we had family ties. Said there weren't that many Harts in the United States." Darrin spoke eagerly, the excitement of the evening apparent in his voice.

"I saw that. You did great with him. In fact, we couldn't have gotten by tonight without you. When the chocolate fountain got clogged, I thought we were in major trouble, but you straightened it out right away. How did you know what to do?"

Bryan, one of the lodge guests from North Carolina, interrupted them. "Hey, Darrin, Cole's challenged me to a race down Bone Crusher tomorrow morning. Wanna get in on the fun?" Bryan had come with Cole to the meet-and-greet.

"Sorry. I already have plans for the morning."

"Too bad, man. This is going to be the race of the season." The tone of Bryan's voice indicated regret, but the excitement lighting his eyes proved otherwise. He appeared happy to tackle the race on his own.

Kelly, one of Stephanie's employees, had joined them at

the same time as Bryan, but when he posed his question, she turned and beat a hasty retreat. Stephanie wondered briefly what that was about.

"You didn't answer my question." Darrin's cool voice broke into her reverie.

"What question?" Stephanie watched Bryan make a bee-line for Kelly. Something was up with those two. Since time-share employees sold to the public, hence the guest, they were encouraged to *not* develop relationships with them.

"Why were you frowning earlier after speaking with the Langstons?"

Stephanie felt her insecurities returning, and she laughed to cover her annoyance. "It was nothing. Just something Papa Langston said about the meeting being a 'surprising' success. As in, if I accomplished anything it would be a shock."

"I'm certain that's not what he meant."

"How can you be certain?" Stephanie had not forgotten that the man standing beside her, feeding her one chocolate-covered piece of fruit after another—she smacked his hand and said, "Stop that"—was the man to whom Papa Langston had confessed his doubts about the success of the time-share program in the first place.

Darrin maintained a wide-eyed innocence till she stared him down, and then burst into teasing laughter. "You've eaten six of those. You weren't even aware of which fruit I dipped."

"It wouldn't have mattered. She loves them all." Bethany stood on the opposite side of the fountain, filling a plate with sandwiches and fruit. "Let's have something to eat, Stephanie, before we start cleanup, okay? I'm starved."

Stephanie hadn't eaten either, preferring to keep clients' plates and glasses filled. "Sounds like a winner to me, although after the six chocolate-covered morsels I ate, I shouldn't be hungry." She rolled her eyes at Darrin, and his laugh was deep, warm, and rich.

They sat at the table together, and Darrin ate what was left on her plate, reaching over, his shoulder occasionally brushing hers, his breath a soft touch on her cheek. No one wanted the evening to end.

Lynzie, the eleven-year-old elf, began a discourse on her dad, Jonas. Everyone relaxed, prepared to listen to the kid. No one was in a hurry for the evening to end.

Darrin propped an arm on the back of Stephanie's chair. Although he wasn't touching her, his warmth wrapped around her like a blanket. She felt a bottomless peace and satisfaction. Tonight there were no shadows flittering across her heart.

Chapter 7

J ust like at college, the four of them, in addition to tonight's guest, piled on a bed and discussed the events of the day. Lynzie, the elf, was the center of attention. Michaela had invited her to spend the night; or, rather, Michaela had caved at the suggestion from the precocious child. That Michaela liked the girl was evident in the undivided attention she gave her, smiling at everything she said. She acted uncomfortable, however, when the child mentioned her father, Jonas. It wasn't long before the rest of them realized why. Lynzie, matchmaker extraordinaire, wanted a wife for her father and a mother for herself. It seemed Michaela was the chosen one.

Bethany poked her leg under the throw they shared, and Stephanie felt her lips tremble with the need to smile. She rubbed the sore spot and waited, knowing one of the others would start the teasing. She didn't have to wait long.

"So, Lynzie," Scarlett began. "Does your dad like blonds or brunettes?"

The child looked from one to the other of them as if

recognizing something momentous was about to happen. She pointed to Michaela. "Her color."

Bethany giggled. "You know, Michaela, you've always loved children. This could be the perfect arrangement for you."

"Girls. . ." Michaela's voice held a friendly warning.

"Really, Bethany?" Lynzie squealed and clapped her hands. "I knew it, I knew it!"

A pillow landed forcefully between Bethany and Scarlett, who leaned against the headboard with Stephanie. "See what you started? Shame on you."

"Yeah, Michaela"—Stephanie had to put her two cents in—"you'd have someone to photograph and I could quit being the guinea pig."

"Lynzie, what does your dad look like?" Scarlett waggled her eyebrows as if that were of utmost importance.

"He's tall and handsome and he's the nicest man in the world."

"*I'll* take him then."

The girls howled at Stephanie's comment until Lynzie's laughing screams of "No, no" finally registered.

"You can't have him, Miss Stephanie—your hair's the wrong color."

Scarlett raised her voice to be heard over the laughter. "Yeah, Stephanie, what were you thinking?"

Bethany wiped her eyes with the end of the throw. "Well, Lynzie, you let us know how we can help you get the two of them together, because our friend Michaela should belong to the nicest man in the world."

Bethany's words had a sobering effect on the group. They all knew the troubles Michaela had had, first with her dad and then a guy who she thought loved her.

"Let's say our prayers, huh?" Michaela linked her fingers with Lynzie's and bowed her head.

Not until she was in her room under the covers did Stephanie remember that she hadn't spoken with Bethany about how to ask Jesus into her heart. She'd find out tomorrow for sure.

Darrin lay on his bed, studying the scripture before him: "Blessed is the man who trusts in the Lord, and whose hope is the Lord." A margin note to the verse, Jeremiah 17:7, defined *hope* as "confidence."

He'd noticed something tonight that puzzled him. Stephanie had latched on to one word in Mr. Langston's praise of the evening. He'd said the evening had been a "surprising success." He could just as easily have meant *pleasant*. But she'd considered the word "surprising" as a negative comment on her abilities. What would make her think that?

And why had she turned him down that morning and then done such an about-face in the afternoon? He was missing something.

He rolled onto his back and placed his hands behind his head. He'd never met a woman as beautiful as Stephanie. Her shoulder-length blond hair hung straight without a curl, and her depthless green eyes could slice and dice you or weaken your heart. Her eyes probed to your very soul. And her skin was as smooth as a peach-tinted cream his mom used.

But something wasn't quite right, and he'd committed all he could at the moment. He'd told her he cared, and he did. He couldn't help himself. It seemed as natural as breathing. But there was a check in his spirit, and he knew that it came from the Lord. Though it might break his heart, if she wasn't the one God wanted for him, he would have to say good-bye. He would not walk the rest of his life without his mate, the one God made just for him. He would always feel like he was missing a part of himself if he did so.

He woke later in the night and pulled the covers over him, not even bothering to slip out of his clothes.

The morning had gone okay, but Stephanie now sat with her head in her hands, waiting on her staff to return to the time-share quarters. They had made it through the free breakfast on schedule, then the clients were paired with a team and they'd all left to visit the cabins that lined the mountain beyond the lodge. It should have taken only an hour, since there was such a small group of clients, but it had already been an hour and ten minutes. A slight worry niggled at the headache she was starting.

"How's it going?" Darrin lounged casually against the doorframe.

"So far, so good." She touched the tips of both forefingers to her temples and massaged.

"Headache?"

"Yep."

The first team noisily arrived and forced him to move. He winked at her and disappeared out the door. On the heels of the first group, all four teams entered the room, and the sales talk began. In less than five minutes, the first couple left. They admitted they'd just come for the free vacation and meal. Two more couples followed shortly thereafter, and things began to look bad. She strolled about, nodding at a few people as she moved, answering a question here and there. Conversation had settled into a subdued murmur, when she looked up to find Darrin strolling toward her. He came close, looking down at her intently.

"I brought you something." He handed her a cup of hot tea and two Excedrin.

"Oh, thanks, honey—Darrin," she hastily corrected herself. Stephanie stiffened, helpless to halt her embarrassment. She felt the heat stealing across her face. "I'm sorry, I—"

"You will take the sunlight out of my day if you apologize." He cupped the side of her face and lifted her chin with his thumb. She looked into dark, earnest eyes and was enthralled by what she saw. He genuinely cared for her.

"Miss Stephanie?" one of the salesmen called out to her. Darrin glanced sideways in surprise. So *he* had forgotten where they were, too. They exchanged a subtle look of amusement and he reached for her hand and squeezed; then he walked out the door.

If Stephanie hadn't known better, she would have thought

the sunlight had hidden behind the clouds.

For the next hour she ran credit applications, refigured loan amounts, and discussed payment options with those who were interested. In the end, instead of the statistical average of two buyers out of every ten prospects, she had six. She wanted to sing and run and shout. She had twenty-six weeks to work with over the six months ahead of her. If she sold six packages on average per week, she would have three of the ten cabins completely sold for fifty-two weeks of the year for life. That's more than she dared hope for, but today she would rejoice in what she and her team had accomplished.

She skipped lunch, working with her staff until someone noticed the time. They made sure every jot and tittle was signed, initialed, and ready for the banks. Because several credit reports weren't perfect, they'd had to use different loan facilities. Two of the couples bought outright, so Stephanie printed the deed and prepared to have it notarized.

She felt exhilarated. She bragged on her staff, praising them for a job well done. She wanted to celebrate. Normally the first people to pop into mind for a celebration would have been the girls, but tonight one set of dark eyes occupied her mind.

"You seem very pleased with yourself. Should we go celebrate?"

We are in sync.

She turned to face him, no longer able to hide her happiness at his presence. She heard his quick intake of breath as she walked into his arms.

Chapter 8

Darrin closed his arms around the woman who had stolen his heart. Her hair smelled clean and fresh as the mountain air, and the perfume she wore was light and breezy. She fit perfectly. The hug was over much too soon, and he waited as she gathered her purse and cell phone, then he followed her out the door.

He'd borrowed the Langston's SUV and made reservations at Mokoto's, a fancy restaurant at Incline Village. They entered and were seated immediately. He slid into the circular booth beside her, neither willing to move very far away from the other. They ordered sesame chicken and steak.

"If you match today's success every week, you'll have at least one cabin sold in six months, right?"

"Three."

"Three cabins? Wow! I'm impressed." He reached for her hand, and as they talked, he examined her fingers and compared the size of her hand to his. "Did you tell the Langstons?"

"I didn't get a chance. You whisked me out of there."

"You didn't want to come with me?" His eyes caught and held hers.

"You know I did."

Their meal came and Darrin prayed for their food, holding her hand on the tabletop. Stephanie realized she was pleased that he had prayed. It felt right. They ate well, eating off each other's plate.

"Are you leaving to go home Christmas week?"

"No, I'm staying at the lodge with Bethany and the Langstons. Are you leaving?" Stephanie dreaded his answer. If he left, she would miss him terribly.

"Yes, I promised my parents I'd be home that week."

"Do you still live with them?"

He chuckled. "No, I haven't for several years. I have three younger siblings who still live there."

"Boys or girls?"

"Both. Emily's twelve and Bianca's fifteen. Eli just turned eighteen. There's a set of twins between me and Eli. Jessica and Jaime are near your age."

"And how old are you?" *Funny the things you don't know about a person till you ask.* Stephanie's mind worked feverishly, ticking off all the things she wanted to know about the man beside her. A tiny glow cheered her. She hoped she'd found someone who would love her unconditionally.

"Twenty-seven. You?"

Caught up in her own thoughts, it took Stephanie a moment

to realize he'd asked her a question.

"Oh. I'm twenty-three, or will be the third of February."

"Any brothers or sisters?"

Stephanie looked up to find him studying her intently. "No, I'm an only child, thank God."

"You didn't want brothers or sisters?" She heard the incredulity in his voice.

"Very much. But my parents lived from hand to mouth. They wouldn't keep a job. I was in six different schools by the time I was eleven." Stephanie heard the old bitterness creep into her voice. "That's no kind of life for a child."

"Where are your parents now?"

"Last I heard, they were in Texas. They dropped me off at my grandmother's place when I was eleven, and I only hear from them sporadically. She died when I was seventeen, and they didn't even come to the funeral." She pulled away from him, fighting back tears. What was wrong with her? She hadn't cried over them since the day they left her.

"Let's get out of here." Darrin raised his hand for the check and then slid from the booth. He held her coat, sliding it up her arms and squeezing her shoulders beneath, offering support the only way he could with an audience. Their coats and scarves on and the bill paid, they entered the cold outside air.

"Would you like to walk for a few minutes? We could use the boardwalk beside the lake." At her nod, he pulled her hand through his arm and they strolled along with the cold air gently pushing against their faces.

"It must have been hard for you. Emily's twelve and she

just now can spend the night away from home. She gets home-sick away from Mom and Dad."

"It was tough but I made it, and now I seldom think about it. I'm not sure what made me so emotional tonight, except in sharing the joys of today with you, I realized I have no one else to share with."

"You have the Lord."

"You sound like Bethany. She always says that."

"You don't believe it?"

Stephanie became uneasy under his scrutiny, and she thought she heard disapproval in his voice. His tone alone set off alarm bells. He believed like the girls; she'd have to watch what she said.

"Of course I believe it. Where would any of us be without the Lord?"

She felt, rather than saw, him relax. She *had* to get with Bethany and find out if there was more to this Jesus thing than she thought. Bit by bit she began to realize there just might be something, or Someone, to fill the big hole in her heart.

They returned to the SUV and drove back to the lodge, riding in silence part of the way. After they pulled into a parking space, Darrin removed a gift-wrapped box from his pocket.

"I bought this before I knew today's outcome. I wanted you to know that whether you sold anything or not, you were a success in *my* book." He lifted a gold locket from the box and laid the chain across her hands.

Stephanie struggled with her thoughts. His words could so

easily be taken the wrong way. Had he been expecting her to fail? There was the whether-you-sold-anything-or-not aspect, but then there was the you're-a-success-in-my-book part. A warning voice whispered in her head, *Don't blow this*.

As casually as she could manage, she leaned forward and kissed his cheek. "It's beautiful, Darrin. I will cherish it."

She placed the locket back in the box and put the top on. She couldn't put it on over her coat, but as soon as she got to the lodge, she would have him fasten it on.

Darrin leaned back against the seat, and she took his hand in her own. She laid her head against his shoulder. Would she ever be able to fully trust? Why did she always question every motive, wondering if something was a setup or if it was sincere? Could her parents have destroyed any chance she might have at happiness with a good man? For the evening to have started so beautifully, she suddenly felt cheated.

Something had happened. Darrin felt it in his soul. He thought back over the evening, examining each action, yet he couldn't put his finger on just when things changed. It had to be his fault, though, because Stephanie had been perfect. Her smile—*aah*, she lit up the room. The dazzling holiday decorations in the restaurant didn't hold a candle to her beauty. She outshone them all.

He wondered what his family would think if he brought her home with him at Christmas. He couldn't wait to show her his home and Green Mountain Manor.

He heard the whisper of a voice and he suspended all movement. He waited for the sound again but it didn't come. He sank down on the bed and stared at the floor. That had been a check in his spirit. He didn't need to wait for it again. He recognized it as the voice of the Holy Spirit, and it could only mean only one thing—he'd been thinking about taking Stephanie home to meet his family and the Lord was saying no.

He fell on his knees beside the bed. *Lord, why? I already love her. She's everything I want in a wife.* There it was again. He wept. Into the wee hours of the night, he alternated between reading his Bible and praying. When the sun touched the horizon, he was at the top of Corkscrew, sweating and weak from the walk up, but determined to get away from the lodge, away from his thoughts.

Chapter 9

Saturday dawned and the girls slept in. Michaela, Bethany, and Stephanie went to Incline Village for lunch and an evening of shopping. They giggled and laughed, then teased Michaela about Lynzie's current strategy to marry off her dad. Michaela retaliated with some news of her own; it seemed that while Stephanie and Bethany had been occupied, Derrick from the church group had been dogging Scarlett's every step.

The conversation turned to the locket Stephanie wore, and when she explained why and when Darrin had given her the gift, more explanations were demanded.

Bethany remained firm on her assertion that nothing had happened between her and the ski instructor, Cole, so they received no new information from her.

At seven they went to the movies to see *Fireproof*, and they cried through several parts. Afterward they went for pizza, arriving around ten thirty at a quiet and apparently retired-for-the-night lodge.

"Where is everybody?" Michaela walked over to the lounge, then shook her head. "Nobody here."

"Hmm. You don't think anything happened while we were out, do you?" Bethany's thoughts were evidently about her grandparents.

"Nothing happens if we're not around." Stephanie tried to lighten the mood, but Bethany headed toward her grandparents' suite. In a moment she returned and pushed the elevator button.

"They're asleep. The lights are out."

The elevator dinged and the night desk clerk exited with a container of ice.

"Sorry to have left the desk, but the ice machine down here isn't working. I needed ice for my drink."

"No problem, Larry. See you later." Bethany waved as the elevator doors closed them in. No one spoke until they entered the suite, and then Michaela surprised them all.

"Girls, tonight I'm going to skip prayer time with you. It's late and I have some private things to talk over with the Lord. Are you guys okay with that?"

Bethany glanced at Stephanie as she said, "It's fine with me, Michaela. We're big girls now. The nightly ritual was to help us through college. I think I'll turn in, too."

Stephanie stood alone in the middle of the small living room. What had just happened? How could they give up on prayer time? This was horrible. She felt a main part of her life slipping away, and a void gaped open, ready to swallow her up. She was afraid to go to her room. Didn't *they* feel the danger?

She needed to tell Bethany how she felt. She crossed the small distance to Bethany's door, preparing to knock, when she heard muffled sobbing. She twisted the knob, anxious to comfort her friend. The door was locked. In all the years they'd been together, Bethany never once had locked her door. She searched anxiously for the meaning of this. Had she grown tired of the friendship the four of them shared? The question was a stab in her heart. Panic like she'd never known before welled up in her throat. If she lost these girls she'd have no one. She pressed both hands over her eyes as if they burned with weariness. With leaden steps, she made it to her room. As she had since she was a child, she turned on the bedside lamp, then curled up on her bed in a fetal position and waited for morning to come.

The next morning, Stephanie's back ached between her shoulder blades, and instead of the usually lively eyes in the mirror, the eyes looking back at her were shadowed with weariness.

She dressed for church, choosing to skip breakfast and arriving at the entrance as Mr. Langston pulled the car to the door. Bethany, Scarlett, and Michaela rounded the pillars of the porch just as Stephanie placed a foot in the car. They were laughing and chattering as if nothing unusual had happened the night before. She all but felt her chin drop. She climbed into the very back seat of the SUV, leaving the middle seat for her friends. Mrs. Langston called a greeting to them, and they were off.

As they entered the church, Bethany hooked her arm

through Stephanie's and smiled at her with such sweetness, Stephanie's heart took flight. Maybe they weren't losing their friendship. She resolved to be better, to be the kind of friend Bethany deserved.

The pastor that morning used as his text Isaiah 53:1–2, and he titled his message, "The Tender Plant."

He spoke of Christ being tender in His infancy, His torment, and then His loving-kindness. Something he said right before he closed found a lodging place in her heart. He said that because of Christ's death on the cross, a lost man can come from death to life. She reckoned that lost "man" would be her. As they stood for the invitation, her legs trembled, and she thought her heart would pound out of her chest. She clung to the bench in front of her. What was happening? She started to ask Bethany to leave, but Bethany had her head bowed with tears running down her cheeks. And then the pastor prayed the dismissal prayer. She sank to the pew in relief.

She watched in confusion as Bethany went forward and took her grandparents to the altar to pray with her. Didn't she realize the service was over? What was wrong in Bethany's life that had her so brokenhearted? Why wouldn't she tell her? They had always shared everything, even when they couldn't speak about it, with Michaela and Scarlett.

They ate lunch at the Lone Eagle Grill, Mr. and Mrs. Langston discussing the pastor's message. Stephanie almost spoke up and asked how a person would go about asking Jesus into her heart, but she didn't want the other girls to know she hadn't already done that.

She hadn't seen Darrin since she'd said good-bye to him yesterday, when the girls left for town. Usually he was in church, but his absence today had her worried. She looked for him in the lounge area but found a youth group enjoying the warmth from the fireplace. She never tired of the beautiful Christmas tree that filled one corner of the room. She walked toward it, mesmerized.

"That's odd. I hadn't noticed that before," she said aloud.

"That there are very few ornaments on the bottom?" Scarlett had come up behind her.

"Yeah."

"We thought it'd be a special touch if each guest would hang an ornament on the tree. Sorta make them feel a part of the Christmas spirit here."

"What a fantastic idea. Scarlett, you are so talented. You really should put all your suggestions into a book. You'd make a fortune."

"That'd be plagiarism since I get all my plans out of books or off the Internet." Her happy laughter stirred a spark of hope in Stephanie.

"You wanna play Scrabble with some of us in the dining room?"

For a moment Stephanie was tempted, just so she could be with her friend, but the sleepless night had taken its toll, and she knew tomorrow she would pay if she didn't rest today.

"Thanks, but I think I'll go take a nap."

"Bethany did, too. Seems she had a rough night."

"I'll check on her."

Stephanie entered the suite, weary of the argument continually waging inside of her. They loved her. They didn't love her. They would leave her. They wouldn't leave her. For once in her life she'd like to belong to someone and know without a shadow of a doubt that they loved her and wouldn't ever leave her.

She entered her room, kicked off her shoes, and changed into her pajamas. On her bed she found a card from Bethany, congratulating her on her time-share sales. She read it then started to toss it on the dresser, when the words in the bottom left-hand corner caught her attention. She pulled the card closer to read the small words: "For he hath said, I will never leave thee, nor forsake thee (Hebrews 13:5)."

The pastor had said everything in the Bible was true. Then this verse had to be true. She would never be alone again.

She left her room and went to Bethany's. The door was unlocked and she found Bethany wiping her eyes. She'd been crying again, and Stephanie almost decided against talking with her. But she had to get the misery out of her own heart before she could help her friend.

"Bethany, I know you're troubled about something and I want to help, but first can you help me?" She waited till Bethany patted the bed beside her and scooted up to rest her back on the headboard.

"Sure. What's up?" The tears started first in her voice then ran down Bethany's face again, and Stephanie stared at her helplessly.

"I'm sorry." Bethany shook her head as she spoke. "I can't put it off any longer." She reached for both of Stephanie's hands. "Stephanie, don't you want to give your heart to Jesus?"

"Yes! Yes, I do, but you said I had to ask Him to come into my heart. Now you say I need to give Him my heart. I don't care which it is, I just know I need Him." Stephanie's body shook with sobs. "But I don't know how to do it." The last words came out in an agonized whisper.

"Oh, you poor girl." Bethany climbed off the bed and sank to the floor. "Come join me."

She fell beside her friend and waited until Bethany had turned some pages in her Bible. The pages refused to open to where she wanted, though, so she closed the Bible and hugged it to her chest. "Stephanie, do you believe that Jesus died so that you might be saved?"

"Yes."

"Do you believe that if you don't accept Him into your heart, you'll die and spend eternity in hell?"

"Yes, I do."

"Do you believe that you're a sinner and need salvation?" She waited for Stephanie's nod.

"Then bow your head and say, 'Jesus, please come into my heart and save me, and make me Your child. Forgive me of my sins in Jesus' name.'"

Stephanie repeated the words, but even before she finished, a peaceful calm settled over her weary soul. She opened her eyes and exhaled a long sigh of contentment. She looked at Bethany whose smile broadened in approval. Bethany opened her arms and Stephanie sat in the embrace of her dear friend, glorying in their shared moment of joy. She felt a bottomless peace and satisfaction.

Chapter 10

When Stephanie finally left Bethany's room for her own, she took Bethany's suggestion and wrote the date in the front of her Bible. A Bible with pages that were not worn, nor were verses highlighted as in her friends' Bibles. She read page after page until her eyes were so heavy, she could no longer keep them open. She slept through the evening, not hearing the opening of her door before the night service, or again at midnight. She slept till five the next morning, and she awoke with a sunny cheerfulness.

Stephanie stared out over the snow-covered mountains and then read her Bible. She read about Ruth and how she'd been a stranger in a foreign land. She read in the Psalms and sang passages she'd sung in church and hadn't even realized they were from the Bible. She prayed her first prayer since her salvation, and this time she meant the words from the depths of her heart.

The sky turned from black to gray, and then the sun

peeked over the horizon. Its rays caught the snow crystals and turned the mountain into a shimmering diamond. *"How majestic is your name in all the earth!"* A phrase from one of the Psalms echoed in her mind. Everything looked new.

She dressed quickly and gathered her clothes to wash. Not many people would be up this early, and she would have the laundry room to herself. She grabbed her journal and threw it on top of the clothes basket. She wanted to record her feelings and the new things the Lord had taught her.

After quietly slipping out the door of the suite, she headed for the laundry room. She loaded the washers and then pulled a chair to the folding table and began her first journal entry. Less than an hour later, she was on her way back to the suite. By now she could hear activity all over the lodge, so she took the back hall, hoping to avoid being seen by anyone. Her pony-tail had slipped and her hair hung loosely around her face; she was wearing her old, raggedy sweats.

She'd almost made it when she heard the dreaded voice of the city inspector. There was no mistaking the woman's shrill laugh, and Stephanie turned to run back the way she'd come, when another voice stopped her dead in her tracks.

"Let me know when you arrive and I'll be happy to show you around." Darrin's voice had depth and authority.

"I sure will. It'll be great to see the place run efficiently and specs up-to-date. I'm sure you do a fantastic job."

"I try to get things right."

Stephanie tried hard not to let the hurt seep into her heart, but though she tried, she was assailed by a terrible sense of loss.

He still wanted her job; he even acted like it was already his.

"*I will never leave you nor forsake you.*'" Her confidence spiraled upward. Nothing could dampen the joy of having Jesus in her life. He would help her find her true love, and if not, she'd be satisfied in Him. She rounded the corner, the torn clothes basket flopping on her hip.

"Good morning, Darrin. Ms. Gibbons. Isn't this a lovely day?"

If she hadn't been so hurt, she would have laughed at the surprised look on Darrin's face.

"Oh, it's you. I didn't recognize you without all the makeup."

"Now that was classic, Ms. Gibbons." She didn't miss Darrin's obvious examination of her features and his approval, but she'd had enough of people like him to last a lifetime. "Since I only wear eyeliner and lip gloss, then your glasses prescription may need updating. But why are you here so early? Our appointment is not until nine."

"It's started snowing again, and we're supposed to accumulate three to six inches today. I didn't want to get caught out here with no way back to town."

"Then *I* will show you the cabins. Have a seat in the lounge and I'll be right down." She made sure she looked Darrin square in the eye when she emphasized who would show the lady around for inspection.

She pressed the elevator button, turning her back on Darrin. She didn't look up as the door slid closed, but she knew he'd watched.

With an odd twinge of disappointment, Darrin allowed Stephanie to leave without uttering a word to stop her. He'd honor the Lord's instructions, but that didn't stop a flash of grief from ripping through him. He wished he knew why the Lord had put a caution sign up. Until yesterday, he'd been with her every day for a month. Maybe just a few moments at a time, but he'd grown used to seeing her beautiful face and hearing her laughter.

He was tired of hiding out on the ski slopes. His muscles complained with every movement, and his ankles ached. Sheer determination kept him from limping and wincing with each step. But that was nothing compared to the misery of not seeing her yesterday.

She knew. He didn't know how she knew it was over, but she knew. She hadn't even looked back at him this morning. Ten more days and he'd be flying home for Christmas. He might call his dad and tell him he'd be home earlier. He'd observed all the time-share proceedings, and he knew it was a risk, but with the right person heading up the program, it could also be a huge success. He understood the concept; he'd just have to hire a good coordinator. There had to be more than one of them on the planet.

For the next three or four days, he visited other resorts and hotels in the area with time-shares. He talked with managers about defaulting on bank loans and how the bank handled foreclosures on a place that fifty-one other people also owned.

He left early in the morning and returned late at night.

He bought presents for his family and had them shipped to his home address. If they were sent to the Manor, Emily would open them, then wrap them again. He suddenly had a fierce longing to see his family, but the pull to stay near Stephanie was stronger. Finally, he called his mother, and, bit by bit, he told her his story.

"You did what was right, Darrin. But remember, a check doesn't necessarily mean no. Sometimes it just means to wait until the directions are clearer."

"You would love her, Mom. She's kind and funny. And when she's excited, her eyes shine like jewels. When she laughs, I get a funny feeling in my stomach."

"And you've not seen anything that would cause the Lord to say wait?"

"No, that's what's so confusing. She goes to church every time the doors are open for services. Her talk matches her walk. She once said one thing that bothered me, but she straightened it out immediately. So I have no idea what the problem is."

"Maybe you should talk to her. It's just been a month, son. You can't learn everything about a person in a month."

"I know that I love her. Shouldn't that be enough?"

"Sometimes it's not." His mother was quiet for a few moments as if pondering her next words. "Get some rest, Darrin, and read Proverbs 31. Maybe you'll find some instructions there."

"Thanks, Mom. I love you."

"I love you, too, son. Take care."

He closed his cell and took the elevator down to the lounge. He took a seat beside the fireplace and opened his Bible to Proverbs 31. But never in a million years could he have prepared himself for what he learned next.

Chapter 11

Two weeks ago, she'd never have believed her life would be so different. She'd begun to realize what God had done for her, and she had such a hunger to learn everything there was to know.

And even though there was much to occupy her time, there were always thoughts of Darrin that would not go away. She could no longer deny that she loved him. In fact, she was shocked at the depth of her feelings. But he had opted not to be a part of her life. The last time she'd seen him had been the day of the city inspection. As had happened often the last day or two, her thoughts winged back to that day.

Stephanie entered the back of the lodge after a friendly wave good-bye to Ms. Gibbons, a.k.a. City Inspector. The last cabin had passed inspection and could be shown to prospective buyers.

She stomped the snow off her boots and shook her coat to loosen a layer of powdery snow before hanging it up. You could scarcely see two feet in front of you out there, due to the heavy snow. Skiing would be fantastic, but it also meant some guests would miss their flights. No guests equaled no sales.

"Stephanie!" The shriek from Scarlett's throat had to have done damage to her vocal chords. "Bethany just told us the news. You're a new Christian!"

Stephanie grunted as Scarlett threw her arms around her, squeezing hard, and tears filled her eyes as she heard her half sob, "I'm so happy for you."

Scarlett drew back and they began to wipe each other's tears away, laughing and talking at the same time. "How do you feel?"

Stephanie poured out her heart. "I want to sing and shout and read my Bible. It's all I can do not to tell everyone I come into contact with, what has happened to me. In fact, I just mentioned it to the city inspector and I think she passed the cabins' inspections just to get away from me." They both chuckled and walked hand in hand to the stairs.

As they crossed the lobby, Darrin stepped out of the elevator.

"Have you told him?"

"Shh. No, I haven't." Stephanie didn't feel he deserved to know. She knew in her heart he'd been avoiding her. Still, she couldn't explain why she didn't want to tell him; she just knew she wanted to understand what had happened herself before sharing the news with Darrin.

They walked past him with only Scarlett calling out a cordial, "Hi, Darrin."

Later that night the girls had one of the best devotional

times in their history together. After many tears and everyone sharing their thoughts about Stephanie's salvation experience, Stephanie remembered to ask about Bethany's problem.

"What problem?"

"You've been crying for two days, Bethany. In all the excitement I forgot, but I want you to know I'm here for you."

Bethany began to laugh and grabbed Stephanie in a bear hug. "You silly girl. I was burdened over *you*. You told me that day sitting in the infirmary that you'd never invited Jesus into your heart. I started praying right then that God would prepare you for salvation. In church yesterday, I felt that you would go forward, but you didn't. I saw that you were under heavy conviction, and I longed for you to be saved. I told God I'd give up peanut M&M's if that's what it took for Him to save you."

They burst into laughter, and Stephanie spoke over the lump in her throat. "Thank God that's not what it took or we'd have to put up with your mood swings." The pillow fight that followed had them gasping for breath, Michaela and Bethany lying on their backs on the floor.

"Seriously, you've been the best friends a girl could have. Thanks, Bethany, for praying for me." Stephanie swiped at the tears that came from nowhere. "Each one of you has shown me what a true Christian should be, so I've had the best examples. I wish there were words to tell you how much I love you. I wish I could tell Jesus how much I love Him, too."

"You can." Scarlett's voice rang with sincerity.

"How?"

"By telling others your salvation experience, so that they might be saved, too. Remember, the Bible says if you're ashamed of Him, He'll be ashamed of you."

Stephanie had not known the Bible said that, but she'd mulled it over constantly the past couple of days. She'd been too embarrassed to tell Darrin that she'd become a Christian, afraid that he'd think badly of her for pretending to be a Christian all the times they'd been together.

Now it grieved her to think the Lord might be ashamed of her. *Lord, give me the courage and the words, and I will tell him. Father, I will shout if from the rooftops. I never want You to be ashamed of me.*

When she and Papa Langston had set the program up, they'd decided to do only one group a week. She had just finished her third week of time-share sales and had invited the last couple to accompany her to the lobby to place an ornament on the tree.

She couldn't believe her eyes. Her heart thumped erratically. Darrin was sitting by the fireplace reading his Bible. She hadn't seen him in days. Had she not heard differently from the girls, she would have thought he'd left already.

She helped the couple choose an ornament then escorted them to the stairs, encouraging them to visit their cabin as many times as they wanted before they left in the morning.

She retraced her steps to the fireplace. *God, give me courage,* she prayed.

"Hi, Darrin."

"Stephanie."

"I need to say something to you, and I want you to listen and not say anything. If you speak, I might not make it through. Do you promise?" Her knees were weakened by the trembling in her limbs.

"I promise. Would you like to sit?" He indicated the sofa across from him.

"No. I'd rather stand." Her brain was in tumult, her thoughts scattered. *Lord, help me.* Her troubled spirit quieted.

"I have been bitter toward you for trying to take my job."

"What?" If she didn't know better, she'd have believed his astonishment at her words. She held her hand up for silence.

"You promised."

He inclined his head, submitting to her will.

"I know it's true because I overheard you telling Papa Langston all the things that could go wrong with my program. Then I heard you talking with the city inspector, telling her you did a good job keeping things up to specs and that you would show her around. I have come to terms with your deception. The Lord graciously saved me two weeks ago, and I have someone now who will never leave me nor forsake me, and He won't treat me badly. So if you want this job, you can have it. My Lord will have something better in store for me."

She turned to walk away, sick with the struggle it had been to expose her feelings to him. She hadn't taken two steps when Darrin stepped in front of her and swept her into his arms, almost crushing her within his embrace.

It took a moment for Stephanie to register what he kept repeating, over and over. "That was the check. You weren't saved."

They withdrew from each other and he cupped the sides of her face with his hands. "That was the check, sweetheart. You weren't saved."

"I have no idea what you're talking about, Darrin. You're confusing me, and it doesn't matter anyway." She pulled his hands away from her face and walked past him.

"Stephanie?" His voice halted her. "I've never wanted your job. Mr. Langston and I were talking in generalities, and the city inspector was talking about my lodge in Colorado."

Stephanie stared at him a moment, recognizing the truth for what it was. That didn't change the fact that he'd avoided her for two solid weeks and that a stranger, the city inspector, knew more about him than the woman he claimed to be interested in. As far as she was concerned, he'd left her. She couldn't deal with that.

"Stephanie, please. . ." His voice was rough with anxiety.

She studied him intently. His eyes widened in alarm when she began to turn away.

"Tell me one thing, Stephanie." She paused, waiting for his question. "Tell me how to win your heart"—his eyes entreated her to help him—"because I don't have a clue."

"I can't entrust my heart to you, Darrin, because you left me. It's taken me a long time, but I finally realize I deserve better than that."

"I didn't leave you. I longed to be by your side every day."

"Then why weren't you here? Why did you let me think you'd found something better in the inspector? And how was I to know you had a lodge in Colorado? You never said a word about it to me, but you found time to tell her?"

"I don't know what to say. I didn't know you thought that."

"That's right. You couldn't know because you weren't here."

"Sweetheart, I told you—there was a check in my spirit. God was telling me to wait. I didn't know why, but I had to obey Him. Now I realize it was because you weren't saved."

"So you're telling me that a God who loves me and knew that being left behind messed up my psyche told you to leave me, too?" She was so furious, she could hardly speak. "I don't believe you, Darrin Hart, and I won't listen to anything else you have to say."

She walked away, her jaw tight with the effort to keep the tears at bay. She entered the lobby to find all three friends staring at her with varying degrees of sympathy. Smothering a sob, she fled upstairs.

Pacing the floor of her room, she replayed the conversation over and over in her mind. Could he be telling the truth? She put on casual clothes and sank onto the bed with her Bible. Maybe she could find the answers in His Word.

She studied and read, only to get up frustrated and begin pacing. She'd put in so many overtime hours, she knew Mr. Langston would not be upset if she didn't return to work. At five, the others returned to the suite and begged her to go with them for pizza. After a while, they realized she was not going to give in, so they left without her.

Her mind kept wandering, so she turned off the old sit-com rerun she'd been trying to watch. She picked up her Bible again and let it fall open wherever it would. She began reading in 2 Corinthians, and while it was interesting, she found no answers—until she came to chapter 6, verse 14: "Do not be yoked together with unbelievers. For what do righteousness and wickedness have in common? Or what fellowship can light have with darkness?" Oh goodness. There it was. Darrin had told the truth.

She raced from the suite, determined to find him. She didn't even know what room he was in. She went to the front desk for the information.

"Mr. Hart checked out this afternoon. He had a four thirty flight to Aspen, Colorado."

As Stephanie's confused mind fought to understand that information, another quick and disturbing thought caused her to grab onto the desk for support.

She had driven away a man who claimed to love her. Had she driven her parents away, too? She felt the blood leave her face and looked for a place to sit down.

"Are you all right? You look a little pale." The desk clerk's voice sounded far off.

The girls chose that moment to return to the lodge, and one look at Stephanie's face, and Bethany had a chair pushed under her with her head between her legs.

"What happened, Stephanie?"

Scarlett placed her scarf, a bit wet from the snow, against Stephanie's neck. The cold wetness revived Stephanie, and she sat upright.

"It's my fault," she whimpered. "I sent him away and now I'm all alone."

"First of all," Michaela said matter-of-factly, "you didn't send him away. He went home for Christmas. He's had that return ticket since he arrived."

Michaela placed her hands on her hips. "I always thought you were the strongest of us, but you're turning into quite a wimp. Now snap out of it and look around. Do you see us? We're here. We're not going anywhere, and if I were a betting person, which I am not, I would say *you* will be the first to leave *us*."

Stephanie's weakness began to evaporate as Michaela's words sank in. Her knitted cap had slid to the side and barely hung on one ear. She still had her outside clothes on, so with her hands on her hips, she looked like a very small hippopotamus.

Stephanie brought a hand up to stifle her giggles. Michaela's eyebrows reached her hairline and she placed her hands in a strangling position against Stephanie's throat. "Stop it. Do you hear me? No one is going to leave you. Don't tar the rest of us with the same brush as your parents'. *They* need help, Stephanie. There is something lacking in them, not you. You should pray for them. They're probably the most miserable people in the world."

"Thanks, Michaela." She reached to give her friend a hug.

They trouped upstairs together, none the wiser when Stephanie sneaked back to the front desk and confiscated Darrin's card from the visitors' desk. Sure enough, his cell phone number was there, clear and legible. She wondered briefly what time it was in Aspen.

Chapter 12

Stephanie returned to her room and dialed the number, then hit the DISCONNECT button. She couldn't get up the nerve to call. She decided to send a text instead.

"Darrin?"

Stephanie waited for what seemed like ages, and then her phone shook.

"Who's this?"

"Someone who's missing you like crazy."

"Oh?"

"And wishing she hadn't sent you away." Stephanie thought he wasn't going to respond, and she laid her head on the bed, the phone close. Then it vibrated.

"What happened that changed your mind?"

In the middle of keying her answer, her phone beeped, indicating she had an incoming call. It was Darrin.

"Hello?"

"I hate texting. My fingers are too big. Can you talk or will it wake up the others?" His voice sounded bigger than life, and she had a hard time picturing him far away in Aspen.

"I can talk."

"I miss you, too, sweetheart."

"So much it hurts?"

"Yeah. At least that much." He rushed right into the big question. "What changed your mind about me?"

"I found the answer in the Bible. It says to not be 'yoked together with unbelievers.' You were standing on His Word. I knew that about you—I just shoved it aside."

"I wish I'd stayed close anyway. I could have led you to the Lord myself. I missed my chance."

"It's okay. You can teach me more about the Bible. I'm an eager student."

"It's a deal."

Conversation lagged and Stephanie laid her head on the pillows.

"Darrin?"

"Um-hm?"

"If you wake up during the night, will you text me and tell me you like me even though you don't like texting?"

"I promise, if you'll do the same."

"I can't," Stephanie stated emphatically.

"Why not?" There was a trace of exasperation in his voice, but the sleepiness had vanished.

"If I text you, I'll have to say that I *love* you, not *like* you."

"Oh, babe. Why do you say things like that when I'm not there to hold you in my arms?"

"By the way, do you want children?"

"Yes, by my wife."

"Got anyone in mind?" Stephanie held her breath, not believing she could be so forward.

"Why? You applying for the job?" His voice had taken on a new tone. It was louder, as if he'd sat up to hear better.

"Am I being offered the job?" She propped herself up against the headboard, the pulse in her neck beating such a rapid tattoo, she could hear it in her head.

"No."

She felt the air whoosh out of her lungs.

"No?"

"Not until I can be there on my knees with a diamond to slip onto your finger."

Oh joy, joy, joy! She jumped to her feet and did the happy dance on the bed.

"Then the answer is yes."

"Sweetheart, you're not supposed to answer till I'm there with you."

"But I can't wait for our happiness together to begin." Her heart fluttered wildly in her breast. He'd asked her to marry him. "Will we have a good life?" She fought hard to keep the insecurities hidden, but every now and then she needed a bit of assurance.

"Do you promise to love me forever, Stephanie?"

"Forever, I promise. I'll be your forever girl."

"Then our life will be fantastic."

"Will you love *me* forever, Darrin?" This sounded strangely like an exchange of marriage vows.

"Till the last breath leaves my body." Her emotions whirled.

"Good night, my love."

"Night, sweetheart."

That telephone call set a precedent for the coming week. Stephanie learned that Darrin wouldn't return until the second of January. That seemed a lifetime away. She filled her days as full as she could and saved her nights for Darrin. She counted the hours, and many nights she could hear the frustration at their separation in his voice. She grew stronger with each declaration of love, and she grew stronger in her love of the Lord. She felt truly blessed.

She shopped with the girls, thankful she'd bought all their gifts before Thanksgiving. Now every time she shopped, she bought for Darrin. There were at least six gifts for him under the tree in the girls' suite.

Christmas Eve arrived and the girls and the Langstons exchanged gifts. There weren't many guests, but Derrick and his family had arrived as well as Scarlett's parents. The atmosphere was festive as they celebrated Christmas and Scarlett and Derrick's engagement. Other than that, it was the quietest Stephanie had ever heard the lodge.

Christmas morning brought more snow, and the girls opened their stockings early so Scarlett could leave to be with Derrick and their parents. Stephanie, Michaela, and Bethany watched a parade on TV, then at noon, they had devotions with the Langstons.

Sitting down to lunch, they heard the snowplow come around the bend in the road and stop. They were pretty much snowed in, unless they wanted to use the snowmobiles to get around. They heard stomping and laughter, and then a big burly man entered the kitchen. Stephanie glanced up, then back at her plate. Mr. Langston would take care of whatever the man wanted. An ice-cold hand descended against her throat, and she shrieked and jumped from her chair.

"Hello, Forever Girl."

She did a double take.

"Darrin?" Then she saw his eyes behind the ski mask. The shriek turned into squeals of delight. "What are you doing here? Oh, praise the Lord—you're here."

His laugh was triumphant as he picked her up and swung her round and round.

"I couldn't wait any longer to be with my girl."

He set her on her feet and then tried to kiss her. The ski mask and cumbersome clothes prevented them from touching. She tugged on his coat, and he slipped one arm out, then the other. The mask and scarf came off next. His hair stood on end, but she didn't care. The minute he was free, he enveloped her in strong arms and kissed her cheek, neck, and forehead.

"I want a *real* kiss." She reached for his head to pull him closer, but he dodged her, laughing at her attempts.

"We'll have our first real kiss in private." His voice dropped to a whisper.

Stephanie looked sheepishly at her friends seated at the table. Their grins proved they knew she'd forgotten they were there. She had completely lost her train of thought.

"Will you guys excuse us?" Darrin didn't wait for an answer. He pulled Stephanie by her hand and led her to the fireplace in the lounge. Down on one knee, he removed the prettiest diamond she'd ever seen from its nest in the box he held and placed it on her finger. "Will you marry me, Stephanie?"

"Oh, Darrin, it's beautiful. Yes, of course I'll marry you."

He gathered her close in his arms, and the caress of his lips on her mouth demanded a response. She went up on tiptoe, wrapping her arms around his neck, and kissed him, lingering, savoring every moment. They pulled apart, and he placed a series of slow, shivery kisses across her forehead and down her cheek.

Her legs were so weak, she'd have fallen if he hadn't held her up. He guided her to the sofa, and she curled her feet under her and faced him. He obviously had some questions for her to answer.

"Please tell me we can be married soon." The huskiness in his voice spoke of the passion he held in check.

"I signed a six-month contract with the Langstons."

"Which we'll let you out of early." Mrs. Langston's voice could be heard from just outside the door to the room.

Stephanie started to giggle, and the rest of the group sauntered into the room, acting as if they had just walked up. She knew better. She could tell from the glistening eyes of her friends that they rejoiced with her. Michaela was right; she would be the first one to leave this family circle. Wasn't it just like the Lord to let her leave first, so she wouldn't have to experience the feeling of being left behind? And He'd saved her, guaranteeing that she'd never be left behind again.

She looked at her future husband and saw that he'd read her thoughts. He leaned over to whisper, and his mouth grazed her earlobe. "I love you."

JEAN KINCAID and her husband, Dale, are missionaries to the Hispanic people in Old Mexico and the Rio Grande Valley. Her husband pastors Cornerstone Baptist Church in Donna, Texas, where Jean teaches the junior girls' class and sings in the Rondalla. They have three adult children and eleven grandchildren. Jean speaks at ladies' retreats and women's events and enjoys all things mission related. Kids believe anything you tell them, so Jean's favorite pastime is sharing stories with her grandkids. Her favorite time of the day is early morning when she spends time in devotional reading and prayer. Her heart's desire is to create stories that will draw people to a saving knowledge of our Lord Jesus Christ. You may contact her at www.jeankincaid.com.

Dating Unaware

by Jeri Odell

Chapter 1

Why did I agree to move all the way to Incline Village, Nevada? Michaela Christiansen questioned her sanity, and not for the first time. Cramming her last box into the trunk of the white Honda Civic, she slowly lowered the lid, hoping it would close. It did. She let out a sigh of relief.

The little four-door had been her faithful companion since her aunt and uncle handed it down on her seventeenth birthday—nearly eight years ago.

Leaning against her car, tears fogged her vision as she gazed at the modest two-story her cousin's family called home. The clapboard siding always had a fresh coat of paint, and in the spring and summer, the grassy knoll was brightened by flowers and manicured grass. Now, however, the beauty vanished as winter knocked on autumn's door. This ten acres was all that remained of the family farm—the farm her grandparents had worked for nearly fifty years. The same farm her grandfather's father and grandfather before him had plowed and planted.

Roots. That's what Michaela longed for, and that's why she had to leave. She had to find her own way, her own life, and a place to settle down, so her future children would have the life she longed for but never had. Thank heaven her aunt and uncle stepped in when they did.

"Why the glum expression?" Her cousin Valerie sauntered down the sidewalk toward her. "I thought this is what you wanted. A new start, a new place, new people, new dreams. . ."

Valerie quoted all the reasons Michaela had rattled off as she convinced herself to leave Springfield, Missouri for some little town in Nevada nestled on the north shore of Lake Tahoe.

She smiled at her petite cousin. The only family resemblance at all was the exact brunette hair color that both of their mothers also shared. Val had the dark Italian eyes of her dad's side of the family. Michaela inherited her father's green eyes and long, lanky form.

"I don't get it." Val was nothing if not direct. "Your roots are here. Our ancestors had Missouri soil in their blood since way back before the Civil War."

"I know. But this feels like your home, not mine. I'll always be grateful that your parents took me in my last two years of high school and helped me through college, but now I want to try out my wings—see if they really work." *Liar.* Truth be told, she'd love to stay here, but being with Val and her family was bittersweet—a constant reminder that her mother married the wrong man.

"I'm sorry your dad didn't make it to your graduation." Val

reached for Michaela's hand and squeezed it.

Michaela gazed out over the bare trees dotting the landscape, and the bareness of her soul echoed within. "He and his new wife were traveling."

"I know his excuse, but it had to hurt."

Her blurred vision was back. A warm tear slithered down Michaela's cheek. "Why is it you are always trying to make me face my emotions?" Michaela laughed and wiped her cheek dry.

"Because you spend way too much time stuffing them."

"Guilty as charged." Michaela glanced at her watch. "I'd better hit the road after breakfast. I've got about eighteen hundred miles ahead of me." Both girls moved toward the house. "You should fly up for a long weekend and try skiing," Michaela added.

Val snorted—a half laugh, half mocking sound. "I don't like to be cold."

Neither do I. Entering the house, the smell of breakfast drew them to the kitchen. A spread fit for royalty covered the round table, which sat in a nook at one end of the large kitchen.

"Did you invite the entire neighborhood or half of Springfield?" Val raised one brow.

"Didn't want to send Michaela off hungry." Aunt Anabelle scooped scrambled eggs from the skillet into a bowl.

Uncle Vinnie came into the kitchen through the back door. "Dogs are fed." He wrapped one strong arm around Michaela and one around Valerie. "How are my girls this morning?" He was a big, muscular man and nearly always jovial. Michaela always felt safe in his hug—secure and protected.

"Morning, Daddy." Val stood on tiptoe and placed a peck on his cheek.

Michaela did the same—only tiptoes were unnecessary.

"It's ready." Aunt Anabelle removed her apron. "Shall we?" She motioned toward the table.

After they settled into the same chairs they always occupied, Uncle Vinnie said grace. Michaela loved the sound of his booming voice. If only there were more men out there like him—dependable, loyal, hard-working, dedicated to his family. *Forget men. I'm through with that species.*

"So our Kayla girl is heading west today." Uncle Vinnie smiled at her. "If you decide that isn't where you want to be, we'll be here."

Aunt Anabelle nodded her agreement.

"Thanks. This is just a temporary gig. I may be back." However, that wasn't her plan.

"It all happened so fast." Her aunt strategically poured syrup over her waffle just so.

"I'd been praying for God to show me my first post-college step. Working part-time for Mr. Ramos wasn't cutting it. Then Bethany called."

"Who is Bethany again?" Uncle Vinnie looked up from his plate.

"She's the one from Republic. Her grandparents own the ski lodge."

Aunt Anabelle solved the mystery. "The curly-headed redhead."

"More auburn," Michaela corrected. Bethany disliked being

272

referred to as anything else.

She placed the first bite of waffle into her mouth, letting the warm, sweet maple syrup bathe her taste buds. "Aunt Anabelle, how will I survive without your delicious breakfasts?"

"Hopefully, you won't be able to. Then you'll come back to us sooner rather than later." Her aunt smiled. "You do what's best for you. Valerie tells us you have a business plan in place."

Michaela nodded, wiping her mouth with her napkin. Of this part of her life she was certain, confident, excited. "Well, you know I minored in photography, and it's my true love."

"We had no idea," Uncle Vinnie joked. "Is that why you are always carrying a camera?"

"Anyway, I'd like to design greeting cards, calendars, posters with beautiful pictures, and prose. I figure my left-brain degree in business will serve me well as I carry out my right-brain passion."

"You've always been so good at seeing the whole picture and planning accordingly." Aunt Anabelle's tone carried admiration.

"I try to cover my bases." Michaela rose and carried her plate to the sink. "Time will tell." She glanced up at the large rooster clock hanging above the sink. "Speaking of time, I've got to hit the road."

They all rose and huddled around her. Uncle Vinnie prayed for a safe journey. They walked her to the car, everyone hugged her again, and Michaela watched through her rearview mirror as they stood on the edge of the road waving good-bye until she turned the corner.

Fighting tears, she raised her chin. "This is a good thing, a fresh start." She spoke the words to reassure the frightened woman staring back at her from the rearview mirror.

"You know, honey, Lynzie is praying for a mom."

Jonas Brooks gazed into his mother's compassionate golden brown eyes. "I know." He placed his elbows on the kitchen table, resting his chin on his fists. Guilt assailed him. "I feel so selfish, but I can't go there—not even for my own daughter. There is not much I wouldn't do for that kid, but I can't marry somebody just because Lynzie wants a mom. It wouldn't be fair to anyone involved."

Mary Brooks sipped her coffee. "No, that would be wrong, but maybe if you'd date, you'd find someone special."

He shook his head. Nobody seemed to get it. "Jill was it—my soul mate." He carried his empty cup to the electric coffee maker and refilled it. Facing his mother, he leaned back against the kitchen counter. "I had my one great love, and yeah, it didn't last as long as I'd have liked, but I had it. Do you know how many people search their whole lives and never find what Jill and I had? What you and dad have?"

She nodded and he spotted the moisture glistening in her eyes.

"I'm content, Mom. I've got a great family, a job I love, and a daughter who's worth her weight in gold. I miss Jill, but I don't want to replace her."

"It's been three years. . ." His mom sniffed. "I thought as time passed you might feel differently."

He shook his head. "If anything I'm more certain all the time that Jill was enough and our love will carry me through a lifetime until I meet her again one day on the streets of gold."

Mary rose and crossed the kitchen, wrapping her arms around her son's waist. "You are a good man, Jonas."

He hugged his mom tight. "Will you help me reinforce to Lynzie that there is no mother in her future? I'm a one-woman man."

"I will, honey. And we'll pray for Lynzie to be content with her God-given circumstances."

Two long, grueling days of driving and six states later, Michaela headed over the pass on Highway 431. *Almost there.* Emotions ranging from anticipation to fear and every nuance in between bubbled inside her.

Starving, she decided to grab a bite before following Bethany's directions to the lodge. It had been almost seven hours since her lunch had been consumed somewhere along Interstate 80.

The Mt. Rose Highway ended and she turned left onto 28. This appeared to be a main drag through the little town. In the dusk, she could see why they called this little town Incline Village. To the north, steep hills stood tall and proud. To her right was a downward drop toward Lake Tahoe. She pulled into a convenience store for directions to a nearby restaurant.

Following the clerk's directions, she turned right on Country Club. Sure enough, there sat Austin's on the left.

Climbing out of her car, she stretched her tight muscles. Man, was she glad that drive was over. Moving toward the quaint gray building, she breathed in the cold mountain air.

Once inside and seated, she removed her coat and scarf. Settling into her booth, she overheard the little girl at the next table.

"I'm still going to pray for a new mom." Determination flowed through each word.

Michaela picked up the menu, trying to focus on the choices.

"Honey, your dad doesn't want to remarry." The attractive lady—probably about her aunt's age—laid down her fork and focused all her attention on the black-haired child.

The thin girl smiled, revealing dimples in each cheek. "It doesn't matter what Dad wants, Gramma. God can work it out if He wants to."

Michaela smiled at the simple faith. *And He can for me as well. God, You can work out things any way You see fit. Out of the mouths of babes, and aptly spoken at that.*

The waitress returned and Michaela ordered a Texas Taco Salad. When the waitress departed, the girl was staring at Michaela. Her grandmother pushed aside her empty plate and stood. "I'll be right back."

She nodded her head, her shoulder-length hair bobbing with the movement, but those piercing black eyes never left Michaela.

As soon as her grandmother disappeared toward the restrooms, the little one made a beeline to Michaela's booth. "You're wearing a Curious George sweatshirt."

Michaela nodded, smiling.

"I'm his greatest fan. May I sit down?" She glanced toward the empty seat across from Michaela.

"Please do." Michaela waved her hand toward the vacant spot across the table.

"I'm Lynzie Brooks." The child held out her right hand.

"Michaela Christiansen." Michaela accepted the bony offering. "Pleased to meet you."

Lynzie slid into the seat across from Michaela. "Do you live here or are you visiting?"

Michaela knew—both from the conversation she'd overheard and the girl's intense gaze—that she was being interviewed for the position of mom. Her heart melted at the fact that this girl considered her mom-worthy.

"Lynzie!" Her grandmother had returned and stood at the end of Michaela's booth, wearing a horrified expression that her precious granddaughter had joined a stranger. The older lady focused her attention on Michaela. "I am so sorry."

At that moment, the waitress returned. On her tray was a salad and two desserts. She placed the salad in front of Michaela and glanced back at the empty table where Lynzie and her grandmother had been. "Oh, you moved." She then proceeded to place the carrot cake and ice cream sundae across from Michaela.

Michaela glanced at Lynzie's grandmother. Her face now

glowed red. Her gaze shot from the dessert to Lynzie—who'd already begun to eat—to Michaela.

Michaela giggled. "Please join me. Otherwise, you may traumatize our already confused waitress."

She smiled. "Thank you. I'm so embarrassed. Please forgive the intrusion."

"No intrusion. Lynzie is delightful. We were just discussing our love for Curious George." Michaela glanced down at her white sweatshirt that had a giant monkey across the front.

"My whole room is Curious George, right Gramma?"

"That it is." The waitress sat a fresh cup of coffee in front of her. "By the way, I'm Mary Brooks—Lynzie's grandmother." She reached her hand across the table, and Michaela knew where Lynzie had gotten the habit.

Michaela introduced herself again. "So, how old are you, Lynzie?"

"Eleven."

"Going on twenty," Mary interjected. "She's an only child, and most of her companionship comes from adults."

"I was an only child, too." Michaela smiled as Lynzie savored her last bite.

"I want a new mom and a sister and brother."

Michaela nodded her understanding. She'd wanted the same, but thank heaven Valerie was the next-best thing.

"Are you married?" Lynzie sat on the edge of her seat, leaning toward Michaela.

Michaela shook her head, dreading the turn this conversation was about to take.

Chapter 2

Neither is my dad." She eyed Michaela expectantly. "My mom died three years ago, and I think it's time he remarries."

Her poor grandmother. The look of horror had returned. She faced Lynzie, a stern expression on her face. "Lynzie, your dad has no plans of ever remarrying." She sent an apologetic glance in Michaela's direction.

Lynzie shrugged as if she were certain God had other plans.

Mary cleared her throat. "Tell us about you. Are you visiting the village or do you live here?"

"Sort of both." Michaela filled them in on her dream job as a photographer and her day job at the lodge. "I'll be setting up their financial, reservations, and maintenance software."

"Sounds like you're in the right place. I don't think there is a more photogenic spot in all the world than Lake Tahoe. Of course, I'm biased." Mary slid her empty coffee cup to the center of the table. "Which lodge are you working for?"

"Snowbird."

"Snowbird?" Lynzie's eyes lit up and she sat up straighter. "We live right next door! I can visit you every day."

Michaela smiled at the child's enthusiasm. Kids always touched a tender spot within, and this delightful little girl immediately captured a piece of Michaela's heart. She loved her faith and saw many similarities to herself at that age. *So much for the seclusion of small-town life.* "I'd be thrilled to see you every day. How close to the lodge do you live?"

"A stone's throw," Mary answered. "We both built on the same ridge. We are on the west edge of our property, and they're on the east edge of theirs. But Lynzie doesn't have to visit every *day*."

"No, I would love it. I'm not mom material, but how about a sort of aunt or big sister?"

Lynzie nodded.

"I've got to go now—I'm exhausted. I've been driving since five this morning, but I'll see you tomorrow. I'll have to unpack my car in the morning. Maybe you can help, since it's Saturday and there's no school?"

They all slid out of the booth and headed for the door.

"I'll be there," Lynzie promised. "I'll bring my dad. He's strong and likes to help people." With that, the little girl followed her grandmother out the door and they vanished into the dark night.

The hope that Lynzie got the loud, clear message that Michaela wasn't available for her dad evaporated as well. Lynzie had a plan and Michaela would have to tread carefully.

"You *what?*" Jonas ran his hand over the back of his head.

"I promised that you'd help Michaela unload her car this morning. She probably has some really heavy boxes." Lynzie shrugged and her expression was a tad too innocent.

Jonas glanced at his mom. She raised her shoulders in a helpless gesture and shook her head. He turned back to Lynzie. "You somehow managed to volunteer me to help a complete stranger—a woman none of us knows—*unpack?*" He rubbed the back of his neck.

"You told me that we should live an active Christian faith." Her raised brows dared him to deny that. " 'Do unto others...' "

He sighed. "What time did you tell her we'd be there?"

"Now."

Jonas walked to the back door and grabbed his coat off a hook. "Please tell me she's an eighty-year-old widow."

Both Lynzie and his mom shook their heads, but neither volunteered more.

Once he and Lynzie were bundled up, they took the trail to the lodge. "You do remember the talk we had only two days ago about any matchmaking schemes?"

"Of course, Dad."

When they entered the lodge, Jonas headed toward the registration desk. Then he heard Lynzie greet this Michaela person. Turning, he caught sight of her and the air left his lungs.

No, there was nothing eighty about her. Their gazes connected—hers held an apologetic expression. She glided toward him, her hand extended.

"Mr. Brooks, I'm Michaela Christiansen." He accepted her hand and realized the last adult female hand he'd held was Jill's.

Michaela smiled and perfect white teeth greeted him. "I only have a few boxes. . ." She glanced at Lynzie.

"It's quite all right. Lynzie likes to help others."

His heart was pounding. How ridiculous. Only teen boys got heart palpitations over a pretty girl, certainly not men over thirty. "Shall we?" He raised his arm toward the door.

He took Michaela's jacket and held it for her as she slipped her arms into the sleeves. That close, he caught the scent of her shiny brunette hair and his senses engaged. She smiled up at him. He took a step backward. Many things he'd tucked into the recesses of his mind came tumbling to the forefront—like the smell of a woman, the softness of their hair and skin, and the grace with which they move. And unknown to him until about five minutes ago, he'd missed all of it.

When they arrived at Michaela's car, she pulled the keys from the front pocket of her jeans. She pushed a button on her remote and all the doors unlocked. Then she opened the driver's door and released the trunk. She handed Lynzie a smaller box, then took two medium ones for herself. She moved aside so Jonas could retrieve a couple of larger ones. Then she led the way back into the lodge.

Jonas followed Michaela and Lynzie.

"So where do you live?" Lynzie asked as they entered the elevator.

"In a suite with three of my friends."

"I didn't know you knew anyone here." Lynzie followed Michaela off the elevator and down the long hall.

"Yeah." Michaela turned into a room where the door stood propped open. "Let's put these in my room and then I'll show you around."

She led them to a yellow bedroom. Lynzie set her box on the bed and commented, "This is so pretty—like sunshine everywhere." While she checked things out, Jonas set his two boxes on the hope chest at the foot of the bed. Michaela had deposited hers on the dresser.

"Pretty nice," she said. "The Langstons did a great job building this place and making it inviting."

He focused his gaze on Michaela. Like Jill, she was very pretty in a wholesome way without tons of makeup.

Jonas cleared his throat. "So you have friends here?"

"Yeah, come on and I'll introduce you." She led the way back into the main living area.

"Guys, this is Jonas and Lynzie Brooks. These are my college buds—Bethany, Scarlett, and Stephanie. Bethany's grandparents own the lodge, and they hired each of us for this winter season."

Jonas greeted each woman. Funny, they were all attractive, but meeting them didn't affect him the way meeting Michaela had. *And she's just a kid—fresh out of college. I'm nearly a decade older than she is. No wonder she called me Mr. Brooks. Good thing I'm not interested, because she is way too young.*

They returned to the car a couple more times—each carrying an armload of stuff. After the last trip, Michaela walked them to the front door.

She faced him. "Thank you so much." Then she focused on Lynzie. "Both of you."

"My grandmother says many hands make light work."

Michaela chuckled and tugged on Lynzie's braid. "And she's right."

"Will you come over for dinner tonight?" Jonas's jaw dropped at Lynzie's invitation. "Grandmother won't mind, will she, Dad?"

He shook his head. Grandmother might not mind, but he did. He'd have to have another talk with his daughter when they got home today.

Michaela smiled and glanced at her roommates, who'd joined them at the front door. "I think we might have plans tonight."

"Nope." Bethany shook her head.

"No plans here," Stephanie assured her.

"I'm washing my hair and going to bed early," Scarlett informed everyone with her Texas drawl.

Michaela's expression mirrored his discomfort at the idea. "Sounds like you're free," he said.

She sent each roommate a *thanks a lot* glare. "I guess I am." Her eyes sent an apology to his.

"We'll walk over and pick you up at six."

Lynzie now grinned ear to ear.

"We don't have to do this."

"My mom won't mind."

Her roommates chimed in. "Go."

"It'll do you good to get out."

"She never did anything but study in college." Scarlett spoke the words directly to Jonas.

He winked at her. "See you at six."

Michaela waited at the front door for Jonas. She paced back and forth, wishing she'd not let herself be pressured into this stupid dinner. He clearly wanted no part of it, and neither did she.

Then she spotted him walking up the trail. He was dangerously good looking—muscular, tall, nice full mouth. *Michaela, don't even think about his lips!* Her cheeks warmed. She stepped out into the cold.

He spotted her and smiled. Her heart did a little dance and she returned his smile. Appealing. Quite appealing. Too appealing.

Taking a deep breath, she walked beside him down the trail. Their cabin radiated a warm glow through the well-lit windows.

They entered through the back door into the laundry room. Lynzie ran and hugged her. Chattering about her room, she took Michaela's hand and pulled her toward the stairs.

Michaela said a brief hello to Mary as they passed the large kitchen. Fifteen minutes later, Jonas stuck his head into Lynzie's room. "Dinner's ready. I take it you got the grand tour?"

Michaela nodded. "Every drawer and shelf."

Mary introduced her husband, Tom, to Michaela. He was an older version of Jonas. Then the five of them settled at a large wooden table. She ended up next to Jonas and across from Lynzie.

Tom said grace and then dished up a bowl of hardy-looking stew, passing the first one to Michaela. "So, tell us a little about yourself. Where are you from?"

Michaela sucked in a deep breath, never enjoying being the center of attention. She'd much rather listen than talk.

"I always say I'm from nowhere, yet I've been everywhere." She accepted the basket of rolls from Jonas, took one, and passed it on to Lynzie. "I was an army brat."

Tom nodded, buttering his roll. "And now you work at Snowbird?"

Michaela explained how they'd all just graduated in May, nobody had landed their dream job, and the timing coincided with needs here at the lodge.

"What was your major?" Jonas laid down his spoon and focused on her.

"Business, with a minor in photography."

"She's going to make greeting cards and stuff—right, Michaela?"

Smiling at Lynzie, she nodded.

"Right you are. This stew is delicious, Mary. And what about you, Tom? What do you do?"

"I'm a forest ranger—just like Jonas."

"Oh." She focused on Jonas. "A forest ranger, huh?"

"And Gramma stays home and takes care of me." This evening, Lynzie wore her shoulder-length hair unencumbered and tucked behind her ears.

"I have the best job of all." Mary reached her arm around Lynzie's shoulders and gave a tight squeeze, pulling the child against her side.

"So do you all live here?" Michaela wasn't sure if Lynzie and Jonas had their own place.

"We do. It's just easier that way since Jonas works odd hours and various shifts. Sometimes he has to travel, so that way Lynzie isn't shuffled back and forth." Mary rose and began clearing the table.

Michaela stood to help.

"Sit down, young lady. Guests don't work in this house." Tom pushed out his chair and helped his wife, leaving Jonas, Michaela, and Lynzie at the table.

"Do you like games?" Lynzie studied her.

Michaela nodded, though she'd never played that many.

"Do you want to play Twister?"

"No." Jonas's answer was abrupt. "How about a board game? That is, if Michaela is willing."

"Uno Attack!" Lynzie jumped up, racing from the room. When she returned, she plopped the game box on the end of the table. "Gramma and Grampa, do you want to play?"

Mary shook her head as she wiped and dried the table. "You go ahead. Grampa and I will load the dishwasher and pop some popcorn."

Lynzie clapped her hands together. "Yeah, popcorn!" She

removed the box lid and unloaded a battery-powered game that spit cards at the players. Then she shuffled cards and passed out some to each of them.

The next couple of hours flew by as they laughed, ate popcorn, and shared small talk. Michaela enjoyed the evening more than she had anticipated.

"One more?" Lynzie asked as they finished the second game. Michaela had miraculously won both.

"No way, kiddo," Jonas answered. "It's past your bedtime and tomorrow's church."

Lynzie faced Michaela. "You want to go with us?"

Michaela glanced at Jonas and was certain she saw dread on his face.

"I'm going with my roommates. Sorry." In truth, they hadn't yet talked about it, but the four of them always attended church together, so it was a safe assumption.

Lynzie's lower lip protruded slightly, but the look Jonas sent her way halted further argument. "Will you at least tuck me in?"

Again Michaela glanced at Jonas for some sort of guidance. "Run upstairs, brush your teeth, and put on your jams. Then we'll see if Michaela is still here."

"Ok." Lynzie sighed loud and long as she left the room.

Jonas smiled and shook his head. "Sorry. I hope she's not driving you crazy."

"Not at all. I mean, as long as you don't mind."

He shrugged but failed to answer.

"I'm done." Lynzie's voice carried down to them from the

top of the staircase. "Can Michaela tuck me in?"

Again, her gaze locked with Jonas's. She wished she knew what he was thinking.

"It's up to you," was all he said.

Michaela rose and climbed the stairs, to Lynzie's delight. They read a story and then knelt together beside Lynzie's bed while she said her prayers.

"God bless Gramma and Grampa, Daddy, and Michaela. Please find my daddy a wife and me a mom. And Michaela needs a family, too. Thank you, God. Amen."

Lynzie climbed into bed and snuggled beneath the down comforter. Michaela touched her cheek.

"Sleep tight." The sweet encounter left Michaela feeling empty and a seed of longing rooted in her heart. She had to find a way to avoid this precious child and her cute dad. They made her wish for things she didn't even want. Or so she kept trying to convince herself.

Chapter 3

While Michaela tucked his daughter into bed, Jonas realized he had a problem, and the way he dealt with problems was head-on. Though he dreaded the task before him, he knew he had to nip this situation in the bud.

When Michaela returned, she appeared slightly flushed and way too beautiful. As he helped her into her coat, his eyes were drawn to her creamy, soft skin. *I'm nipping this in the bud, remember?*

"Would you like me to drive you home? It's pretty cold."

"I can walk." She seemed to sense his discomfort. "Thanks for a nice evening. Tell your mom the dinner was wonderful." She moved toward the door.

"Wait. You're not walking alone."

Shock settled on her features. "I'm not?"

"I'll see you home." He pulled his coat on and they headed out the back door. Neither talked during the three-minute walk, but both were shivering by the time they reached the lodge. He followed her in through the large double doors.

"How about some hot cocoa?" His request clearly surprised her.

"Sure. I'll be right back."

He settled into the conversation pit in front of a roaring fire. No one else was around, but he knew the Langstons tried to keep the fire going strong until almost midnight. They wanted their guests to have every convenience.

When Michaela returned, she carried two mugs; each had steam rising and a dollop of whipped cream peeking over the top. He met her halfway and accepted the rich-scented chocolate drink. Leading her back to the fireplace, he settled into an overstuffed chair. She took the end of the sofa nearest him and held her mug between both hands.

"I'm not good at dancing around things."

Michaela's eyes widened slightly, but she said nothing.

"Lynzie has this notion that I should remarry."

Michaela nodded.

He wished she'd say something—anything. Now it just felt like he was about to give a speech.

"Me? Not so much." He cleared his throat.

Michaela stared down at her hot chocolate. Was she disappointed?

"Anyway, I just wanted to be up front with you. I have zero interest in pursuing Lynzie's idea. None. I'm very content with my life."

She raised her gaze from her cup to the fire. *Come on, Michaela. Say something.*

"As you can probably imagine, being Lynzie's dad is a full-time job—and the best job on the planet, I might add. Then I'm busy at church. I'm a deacon and teach the high-school boys." *I'm rambling.* He paused, hoping Michaela would fill the silence. But no, the silence lingered on.

"My job's pretty demanding, too. Some seasons require a lot of extra hours."

At least she'd finally made eye contact. Was her expression boredom?

He decided to make it personal. It seemed to him Michaela just wasn't getting what he was saying. "You seem really nice and all."

"Oh, I am."

Great, now where did he go from there? She bit her bottom lip, and he almost expected her to burst into laughter.

"No need to complicate things, right? I thought it would be better to lay my cards on the table—"

Michaela erupted with laughter—hard, loud, tear-filled amusement. "Are you breaking up with me?" The words sort of tumbled out between gasps of air and more snickers.

Is she some sort of psycho?

"I've only known you a day." His words held a defensive edge.

She sucked her lips inward and took a deep breath. "Precisely." Her tone shifted to annoyance. "I don't know what planet you're from, Mr. Brooks, but maybe not every woman who meets you wants to sign on as your wife."

She rose, hands on her hips, facing him. "For your information, I already told your daughter that I'd love to be her friend or sort of a big sis, but I'm not interested in being your wife."

Boy did she put him in his place. Her eyes shot fire his direction. He stood to put them back on more even footing.

"I'm really sorry. I didn't intend to offend you. It's just, most women—"

"I am not most women! I'm not on a husband hunt, but if I were, you wouldn't even be a contender!"

"Point taken." He moved a couple of steps toward the door. "Again, I'm sorry. Please forgive any assumption I implied. I'll let myself out." He made quick work of getting out the door and on the path toward home. He was trying to be a good guy, and now he felt like an idiot.

Michaela crossed her arms, let out an incensed sigh, and plopped back on the couch. Too annoyed to enjoy the fire, she carried her now-tepid drink to her suite. There, of course, she found three sympathetic pairs of ears and poured out her story.

"You've got to be kidding! He didn't sound like the arrogant type." Scarlett shook her head, her curls bouncing this way and that.

"Are you sure you didn't take it the wrong way?" Bethany—always the sweet one—struggled to believe anyone ever had a bad intention.

"The wrong way?" Stephanie spoke up. "He sounds full of himself."

"You know what I think?" All heads turned toward Scarlett. "Thou dost protest too much. That stinker is attracted to you, and it is scarin' him to death."

"You might be right." Bethany nodded her agreement.

"And you know what else I think?" Scarlett's gaze bored into Michaela's. "I think the attraction might be mutual."

Now three pairs of eyes stared in her direction.

Michaela raised her chin. "No way."

"Did you see those muscles, girl?" Stephanie winked.

"And that was a nice head of chestnut hair. Imagine gliding your fingers through that." Scarlett giggled.

"He was very nice looking, Michaela. You have to admit that." Bethany's look dared her to deny those facts.

"Just 'cause the guy had a few nice attributes doesn't mean I was hoping to sign on as *Mrs.* Muscles."

They all cracked up.

Then Bethany grew serious. "It's time, Michaela. You haven't dated since freshman year. Since"—she paused as if afraid to say the two-timer's name—"Tad."

"First my dad and then Tad. Fool me once, shame on you—fool me twice, shame on me. I'm not giving a third man the power to break my heart and devastate my life. I'm just not."

Stephanie shook her head. "How realistic is that?"

"Totally. Lots of single people live rich, full lives. Husbands and boyfriends aren't the only road to happiness."

"But who wants to grow old alone?" Scarlett raised her well-shaped brow. "Not me. I'll tell you that for sure. I'm gonna find me a big ol' Texas man and give him a houseful of kids."

"And you love kids," Bethany reminded Michaela.

"I do, and I've been thinking that once my business plan is in full swing, I'll adopt. Single people do that often these days."

"But is it fair to raise a child without a dad?" Bethany's life was steeped in tradition.

"Isn't one parent better than none?" It seemed logical to Michaela. "You guys aren't talking me out of my dream. I know where I'm heading, I know what I want to do, and I know who I want to do without."

"A man." They said it in unison and laughed.

"There are days a male-free existence sounds pretty good." Stephanie rose from their plaid sofa and stretched. "How about if we all hit the slopes tomorrow after church?"

"The slopes? Ya'll know I don't ski."

"Time you learned, Scarlett girl. Why live at a ski lodge if you have no intention of enjoying the runs?"

***

"Dad, did you even say hello to Michaela and her friends at church this morning?"

Somehow he knew Lynzie would never miss his blatant choice to ignore them all. "I was busy with my boys. By the time I finished up, they were long gone." Truth be told, he made sure it played out that way. Not only had he dodged conversation, he avoided eye contact as well.

"I think we should go skiing today," Lynzie announced out of the blue.

Jonas was looking forward to a lazy afternoon filled with football and a recliner. Rarely did he even get a chance at a do-nothing day. "Skiing?"

"Yeah, I'd like to go to Snowbird."

Suspicion rose, and he studied Lynzie. "Come here." He patted the arm of his favorite chair.

Lynzie did as she was asked. In his estimation, her expression was a bit too innocent.

"Lynzie, Michaela and I have no interest in each other."

She raised one shoulder like she couldn't care less.

"None, zilch, zero, nada." He said it every way he could thing of.

"Is that all you wanted?"

Jonas nodded.

Lynzie rose. "I figured that out yesterday, Dad. No big deal, but can we still be friends?"

"You and me? Sure, we can still be friends."

She let out a loud sigh and rolled her eyes with that pre-teen attitude she was quickly attaining. "Dad! I meant me and Michaela, not me and you."

He laughed. "You can be friends with Michaela as long as you have the whole hooking us up idea out of your head for good."

She nodded. "I think you'll be sorry one day. I'll grow up and get married. Gramma and Grampa will get old and join mom in heaven. What'll happen to you?"

He grabbed her arm, pulling her down on his lap. He wrapped her in a tight hug. "You won't go far, or you'll miss me too much."

She wrapped her long, lanky arms around his neck and kissed his cheek. "I love you, Dad. I just worry about you, that's all."

He kissed her back. "That's my job—the worry thing. You're not allowed to worry about me." His heart felt like it might explode with all the love he had for her.

She rose. "So are we going skiing?"

"Sure."

Not fifteen minutes later, they both came out of their rooms all decked out in ski gear. Jonas laid their skis in the back of his pickup. The drive to Snowbird was longer than the walk. He parked away from the lodge, hoping to avoid Michaela. He'd not spoken to her since that dreadful breakup scene. Thinking about it still brought a warmth to his face. *Talk about being an idiot.* Yep, for sure, he could live the rest of his days and never see Michaela again. But with Lynzie around, there wasn't much hope of that.

They slid into their boots and snapped them into place. Carrying skis and poles, they headed toward the lift.

He spotted her immediately. Michaela and two of her roommates stood in line for the lift. He blew out his breath, squared his shoulders, and followed his daughter straight to them.

"Lynzie!" Stephanie and Bethany both hugged the little girl. Michaela appeared as horror stricken as he felt. She turned quickly, and their gazes locked. Jonas forced a smile. She did the same.

"Hello." He strove for nonchalant but sounded anything but.

"Hi." She turned her gaze back to her roommates.

So now what? Lynzie and the roommates chattered away, leaving the two of them feeling uncomfortable and silent.

After they'd all purchased tickets, they waited for their turn on the lift. It was an open, swing-type chair, so only two adults would fit comfortably. He assumed Michaela would ride up alone.

Just before Stephanie and Bethany boarded, Stephanie grabbed Lynzie's hand. "We'll take her with us. That way we won't need three chairs."

Mouths open, Michaela and Jonas watched the three of them hop into the moving seat and be whisked away upward. Then the attendant motioned for them to stand in the pre-marked footprints as the next chair bumped their legs and they slid into the seat.

"I'm sorry." She spoke loud to be heard above the wind. "I had nothing to do with this—in case you are wondering."

"I have no doubts after our last conversation."

Michaela chuckled. "I'm sorry about that. I think I may have overreacted."

"I'm sorry, too. I didn't mean to come across so pompous."

Michaela laughed and he joined her. "I guess neither one of us presented well."

"I've had brighter moments," he assured her. "So who burned you so badly that men are off the grid forever?"

He watched her intensity, but her gaze never met his. She scanned the horizon. "My dad and then a boyfriend."

"No third strike, huh?"

She finally looked at him. "What do you mean?" Her forehead crinkled.

"Not a baseball fan?"

She shook her head.

"You know, players get three tries to hit the ball. You only took two of your three swings at bat. Plus the old adage that three is a charm. Maybe the next guy would be the one."

Chapter 4

The one?" She doubted such a person existed.

He nodded, a knowing glint in his eye. "Jill was my soul mate, and I wouldn't have missed her for the world."

Oh to be loved like that. "You're a lucky man then. Even losing her was worth the short time you shared?"

"Absolutely. Yeah, it hurt like crazy and I miss her still, but life is a series of valleys and summits. One would be meaningless without the other."

"I had no idea you were so philosophical. How did you meet Jill?"

They'd almost arrived at the top, and Jonas unhooked the belt that ran across the full width of the seat. "I met Jill Brown in kindergarten. However, it was not love at first sight. I knew that she and all girls had cooties."

Michaela giggled. She stepped off to the right and Jonas to the left. "Cooties, huh?"

Jonas trudged to a nearby bench and adjusted his skis.

"Turns out we were even in the same church nursery as babies."

"So you grew up here?"

He nodded. "A simple man with a simple life. Hey, I wonder where the rest of our party disappeared to?"

Michaela looked around, but they were nowhere in sight. She longed to hear the rest of Jonas's story, but he rose and slipped his goggles into place.

"I'm taking Rouge."

"A black diamond?"

He nodded.

"I'll see you at the bottom. I'm starting with an easy run. I haven't been skiing in several years."

He waved and was off. Michaela glided over to Sidewinder. She snowplowed her way down, keeping her speed to a minimum. She thought about Jonas as she glided past pines. His brown eyes and wide smile made an attractive package. But even better than his looks, he was just an all-around nice guy with strong family, church, and community ties.

"If I was ever looking for a third at bat, he'd be a good candidate," she mumbled softly to herself. When she got to the end of the run, Jonas waited near the fence for her.

"Any sign of Lynzie or my friends who apparently ditched me?"

He pointed to the lift. Sure enough, the three of them were on their way back up again. "Lynzie got them on a black diamond. Now they're going for round two."

"And you're stuck with me. Sorry."

He shrugged. "Lynzie is having a great time. I like her to be around women whenever possible, so she gets the female influence."

They slid back into another lift seat and started the climb. "Your mom does a great job with her, too."

"That she does, and I'm so grateful to have her. I don't know how single parents do it without family to share the load."

"Me either." She paused. "So, if you don't mind, tell me your and Jill's story."

A slight smile touched his lips. "I don't mind. Lynzie loves to hear it all the time, and it helps keep the memories alive. She is so afraid she'll forget her mom."

"I understand that. My mom died when I was twelve. That was half a lifetime ago. The memories are fainter. It's hard to see her face anymore. I have to keep looking at her picture to keep the image sharp and fresh."

He studied her, and she looked away under his scrutiny. "I didn't realize you'd lost your mom, too."

Michaela nodded and decided a subject switch was in order. "When did you figure out girls were cootie free?"

He laughed. "High school. One day Jill Brown was as annoying as a fly at dinner, and the next, she was the most beautiful girl I'd ever seen."

"That's so sweet."

"We'd actually become friends in junior high, and at her sweet sixteen, she stole my heart. Turns out she'd had her eye on me the whole time.

"A few months later, she was diagnosed with leukemia. We got married a week after graduation because we had no idea how much time we had left and wanted to spend every second of it together. Never take time for granted—that was our motto. Two years later, we adopted Lynzie."

"Lynzie's adopted? I had no idea."

"I figured you could tell. She's from Guatemala."

"I just assumed Jill was Hispanic or something."

He shook his head. "Jill was a natural blond with the bluest eyes you'd ever want to see." There was a longing in his voice.

"Anyway, the disease returned when Lynzie was five. Jill fought long and hard but barely made it to Lynzie's eighth birthday."

Michaela swallowed, hoping to dislodge the lump pressing against her windpipe. "I'm sorry you lost her."

"Me, too, but we had a dozen great years. More than a lot of people ever get. Well, here we are, back at the drop-off point. You ready to up the ante?"

"Not yet. Maybe later today, but not now."

"See you at the bottom." He waved at Michaela and headed for another black-diamond trail. This time he'd try Bucking Bronco. *Jill, my one great love. You'd be so mad at me for refusing to think about remarrying—or even dating.* She'd had the talk with him, telling him he needed to keep living and experiencing life. She wanted him to start over, but he just couldn't. What he shared with Jill was too special to ever replicate.

He whizzed down the trail with the precision of a man who'd made this run many times before. When he reached the bottom, he was slightly breathless but fully exhilarated.

As he waited for Michaela, he was glad he'd shared his high school sweetheart story. Maybe now she'd understand the speech from yesterday.

Stephanie, Bethany, and Lynzie flew toward him, each making a quick turn before nearly plowing into him. All three of them sent a spray of snow his direction. They giggled as he brushed himself off.

"We're starving," Lynzie announced. "Where's Michaela?"

"Here she comes." They all turned to see her weaving slowly down to the end of the trail.

Lynzie skied over and grabbed her hand. "We're going to eat at the outdoor restaurant. Come on."

They all glided across the fresh powder to a designated spot and removed their skis, placing them into a rented locker. Then Bethany and Michaela found a table, while Stephanie and Jonas went up to order.

As he approached the table with a tray loaded with burgers, he heard Michaela say, "If you guys are behind this, you need to knock it off." Michaela's back was to him, so she had no idea he was right behind her.

Bethany glanced at him and he nodded his agreement. He mouthed the words, *Knock it off.*

"Us?" Bethany asked with all sweetness and innocence. Maybe a little too much of both.

"There is no reason to give Lynzie false hopes. Jonas and

I are in complete agreement. We aren't interested in each other, nor are we interested in dating—or the opposite sex for that matter."

Jonas emphatically nodded his head with each statement she made, and Bethany cracked up.

Michaela glanced behind her, and he watched the red hue light up her face. He winked at her and claimed the chair next to hers.

"Everything she said is true." *Though something about her does intrigue me. That only makes her more dangerous.* "Lynzie is quite taken with Michaela, and we'd both be grateful if that line of thinking isn't encouraged. I'll just end up with one very sad little girl."

Stephanie and Lynzie joined them, carrying the fries and drinks. The conversation was dropped but he hoped not forgotten.

Once the food was passed out, he asked, "How long have you girls been friends?"

"We all met our freshman year of college at SMS."

"SMS?"

"Southern Missouri State."

"For some crazy reason, we were all in the same hall and hit it off. The following three years, we roomed together." Stephanie filled in some of the gaps.

"Lynzie, what about you?" Bethany asked. "Where would you like to go to college?"

"My dad and mom both went to college right here at UNR. I might do that." She dunked her fry in ketchup.

"It's so much fun to go away from home, though—live in a dorm and truly experience the college life." Stephanie encouraged Lynzie to think outside her box.

"You meet new people and have new life experiences." Bethany smiled at his daughter.

Jonas wasn't sure he liked the direction this conversation had turned. College, yes. Far away from home? His gaze ran over the little girl he'd raised since infancy. He hadn't considered that possibility.

"You know, Lynzie. . ."—Michaela reached across the table and squeezed her hand—"there are good things about staying home, too."

Thank you!

"You just have to figure out what is right for you. We had to do that, too." She sent a pointed look to each of her friends. "God made us all different, and what works for some of us may not be the plan for everyone." Michaela glanced at Jonas.

He gave her the thumbs-up. "Well said. Jill and I were already married, so staying here made sense for us."

Then he focused on his daughter. "You have awhile to think about that decision. Now, are we heading back out to those slopes or what?"

❧

Michaela had managed to go an entire week without seeing Jonas—though she'd thought about him and Lynzie many times. Perhaps her roommates got the message to butt out.

Speaking of those dear souls, they were probably waiting

for her. She glanced at her watch, grabbed her purse, Bible, and coat, and headed out of her bedroom.

"Hey, slowpoke," Scarlett drawled. "Let's go."

They rode with Bethany's grandparents to church. Lynzie greeted them the minute they stepped into the vestibule. "I saved seats." It was so cute the way she thought they were all best friends.

They followed Lynzie to the third pew on the left. Jonas stepped out as one by one they paraded in front of him. Michaela intentionally placed herself last in line, assuming he'd slide over and they'd have an entire entourage between them. When he stepped aside instead, that put the two of them smack-dab beside each other. And the pew was crowded. It was impossible for her shoulder not to press against his broad one.

He smelled masculine and outdoorsy. The choir came out and took their places onstage. Michaela caught a glimpse of his mom and dad. How cute. She wondered if Jonas and Jill had ever sung in the choir.

As the first song began, the rich timbre of Jonas's voice praising the Lord touched her heart. To her there was no greater joy in the house of God than the men singing their hearts out to their heavenly Father. Maybe because her father never did. He stood stoic and silent beside her mother.

When the singing ended and the sermon began, Michaela tried hard to ignore the man beside her and focus all her attention on the pastor. But an awareness of Jonas kept returning.

She noticed the cadence of his breathing and the large

hands that opened his well-worn Bible. Each page had scribbles and underlining—the man obviously used his Bible! He turned quickly to each verse the pastor referred them to. Not only did he use it, he knew it.

A godly man. A real honest to goodness man who did more than show up on Sunday. Nothing could have impressed Michaela more, because she'd convinced herself they didn't exist. Tad planned to be a preacher, for goodness' sake, but he thought nothing of breaking their engagement and her heart to date another girl. Somehow, deep inside, Michaela knew Jonas Brooks didn't take promises or commitments lightly. If he committed to somebody it would be forever. *Forever*—the word filled her heart with a longing she couldn't afford to have.

When the service ended, Jonas turned to her. "How was your week?"

Light banter, Michaela, friend to friend. "Busy, but I managed to sneak away a couple of times with my Bible and my camera and get some great shots. Your mom told me this is the most beautiful spot on God's green earth, and I might have to agree."

"You'd get no argument from me." When he smiled, a dimplelike line appeared in his left cheek.

"How about *your* week?"

"Not too bad. I can't believe Christmas is only weeks away."

"Me either."

"Are you going home for Christmas?"

She shook her head. Her dad would be on some South Pacific island with Babette. Jonas moved into the aisle and she followed. Lynzie and Michaela's roomies were long gone. They'd all exited out the other end.

"Is this the church you grew up in?"

"It is." They moved toward the back, where groups of people gathered. "Nursery, Sunday school, my baptism, Awana, our wedding, Jill's funeral. Every big event in my life has happened here."

"You're lucky. Roots are a good thing." She felt teary and sentimental.

"Considered boring by some."

"Ah, but not to all." She chose a lighter tone. "How old were you when you gave your heart and life to Jesus?"

"About seven. You?"

"A freshman in college. I worked a couple of years before going to college so I could build up some savings. Therefore, I was an older freshman. Nineteen actually."

"Your conversion was probably more dynamic than mine at seven. Not much changed for me." He chuckled.

Lynzie rushed up and tugged on his sleeve. "Dad, can we go to lunch with Michaela and her friends?"

"Not today. I've got things to help your Grampa with at home." He turned to Michaela. "Sorry."

"Don't be. I didn't know anything about lunch. I need to get back to the lodge. I want to finish a software installation so I can move on to phase two tomorrow morning."

"See that?" he said to Lynzie. "You're not missing a thing."

He wrapped an arm around her drooping shoulders. "See you later."

Nodding, she tried to ignore all the longings that had arisen. Longing for a life like Jonas and Jill had lived. Longing for a man like Jonas and yet not wanting a man at all. And longing for roots, a place to plant them, and people to plant them with.

Chapter 5

D ad, some of my friends are going ice skating down on Miller's Pond. Can we go?"

Jonas glanced up from his open Bible on the desk to his daughter standing before him with her ice skates dangling by their laces from her shoulder. He gazed back down to the prep work he was doing for next Sunday. His longing was for these boys to "get it"—get how much God loves them, the great price He paid for them, and how wonderful life can be, walking with Him one day at time.

"Please, Dad?"

He smiled at the kid he loved more than life itself. "Being an only child and a social butterfly isn't a good mix, is it?"

She shook her head. He rose and stretched. "Give me five." He hugged her on his way out the office door.

True to his promise, they were on their way in a few short minutes. This time of year a four-wheel-drive was a requirement to even get to Miller's Pond. He drove slowly, but his big Dodge Ram handled the challenge effortlessly. When they got back to the pond, Jonas searched the area for some familiar vehicles but spotted only an unfamiliar one. As he parked by the Toyota Four Runner, he spotted Stephanie, Bethany, and Michaela with two men he didn't recognize. Suddenly, this felt like a setup. He turned in his seat to face his daughter, who was halfway out of the cab.

"Wait a minute. Where are your friends?"

She batted her eyes. "Oh, you thought I meant my school friends? Sorry, Dad—I meant the *girls*."

"*The girls*?" He overannunciated as he repeated her phrase.

She shrugged. "You know—Bethany, Stephanie, Michaela. Are you coming?" She slid down to the ground and tightened her scarf around her neck.

He'd been had and by an eleven-year-old. "Be right there." Tonight they'd have the talk about omission and how it still was considered lying. But for now, he'd keep his promise.

Grabbing his skates from behind the seat, he joined his daughter and Michaela on the nearest bench. "Hey."

"Hey yourself." Michaela appeared to be embarrassed. Did she have something to do with this little setup?

After he had his skates tied, he followed Michaela over to meet the guys. "This is Darrin—he's from Colorado—and this is Cole. Guys, this is Jonas Brooks, and he lives here—in fact, right next door to the lodge."

Jonas shook each of their hands. Then they paired off. Bethany skated with Cole and Stephanie with Darrin. And there stood he, Michaela, and Lynzie.

He shrugged. "Shall we?" He took one of Lynzie's hands, and Michaela grabbed the other. The three of them skated round and round the pond, Lynzie doing most of the talking.

"I didn't know Bethany and Stephanie had boyfriends." Lynzie's curiosity had been peaked.

"They don't actually have boyfriends—at least not in the way you mean. They have friends who are men, but they aren't dating if that's what you think." Michaela's voice held a defensive edge.

"Kind of like you and my dad are friends but not dating?"

He glanced over at Michaela, and her expression would best be described as mortified.

"I mean he's a boy and you're a girl. You're kind of friends, but not boyfriend-girlfriend kind of friends. But you like each other okay."

"Well, sort of." Michaela watched as Cole planted a playful kiss on Bethany's cheek. "Someday one of their friendships might grow into a romance."

"And that will never happen with Daddy and you. Right?"

She nodded, but her smile looked forced. "Never."

"So you never want to fall in love?" Lynzie focused her full attention on Michaela. "Or just not with my dad?"

"Not now and not for a long time."

"Why?"

"Lynzie, some things are none of your business." Jonas jumped in to save Michaela from being forced to succumb to Lynzie's curiosity.

"How about you, Dad? Why don't you ever want to fall in love again?"

Jonas weighed which direction to take. He could either insist on a change of subject or he could reiterate—for the sake of all three of them—his reasoning. After thinking through both options and their repercussions, he plowed ahead.

"Here's the thing, Lynzie. I've been in love, and it is the greatest. What your mom and I shared can't be duplicated. I'm a one-woman man, and your mom was my one."

They skated in silence; Lynzie seemed to be content with his answer. He glanced at Michaela, and she, too, wore a peaceful expression. *Good. This issue is finally settled once and for all.*

"How did it happen that Lynzie and Jonas showed up at the lake today?" Michaela asked her two friends on the drive back to the lodge.

"I must have mentioned that we were going skating this afternoon to Lynzie at church on Sunday." Bethany glanced back from the front seat.

"Please don't do that again." Michaela sounded harsher than she intended.

"She thinks we're all gal-pals." Stephanie was scrunched in the middle between Michaela and Cole. "You don't want us to hurt her feelings, do you?"

"She's eleven. We're not buddies with her. Just don't give out any information to her—that's all I'm asking. Just one simple request." Frustration laced each word.

"We'll try." Bethany's soft voice soothed Michaela. "But

she asks some pretty direct questions. You don't expect us to lie, do you?"

"Of course not, but here's the thing: I don't want Jonas assuming I'm arranging these rendezvous. He made it clear—again today—that he loved one woman, she's gone, and he has no intention of loving another. Not now, not ever! And yet I'm always being shoved in his direction."

"Shoved? I think you're being overly sensitive," Stephanie pointed out.

"No man likes to feel like a woman's throwing herself at him," Cole agreed.

"All right, all right," Bethany begrudgingly assented. "Time for a subject change. My grandparents are arranging for an all-day drive around the lake next Saturday. Who's in?"

All five agreed it sounded like fun.

"The van will stop at all the best tourist spots for pictures, food, hikes, and so on. I'll put all five of us on the list. That way we'll have a seat for sure."

❦

Michaela spent the next few days with Jonas in the forefront of her mind. No matter how much she fought it, that man appealed to her senses—the way he looked, the cologne he wore, the rich sound of his voice. . . Her heart was ignoring all the logical arguments of her mind.

God, is there a man like him for me? Being with Jonas and Lynzie made her realize how much she did want a husband and kids. She admired his loyalty and how deeply he loved. He was more faithful to a woman who'd been gone for three years than her dad or Tad had ever thought about being.

Saturday arrived and Michaela threw on her favorite pair of faded jeans and an olive sweeter that complemented her eyes and hair. She grabbed her down jacket, gloves, and scarf before running down the stairs to board the van. No matter how hard she tried, she never beat her roommates out the door. They always ended up waiting on her.

When she hit the lobby, she spotted Jonas and Lynzie going out the front door. Stopping at the registration desk, she asked Sarah for the sign-up sheet. Two of her three roommates, Cole, Darrin, her, Jonas, and Lynzie. She groaned, crossed her name off the list, and headed up the stairs. Returning to the front desk, she told Sarah, "Let them know I have a headache and won't be joining them."

Sarah nodded, but Jonas walked in before Michaela had a chance to disappear back to her suite.

"Did I hear you say you're not going?" In her opinion, Jonas looked relieved.

"Headache," Sarah said.

Michaela nodded and turned to leave. "Have a good time."

She pushed the elevator button, not feeling energetic enough for the stairs. The doors opened. She stepped in. Good. No scene with Jonas. She pushed the Up button. The doors began to draw together. A large hand stopped them.

Michaela's heart dropped. Almost. . .she'd almost escaped without questions or explanations.

The doors reopened. Jonas stepped inside. He pushed the

Door Close button. Suddenly, the elevator felt very small.

"Headache, huh?"

Michaela nodded and sighed. By now she really did have throbbing temples.

"You sure?"

"I think I know when I have a headache." Her words were clipped and annoyed.

"Did Lynzie and I going give you the headache?"

Michaela had two choices—get mad or cry. She settled for the path of least humiliation.

"Remembering ice skating gave me a headache." She reached around him and pushed the Up again.

"That's fair, and I'm sorry."

The door opened and they were on her floor, but neither moved. He stood on one side of the small space and she was across from him.

"Let me ask you a question. Why do you keep slamming me with the same message? You're not interested. I'm not interested. How many times do the facts have to be restated?"

"For Lynzie's sake, often."

"Well, for Lynzie's sake, I'm staying home." She left him on the elevator and didn't look back. Ice skating had been uncomfortable at best. She'd have a better time alone, doing her laundry.

Jonas felt like a heel. He made his way back out to the van. If not for Lynzie and the fact that he was the designated driver since Jackson wasn't free, he'd have gone home himself.

He spent the day half listening to Lynzie's incessant chatter and reliving the day at the pond.

He noted that each of Michaela's roommates seemed to have deepening relationships with their respective men. And then there was Jonas, Michaela, and Lynzie.

His blatant and constant rejection of her might have felt personal. After all, even though he never planned on another relationship, he didn't mind if the fairer sex found him appealing. He needed to take Michaela at her word, let down his guard, and just be her friend—without reservation. She already knew where he stood. Maybe they could have a beautiful friendship. Can men and women even be just friends? He had no idea but was determined to find out.

At church the following morning, Michaela sat with the Langstons. The roommates were spread around, each sitting with her guy. He and Lynzie had been quickly forgotten.

After church, they all gathered in the fellowship hall for the monthly potluck. He held back and waited for Michaela to take a seat, then he went through the line and joined her.

Her eyes shouted surprise when he slid onto the bench next to her.

"This seat taken?"

"Nope. Where's Lynzie?"

He pointed across the room to a group of girls, all about the same age. "I've been an idiot—again. Seems I'm always apologizing to you."

She smiled and raised her brows. "You think?"

Relief washed over him. Not only was she sweet and kind, she was forgiving. He should have known she would be. "I do think. I've never had a woman friend before. Guess the idea kind of scares me."

Michaela laughed. "I understand. Frankly, it scares me a little, too. And like you, I don't want to give Lynzie the wrong impression or hurt her in any way."

He raised his iced tea glass. "Here's to a beautiful friendship." She clanked her water glass against it. *And here's to no broken hearts at the end of this road,* he thought.

Chapter 6

The lodge was hosting a hot dog and marshmallow roast on the back porch. There were several roaring fires in the outdoor pits. Michaela wondered if Lynzie and Jonas would come, but she hadn't asked.

When she came back inside to grab more marshmallows, Jonas and Lynzie had just stepped inside the front door. Lynzie ran to her, giving her a tight hug. She wrapped her arms around the little girl and squeezed back. The familiar longing came with the bear hug. *Lord, I'm just giving this to You and trusting You. Someday. . . .* She'd found a lot of peace lately in handing over her desires to God.

"I wondered if you two would come. Grab a colored ball, and we'll each place one on the Christmas tree." Lynzie searched through the bowl until she found a yellow one, Michaela took red, and Jonas blue. They each hung their ball in an empty spot on the tree.

Michaela stepped back, admiring the lovely tree. "Didn't Scarlett and Derrick do a terrific job decorating the tree?"

Jonas stood next to her. "Seems to me they missed a spot or two—like most of the bottom half."

Michaela laughed. "That was intentional, so each guest that visited Snowbird had the honor of helping decorate the lower portion."

Scarlett breezed through the room, carrying the marshmallows Michaela had neglected to obtain. "I do believe you two are standing smack-dab under a spray of mistletoe."

They both looked above them. Sure enough. Lynzie jumped up and down, clapping her hands and squealing, "Kiss her, Dad. Kiss her."

He turned slowly, facing Michaela. "Guess I have to." He winked.

Her heart pounded. He moved toward her at a snail's pace. She had no idea if he'd actually kiss her or not. Did friends kiss friends?

Though her lips longed for contact with his, that didn't happen. He veered off at the last second, placing a tender peck on her check near the corner of her mouth. She'd wanted more and hoped he wouldn't see that yearning in her gaze.

His eyes sparkled and danced with mischief. She wondered what he was thinking. For certain he'd not have longed for the real thing, as she did. He'd told her otherwise too many times for her to have even a spark of expectation.

"Dad, I don't think that counts as a real kiss." Lynzie seemed as disappointed as Michaela felt. "Let's just go outside."

Lynzie headed straight for the fire pit, where Michaela's roommates were gathered. "Hi, girls." She hugged all three of them. "My dad and Michaela just kissed under the mistletoe."

Michaela's face warmed quickly and not just from the blazing fire.

"Not a real kiss, though," Lynzie continued. "The on-your-cheek kind."

Everybody laughed.

Jonas stabbed a hot dog with an unfolded clothes hanger. He passed it to Lynzie, and she held it over the flames. Then he hooked another one for Michaela. By the time his was ready for the fire, Lynzie's was toasty brown.

Derrick helped Lynzie get it loose from the hanger and into a bun. Soon all three of them were busy devouring the charred dogs and listening to the other couples share stories of their favorite Christmases.

Jonas seemed to sense Michaela's discomfort. "Do you want to get away from here?"

With gratitude, she rose. "We're taking a little walk."

"In this frigid weather?" Stephanie sounded astounded by the notion.

"Yep." Jonas didn't defend their decision. "Lynzie. . ." He motioned for his daughter to join them.

"Do I have to go?" She'd just slipped a marshmallow onto her hanger.

"We don't mind keepin' an eye on her," Scarlett assured.

"Please, Dad. . ." Lynzie shot a pleading expression in Jonas's direction.

He nodded. "Behave."

Lynzie squealed. "I will. I promise."

Jonas took Michaela's elbow and guided her away from the porch and into the dark night.

"Thanks," she whispered, shivering already.

He wrapped an arm around her shoulders, drawing her close. "I don't want you to freeze to death," he said.

Michaela felt the need to say something—a small explanation. "My childhood wasn't the greatest. I don't have a lot of happy family stories."

"I'm sorry, Michaela. Every kid deserves a blissful, carefree childhood." He'd guided them around to the front of the lodge. He led her to the large indoor fireplace in the conversation pit, and they both settled on the hearth, only a foot or so from the hot blaze. The room was quiet, everyone else still outside.

Her shivers slowly subsided.

And he waited, not pushing. Minutes passed. Finally, he cleared his throat. "If you ever need to talk about your past with somebody, I'm here." The compassion in his eyes nearly did her in. *Oh for a man like you. Lord, that's the desire of my heart.* She'd quit trying to fool herself into believing she wanted to live and die alone, fulfilling only her professional goals.

She smiled. Tender feelings flooded her heart like new shoots on a plant. "Thanks for your kind offer. But I'm here for a fresh start, a new beginning. 'Forgetting what is behind. . .'"

He nodded his acceptance. " 'And straining toward what is ahead.' " The tenderness in his voice was something new and made fighting the growing feelings even harder.

He reached for her hand, squeezing it in an encouraging

way. His hand was strong and wrapped hers in comfort, reassurance, and security.

Lynzie barreled through the door. "Dad! Dad, are you in here?"

Jonas jerked his hand back. Michaela understood, but the action still stung. He jumped up. "Over here." A hint of panic laced his tone. "What's wrong? Are you all right?"

Lynzie waltzed over. "I'm fine." Her eyes shone bright with excitement, and the color in her face had heightened. "Tomorrow they're going on a sleigh ride! Can we go? Please, please, please?"

Michaela watched the uncertainty play out over his face.

"Do friends take sleigh rides together?" she whispered.

He relaxed, and she knew he understood the message. The compassion he'd shown tonight didn't redefine their relationship.

"They do. And we will." Refocusing on Lynzie, he continued, "Go tell them we're in, kiddo."

* * *

Jonas sat on the edge of Lynzie's bed. "What do you mean you don't feel well?" She'd felt fine all day.

"I don't know, Daddy. My head hurts, my stomach hurts, and I just feel yucky."

He laid his hand across her forehead just like his mom did when he was a boy. "You don't feel warm."

"I'm sorry, Daddy. I just can't go tonight." She rolled over on her side, pulling the covers tighter around herself.

"I'll call Michaela. She'll understand."

Lynzie rolled back over to face him, her eyes wide. "No. Gramma will watch me."

"You know I don't like pushing my parental responsibilities off on Gramma just because we live here."

"I know, Dad. Gramma is only responsible for me when you're at work—otherwise you're the dad." She quoted his mantra that he'd said aloud more than once. He'd put that boundary in place when he and Lynzie moved in with his parents after Jill's death. He wanted Lynzie to have clear delineation between her parent and grandparents. They'd raised him and his brother Tom, and he wanted them to enjoy the grandparent role, not have to raise a third child.

"But don't you think this one time would be okay? Michaela's never been on a sleigh ride, and she's really looking forward to it."

"She is, is she?" He remembered last night that the two of them had talked extensively about it.

"She'd be so disappointed." Lynzie yawned and rolled back over. "I need to go to sleep now."

He bent over and kissed her cheek. "See ya later, kiddo."

She looked back over her shoulder. "Does that mean you'll take her?"

He smiled and nodded. "Yeah, I'll take her."

Jonas decided to actually arrive a few minutes early and walk up to Michaela's suite. When she walked into the room, he noticed she looked extra good. His heart thumped to life in his chest.

"Hi!" she said. Her greeting was breathless.

He smiled, trying to play it cool. "You look nice tonight. Did you dress warm enough?"

"Long johns and all. Where's Lynzie?"

"Home—sick."

"We don't have to go. If you need to be with her, I completely understand." Her kind offer made him relax a little. *See, we are still just friends. She's not thinking or expecting more.*

"My mom's with her. She'll be fine."

"If you're sure." Michaela shrugged. "Are you ready then?"

He nodded, and she grabbed her coat off the hall tree on the way out the door. She carried it over her arm until they reached the front door to the lodge. When he helped her into it, he caught a whiff of her perfume—subtle and sweet. He tried to remember what Jill used to wear to compare, but suddenly he could no longer recall her scent. Now he was fully aware of another woman. The shock of it hit him hard.

The rest of their group gathered, excited conversation flowed, and he joined in, not wanting to analyze what this new discovery meant. Scarlett and Derrick were rather subdued. Apparently it was his last night in town. He'd be leaving the following day. Seemed to Jonas that they'd fallen fast and hard.

The sleigh pulled up to the front door and everyone bundled up before heading out into the cold. Eight of them made for a tight squeeze. Jonas wrapped his arm around Michaela, and she fit against his side like a puzzle piece. She drew a blanket over their laps.

At the beginning of the ride, everyone was chatty and laughter flowed. As time passed and the cold settled in, each couple drew closer and the conversations grew quiet, personal, intimate.

Couples. This wasn't a setting for friends. He wasn't even sure he still thought of Michaela as simply a friend.

"I'm sorry. This is awkward and wasn't a good idea." Her breath danced across his cheek as she whispered near his ear.

Her eyes—so sincere—gazed deep into his. A yearning to kiss her welled up inside of him, but he fought it, turning his gaze to the night sky instead.

"Beautiful night, isn't it?"

She leaned her head against his shoulder and gazed up. "That it is." A contented sigh escaped, only adding additional concern to Jonas.

Men and women cannot be friends. What was I thinking? Why did hanging out seem like a good idea?

When the driver turned toward home, relief came.

"I'd move over if I could," Michaela whispered. She must have sensed his discomfort.

"You're fine." He studied her face and realized for the first time that she was a beautiful woman with a beautiful heart. Had she always been this pretty? He wasn't sure.

All sorts of feelings and emotions that he hadn't dealt with in years surged through him. In her eyes he saw questions and uncertainties. All the same things he was dealing with.

The sleigh glided to a halt and they'd returned to their

327

starting point. Each couple quietly gathered their belongings and disembarked.

Jonas climbed out and lifted Michaela down. They stood next to the sleigh, his hands on her waist, hers resting on his forearms. The three other couples headed inside, and the driver pulled away into the night.

"Good night, Jonas." Michaela leaned in and placed a kiss on his cheek. "Thanks for being my escort for the evening." He knew it was for his sake that she kept reiterating the no-strings-attached friendship.

He didn't loosen his hold, nor did he move closer. He studied every detail of her face, but all he thought about was kissing her. Should he? Shouldn't he? He knew friends didn't kiss, at least not the way he wanted to kiss her. It had been on his mind since the mistletoe incident.

Then he decided. One kiss. Just one. Ever so slowly, he began to draw her toward him. With no resistance, she came. One kiss and he'd put her and it out of his mind.

Her eyes were warm and filled with anticipation. His heart pounded in his rib cage. Could she hear it? He removed his hands from her waist and pulled her into an embrace. She wrapped her arms around his neck, leaning in. He leaned down. Their lips touched. He took his time with the kiss, lingering over the softness of her lips, tasting their sweetness.

When he lifted his head, her dazed expression of affection brought him back to reality. Guilt with the force of a gale wind hit him.

"I'm sorry, Michaela. That kiss should never have happened." He'd been wrong—so wrong to mislead her.

Her arms dropped from around his neck and her expression hardened. "No, it shouldn't have." She turned and ran the few feet into the lodge.

Chapter 7

All three couples stared as she ran past them and up the stairs to the girls' suite. Michaela didn't stop until inside the privacy of her bedroom. She shut the door, threw herself across the bed, and sobbed.

Why, why, why did he have to go and kiss her? Now the illusion of friendship was ruined.

She heard a knock at her door. Stephanie called out her name.

"What?"

The door opened. All three of her roommates came in. Bethany headed to the bathroom and returned with a box of Kleenex. Stephanie and Scarlett settled at the foot of the bed. Michaela leaned against the pillows resting on the headboard. Bethany joined her at the head of the bed.

"What happened?" Scarlett asked.

Michaela wiped her eyes on the tissue. "He kissed me." She sniffled a couple of times.

"Was it that bad?" Concern lined Bethany's face.

Michaela shook her head and cried harder. "It was wonderful."

"Then why in the world are you crying like a baby?" asked Scarlett.

"He said it was a mistake—should never have happened." More tears fell.

A quiet "Oh" slid from Bethany's lips. "This is our fault."

The other two nodded. Scarlett came around and hugged Michaela. "We are so, so sorry."

"It's not your fault," Michaela reassured them.

"Yeah...I'm afraid it is," Scarlett drawled. "You see, the three of us decided you needed a push in the dating direction."

Horror struck Michaela. "You guys didn't. . ." Had they paid Jonas to date her or something just as degrading?

Compassion filled Stephanie's green eyes. "Jonas seemed like the perfect guy to get you back in the game again. I mean, he's great looking, smart, and sensitive."

Michaela sniffed again. "Reciting his wonderfulness isn't making me feel any better."

"Sorry." Stephanie lowered her gaze to the bed.

"So how did you get him to agree to this scheme?"

"Oh, he didn't," Scarlett assured her. "This was our doing, with a little help from Lynzie. You two were—"

"Your pawns?" Michaela didn't like the feeling of being manipulated, but at least Jonas had not been party to their plan.

"No. Not at all." Bethany picked at the quilt. "You seemed so well suited."

Stephanie shrugged. "We just wanted you to be happy."

"Do I look happy?"

All three shook their heads.

"Now it all makes sense. Every time I went anywhere, I'd run into Lynzie and Jonas. What did you do, call her every time I left the house?"

"Pretty much. It doesn't sound so nice now," Scarlett admitted.

"Did you know that last week alone, I ran into them at least four times—church, the drug store, when I was on a walk, and even when I was doing some photography." Her gaze rested on each roommate. "But of course you know. It was all part of your plan—your evil, sinister plan."

"We intended it for good," Bethany said.

"How can lying and manipulating be for good?"

"That was not the way we looked at it." Now Bethany's tone held a defensive edge.

"Some days the accidental meetings were so frequent, I falsely hoped I was growing on him or that he wanted to see me but wasn't ready to admit it!"

Michaela got off the bed and paced to the door. Turning, she stopped. "You used an eleven-year-old child for your plan and fed her information so she could manipulate her father into going where I was?"

They each nodded.

"Said that way, it sounds so ugly. We meant no harm. Honest, Michaela." Stephanie's eyes reflected her sorrow.

"We were overzealous and may not have thought things through, but you and Jonas need each other." Scarlett had her hands on her hips, daring Michaela to deny the facts. She continued, "There is chemistry between you two. We all spotted it a mile away." The other two nodded their heads. "You're both just too stubborn or stupid to see the truth, so we thought we'd help you out a little. We messed up, and we are sorry you got hurt, but our hearts were pure."

Bethany searched Michaela's face with a probing gaze. "Will you forgive us?"

Michaela let out a sigh. "Yes, I'll forgive you, if you promise never, ever to mess in my life again."

"We promise," they answered in unison. Then they all hugged.

The question was, could Michaela forgive herself for giving her heart to a man who didn't want it?

"I cannot believe this," Jonas said, talking to his reflection in the mirror the next day. "Ouch." He grabbed a tissue and held it against the knick he'd just carved into his chin with his razor.

He was off today and needed time alone—to think. Lynzie had boarded the school bus not ten minutes earlier. As soon as he finished his shower and shave, he planned to hit the slopes. He hoped the exhilaration would clear his head.

Thankfully, the trails would be fairly empty since most people were at work or school. Empty was good. He needed the quiet to process his crazy feelings that started running out of control under a sprig of mistletoe with a certain green-eyed brunette.

He'd avoided the kiss that time but hadn't escaped last night. Something inside him awoke. Some sleeping giant who'd slumbered since Jill's death.

He'd convinced himself that keeping his heart at bay would be an easy feat, and it was—that is, until Michaela waltzed into his life.

Because the slopes were as uncrowded as he'd hoped, he got his own chair on the lift. He bent his neck back and stared up into a cloudless, bright blue sky. "God, I really messed this up. I've got feelings. I'm pretty sure she's got feelings. Men and women cannot be friends. Now how do I undo this mess?"

The only answer he came up with was avoiding her. He'd been right in the first place and should have stuck to his guns. What sane thirty-one-year-old lets an eleven-year-old run his life?

He closed his eyes and tried to bring Jill's image to the forefront of his mind, but Michaela was the one he saw. She'd stolen Jill's scent and now Jill's face from his memory. And he hated himself for letting it happen.

One more run down the slopes, and he'd call it a day. His resolve had returned. His plan—run fast and far from Michaela or any other female—was back in place.

Then he changed his mind. He'd go home early and process this mess with his mom. She always helped him sort through his tangled emotions in a logical way.

On the drive home, he decided he needed a course in Avoiding Women 101, because he'd failed miserably. And he'd hurt Michaela in the process. The crushed expression she wore when he'd apologized for the kiss had haunted him ever since. She'd done nothing to deserve that. She had, however, planted herself firmly in his heart, and he had no idea how to pluck her loose.

When he entered the kitchen, his mom glanced up from chopping celery. "Stew tonight. Were you off today?"

"Yeah. I spent the whole day out on the slopes." He settled onto a barstool across the counter from where his mother was working.

"Everything okay?"

He chuckled. "You know me too well."

"It's been your pattern for more years than I can count. Whenever you have something heavy to deal with in your life, you head for the slopes." She smiled.

"I don't think Lynzie was sick the other night." He stated one of several concerns.

His mom moved to the sink. "I don't think so either."

"Every time she drags me anywhere, we run into Michaela." Jonas sighed. "She's been manipulating me, hasn't she?"

His mom dried her hands on a dish towel and pursed her lips.

"I know you pretty well, too," he said. "You know something, don't you?"

She hesitated. "This is hard. I don't want to damage my relationship with Lynzie or break the trust she has in me."

"Tell her I asked and you couldn't lie."

His mom leaned back against her counter, facing him. "I caught Lynzie on the phone the other night after you left for the sleigh ride. She is apparently in cahoots with Michaela's roommates."

"You've got to be kidding me." He shook his head, both stunned and relieved by the news. "Sometimes I found myself wondering who was putting whom up to what. I didn't want to believe Michaela was one of those manipulative females."

"She's not, but your daughter and Michaela's roommates are another story. According to Lynzie, the two of you didn't have a clue. She had her own agenda and roped Michaela's roommates into helping."

"She'll be grounded till she's twenty. My little girl—the conniver."

"For whatever reason, she desperately wants a mom."

"I didn't think I'd ever meet anyone who could replace Jill."

His mom focused her gaze on him. "No one will ever replace Jill for either you or Lynzie. But Jill's gone, and you guys are still living."

"I know, but what we had was so incredible. What if I were to remarry someday and it was horrible?"

"A relationship is the sum of the two people involved. If you choose wisely with God's help, your marriage can be just as good—different, but just as good—as the one you and Jill shared."

"You think so because I've developed feelings for Michaela, and now I feel guilty for falling for her, for replacing memories of Jill."

His mom came around the bar and placed an arm around

his shoulders, giving him a tight squeeze. "Memories fade over time and are replaced with new ones."

He laid his head in his hands. "I don't want to forget her, Mom."

"You won't forget everything. I promise."

"Now it's Michaela I think of instead of Jill." His tone was guilt ridden.

"Because Michaela is here in the present. You can see her and touch her and smell her."

"Boy, are you right about that." He raised his head and smiled.

She returned his smile. "No one—except maybe Lynzie—wanted you to remarry more than Jill did."

"So you think it's okay?"

A wide grin split her face. "More than okay—wonderful, exciting, a gift from the Lord."

"So you like Michaela?"

She nodded. "Very much."

"How can I be sure, though? I don't want to make the biggest mistake of my life."

"I've been reading a book about fasting. In the Bible, when men and women were faced with a tough decision, they fasted to hear from God. As a matter of fact, in Genesis 24 the very first fast is recorded, and the purpose was to find the right wife for Isaac."

"I'm not off again until next week. It would be hard to spend a day in prayer while I'm working, so I'll schedule it next Wednesday—two days before Christmas."

"As you know, I don't believe in rushing important decisions, and that will give you this week to pray about it. Your dad and I will be praying with you."

"I'm not going to mention this to anyone else, just in case this isn't God's will. I've already hurt Michaela enough."

"Sounds like a good decision."

He hugged his mom and headed out the door to meet Lynzie's bus. He felt much better. He hoped Michaela was part of God's plan for him.

Chapter 8

Michaela would make the big announcement tonight at dinner. Boy, would they all be surprised. She'd been working day and night to get the lodge up and running, and now she had!

The roommates decided to go out to dinner tonight and celebrate Christmas—just the four of them. It was a few days early, but they wanted the chance to all celebrate together, so Michaela drove them into town and parked in front of Austin's.

They were all dressed in red and carried packages and bags into the restaurant. The air crackled with excitement. Michaela loved this time of year, and this Christmas was the fifth that they'd all celebrate together. Then Bethany would fly home, but the other three were staying in Nevada.

They settled at the table, each ordering her favorite dish. Michaela got the grilled Portabella. Once the waitress had taken their orders and delivered their hot tea, they passed out presents. Each onc oohed and aahed over scented bath gift packs, slippers, and candles. Michaela gave each of her friends a devotional for the following year.

Dinner was delivered just as they finished unwrapping their gifts. They cleared the table and shoved stuff under their chairs to make room for the food. After Bethany prayed, they all dug in.

About halfway through dinner, Michaela cleared her throat. "Ladies, I have news."

All of their eyes grew wide. "You're getting married!" Scarlett blurted out.

Michaela smiled. "I'm moving."

"What?" It was Bethany's question. "You can't leave! What about your job?"

"I'm finished. I've done what your grandparents hired me to do. The lodge is completely computerized—fully automated."

"I thought we all agreed to stay for one season," Stephanie said, apparently questioning Michaela's loyalty to the plan.

"I've talked to Mack and Elizabeth, and they both gave me their blessing to leave early." Michaela shrugged. "I did what I came to do."

A tear rolled down Bethany's cheek. "We'll never all live together again."

Michaela fought getting sentimental herself. "No, I guess we never will. Part of growing up, I suppose, but if my hunch plays out, I'll see you all within the next year for a wedding or two."

Each of them was twitterpated and probably hoped it would be them. Truth be told, Michaela wanted the same thing.

"Why are you doing it?" Scarlett asked.

"Jonas. I did fall for him, just as you guys hoped. Problem is, he didn't fall for me. I can't keep running into him—it hurts too much. And I don't want to hurt him or Lynzie. It'll be easier for everyone concerned if I vanish. Then they can forget me and get on with life.

"I've spent the last week looking over my shoulder and avoiding him and Lynzie like they have some contagious disease. I've ducked down aisles, turned my car into alleys, laid across my seat in hiding just so I don't have to face them. But it's not working, nor does it stop me from missing them. I need to get away somewhere where they aren't lurking around every corner."

"Where will you go?"

"I haven't decided, but that's sort of the great thing about this. I can go anywhere in the world. Nothing is tying me down or holding me back." All the words were true, but they did not at all reflect how Michaela honestly felt. She was the girl who ached to settle in one spot for the rest of her life. At least one spot was off her list of possibilities—Incline Village, Nevada, was not the place for her.

On their way out of the restaurant, Lynzie called to them, darted across the crowded room, and hugged each one. Michaela wished the floor would swallow her up when Lynzie told them over and over again how much she missed them.

Michaela's gaze wandered across the room until she spotted Jonas. He waved. Her heart ached inside with an almost unbearable pain, but she smiled a carefree smile and waved back, hoping he couldn't see the hurt she carried. Most likely, this would be the last time she'd ever see him face-to-face. Ah, but the memories—they'd haunt her forever. Tears pooled in her eyes as she gave Lynzie a last hug.

"Maybe Dad and I will see you around sometime." The longing in the little girl's voice stabbed Michaela's heart with yet more pain.

"Maybe." Michaela rushed out the door. Tears ran freely down her cheeks. Scarlett drove them home, and Michaela cried all the way.

"Now you see why I have to leave."

No one argued the point. They loved her and ached over her pain.

Jonas knocked on the door. Scarlett answered. Her stunned surprise led to a gaping mouth.

"Is Michaela around?" He sounded so normal for a man with a knot the size of Texas lodged in his gut.

Scarlett nodded. He'd never seen her so quiet.

She left him standing in the open doorway for what seemed like an eternity. He heard whispering and people moving about but couldn't see what was going on without actually stepping into the suite, which he opted not to do.

Finally, Michaela stood in front of him, wearing sweats, a sweatshirt, no makeup, and her hair pulled back into a ponytail. "I wasn't expecting you." She looked down at her attire, obviously embarrassed.

"You look beautiful to me." Whether it was what he said or the huskiness of his voice, he didn't know, but she looked as stunned as Scarlett had.

"May I come in?"

"Oh. . .yeah. Sure." She was rattled—of that he was certain. She opened the door wider and stepped aside.

He entered, shut the door, and pulled her into his arms. The kiss he'd given her the other night was nothing compared to this one. This one contained every ounce of his love.

When the kiss ended, she smiled and whispered, "Wow."

"That's only a sneak preview of what's to come."

Confusion creased her brows. "I don't understand."

"I only *thought* I was content with my life." He kissed the tip of her nose. "Then you came along and were an unwelcome, yet at the same time *welcome*, daily distraction from my so-called contentment."

"I was?" She seemed to have a hard time believing or accepting his words.

"Then you quoted that verse about 'forgetting what was behind and straining toward what is ahead,' and I knew God wasn't just speaking to you through His Word, He was speaking to me from the very same passage."

Her smile widened. "Do you mean that I'm your ahead?"

"If you say yes. The truth is, Michaela, I'm in love with you."

"You are? I just can't believe this is happening. I mean, you were so adamant about. . .everything."

"Instead of being content, I think I was afraid to love again. I never wanted to experience again the depth of pain I felt when Jill died, but the thought of never seeing *you* again brought the same sort of pain."

"That's why I was leaving. I couldn't stand the thought of seeing you every day and not being part of your life."

"Is that your way of saying you love me, too?"

She shook her head. Had he misread her? Wrapping her arms around his neck, she spoke in a sure voice. "Jonas Brooks, I love you. So much, in fact, that I'm going to quit running and spend the rest of my life right here with you and Lynzie."

"Why, Michaela Christiansen, is that a proposal?" He raised his brows.

She shook her head again. "It's an answer to yours, whenever you're ready to ask."

He pulled her back against him. "How about now?"

"Then how about yes."

He kissed her again. This one ended with claps and cheers from her roommates.

Michaela left his arms for theirs. They all cried, hugged, and cried some more.

"Is this what I have to look forward to?"

"Probably," they all agreed.

JERI ODELL is an Arizona native. Married to her high school sweetheart, Dean, for thirty-six years, they have three adult kids and three grandchildren. Jeri works in the finance department at her church and teaches women's Bible studies there. She loves the Lord, being Grammie, time with family, and encouraging women in their faith walk. God gave her the privilege of writing eight novellas, eight novels, and one nonfiction book—to Him be the glory!

A Letter to Our Readers

Dear Readers:

In order that we might better contribute to your reading enjoyment, we would appreciate your taking a few minutes to respond to the following questions. When completed, please return to the following: Fiction Editor, Barbour Publishing, Inc., P.O. Box 719, Uhrichsville, OH 44683.

1. Did you enjoy reading *Christmas Love at Lake Tahoe?*
   ❑ Very much—I would like to see more books like this.
   ❑ Moderately—I would have enjoyed it more if _____

_____

_____

2. What influenced your decision to purchase this book?
   (Check those that apply.)
   ❑ Cover   ❑ Back cover copy   ❑ Title   ❑ Price
   ❑ Friends   ❑ Publicity   ❑ Other

3. Which story was your favorite?
   ❑ *The Christmas Miracle*   ❑ *Tinsel, Tidings, and Time-share*
   ❑ *No Thank You*   ❑ *Dating Unaware*

4. Please check your age range:
   ❑ Under 18   ❑ 18–24   ❑ 25–34
   ❑ 35–45   ❑ 46–55   ❑ Over 55

5. How many hours per week do you read? _____

Name _____

Occupation _____

Address _____

City _____ State _____ Zip _____

E-mail _____

If you enjoyed

CHRISTMAS LOVE AT LAKE TAHOE

then read

CHRISTMAS HOMECOMING

Silver Bells by Debby Mayne
I'll Be Home for Christmas by Elizabeth Ludwig
O Christmas Tree by Elizabeth Goddard
The First Noelle by Paige Winship Dooly

———————————————————

If you enjoyed

CHRISTMAS LOVE AT LAKE TAHOE

then read

WILD WEST CHRISTMAS

Charlsey's Accountant by Lena Nelson Dooley
Lucy Ames, Sharpshooter by Darlene Franklin
A Breed Apart by Vickie McDonough
Plain Trouble by Kathleen Y'Barbo

Available wherever books are sold.
Or order from:
Barbour Publishing, Inc.
P.O. Box 721
Uhrichsville, Ohio 44683
www.barbourbooks.com

You may order by mail for $7.97 and add $4.00 to your order for shipping.
Prices subject to change without notice.
If outside the U.S. please call 740-922-7280 for shipping charges.